LOST CANYON

CROW'S NEST

PROFILE POINT

ROCKSLIDE

PLATFORM

DANIEL MOON'S

THE GOBLINS

RABBITS HEAD

1ST BATHOUSE

2ND BATHOUSE

3RD BATHOUSE

DEEPLICK

FARLEY'S CANYON

NESTER DAVIS'

THE GATE

ARMCHAIR CANYON

never past the gate

a novel by
emma lou thayne

never past
the gate

A ➜ Peregrine Smith Publication

The first four lines of the poem, "The Centaur" by May Swenson, are used as
an epigraph by permission of the poet from her collection, TO MIX WITH TIME,
copyright © 1963 by May Swenson and Charles Scribner's Sons, New York.

Library of Congress Card Catalog Number: 75-33580
ISBN: 0-87905-047-0

Manufactured in the United States of America

To those who love it too.

"The summer that I was ten—
Can it be there was only one
summer that I was ten? It must
have been a long one then—"

"The Centaur," by May Swenson

CHAPTER ONE

They never told anyone about their plans for that climb, and certainly not Mother. She had said, "If you hike the mountain behind the cabin and go past the grotto, you'll run into more rattlers than you can handle. Uncle Wooster-with-the-Long-Beard found so many there that he brought a pig up to root them out. Pigs are the best there is against rattlers. They wade in and tromp them to death. But children can't do that, even in high boots or with a hiking stick, so just keep your eyes peeled and stay clear."

Despite the warnings, Wid and James and their cousin Smithy had gone anyhow. But when they came panting down to the spring where Katie and Jody Sue were arcing thin sprays through their bottom teeth, they were as pale as oatmeal. Smithy had lost his stick, and Wid kept hitting his against the ground and mumbling, "I just can't figure how come that didn't hold him down. Heck, it's the toughest around—mountain mahogany—and it didn't do a thing."

Katie knew they had figured on using the hiking sticks. One of them would pin a snake with his stick, and the others would pound it with theirs. They were peeled smooth as axe handles and cut to fit like long canes under their hands as they hiked. Back from the hike, James had sat crouched with his fingers in the spring for a long time, his stick under his arm, unaware of Katie pushing sand into the beginning of the stream with her own hiking stick that was still untested.

After dinner when she and James were throwing out dishwater behind the cabin, Katie found out what had happened.

"Did you go to the grotto?" she braved.

"Sure."

"Well—you must've seen some."

"Uh huh."

"How many?"

"More'n you'd ever think there ever were."

"How many? Ten? A hundred?"

"I don't know. They were all curled up together moving —kinda like grayish tan mud."

"Well, didn't you even try to kill one so you could skin it like always?"

"Wid did. There was one coming out from under the rocks. You know how the rocks all fit on each other up there and make a sort of cave right out in the open?"

"You know I've never seen it," she said accusingly, "but I've heard about it."

James ignored her jab and went on, "Well, there was a tunnel under one side and this big one came out — slow, straight — straight as a pulled rope. You know how rattlers never curve like other snakes when they move." Katie nodded. "Well, this one came out with his head kind of up and those big jaws out in front of him—like a fat arrow head."

"Did he see you? Was he rattling?"

"No. Quiet as air. We all just stood there sorta hypnotized. I didn't much want to move. But I knew Wid would. He was right above him on the loose rock. We were about this far below." James suspended the tin dishpan in one hand to show with the other the full length of his stretched-out arms. "I knew if Wid pinned him it would be up to me to smash his head, so I just waited and started to move my stick up to where I could plant it down hard. Wid got his about to his waist and started to swing it down over the snake. But

2

the rocks slid and he slipped."

"Into the snake?" Katie's blue eyes opened like a bird's, waiting.

"Almost. I thought he would for sure. His stick sort of grazed the snake right behind its head, and rocks started rolling toward it."

"Did Wid fall?"

"No. Just did a little dip and sat down with his hands to brace him. Landed on his stick. Then he got right back up and tried to pin the snake, but his stick didn't hold it at all."

"Did the snake strike?"

"Boy, it tried. I smacked it with my stick, but it coiled up so fast it felt like solid cement when I hit it. Its head sat up like an S curve and it started to fly at Wid's boot. Just sort of a flash."

"Could you see its fangs?"

"Sure. White back of its tongue. The tongue kept flashing around. Black and thin. Black on the ends, pink behind. And fast. Like the needle on Mother's machine when she's pumping her hardest. Only sort of twittering and waving. I watched really hard. Then I tried to hit him a couple more times, but Wid said 'Run,' and we all did."

"Did it chase you?"

"I haven't got any idea. We just tore down that mountain. Far as I was concerned, the whole grotto came after us. All I could think about was Mother telling about those pigs and wondering how they could stamp anything with their little twinky feet."

"How about Smithy? Where was he?"

"He lost his stick. He might've been pounding up there like I was, but I don't remember anything about him. And we've never talked about what happened."

"Will you go back—ever?"

"I doubt it. But Wid will. Probably not soon. Not this summer. But sometime. It really got him not to be able to pin that one."

"I want to go."

"*You* want to go?"

"Sure. And I will. Just watch."

That had been up the canyon in late August the year before.

Now, in the city, the back screen door at Crystal Avenue slammed and the summer of 1935 began, Katie's tenth. She was using the ice pick to fit wet chunks between long quarts of milk in the wooden box labeled DAIRY THINGS. In just less than an hour she'd be in the canyon getting ready to whittle kinnikinick flippers and scour out borrowed lumber for secret huts. There'd be Tony to find—and Shadow. And she'd get to the grotto, this year for sure.

"Hey, Bruv, don't forget the brown paper for maps," James said to Wid in their last minute jamming of pockets. "And the magnifying glass for starting fires, and the extra heavy string for tops—oh, and your rat poison."

"Don't worry, Bruv, I never forget."

But James kept naming his packing, knowing that his big brother could be deflected at any time. "Maybe he is dreamy—like Mother says," he thought as he watched Wid hang over the edge of his bed and try different combinations on the lock to his scout box — upside down to make it a challenge.

"Tug the corners tight," Mother cheerfully reminded Lena, who, after seven years of "living in" with the Bartons, already had. They billowed old sheets over the living room furniture to leave it as shrouded as in spring housecleaning when pink and black worms of wallpaper dough settled on its cemetery.

"I speak a window," six-year-old Davy called over the bedding he thrashed into the back seat of the Hupmobile.

"You're too little," Wid said with authority. "Maybe later."

"Six is crummy!" Davy mumbled. "It's stupid! I bet you and James were never six! You gotta be so big!"

"Hand me the brown suitcase. And the shoe bag. And we can slip another food box in right here." Father squinted and shoved to make all of it fit, no matter what Mother sent out. "And Katie-bug, don't get your hair mussed up, whatever you do." He rubbed his hand over Katie's light brown ringlets and grinned as she pushed her box toward him. "If there's anything I like it's a nice prim little lady!"

Katie banged his hand away and grinned back, "Oh yes, and I know just how prim, Mister Heathcliff!" She darted past him and into the house with Father charging after her.

"Did you lock the clothes chute, Candland?" Mother called into the broom closet in the kitchen where a trap door opened and her voice could carry down the chute to Father in the basement.

"Yep, Flossie. And I checked the coal chute and shut all the dampers and secured the transom and lowered all the upstairs blinds to six inches and locked the windows and put all the keys to everything on the Diatta by the bread drawer. We're tight as my scalp before an Aunt Elizabeth head rub."

Mother smiled and shook her head. "Are the kiddies in the car?"

"Pretty near. All but you, you cute little customer. If you'd just give the barometer a last minute tap and see what kind of day we're going to have, we could mosey on up to the green world."

Twelve miles east of Salt Lake City, in its quarter-mile deep ravine hugged by six steep mountains that spread their hips and stomachs like a loop of paunchy generals, the green world waited. On the farthest ridge, the granite Armchair shone like a crescent haze as it reached its fat arms, still full

5

of snow, toward the canyon that bore its name. In it, summer would begin with Katie Barton and her three brothers, Mother, Father, and Grandma Ruskin, and a flock of cousins whooping into cabins along its stream and up two sides of L.G. Mountain. Since 1869 it had known how to let the footprints of the Ruskins multiply in its red dust. From Grandma's as a bride to Katie's, a history of adventures sank upon each other and expected more.

The only human being in the canyon waited differently. Mister Davis made his deliberate way down the road and past the empty cabins. Aspen twittered into the soft sway of the maples by the icy Spring. Squirrels chittered in the pines by the Platform. Birds sent shrill explosions out of the cottonwoods. A porcupine lumbered ahead of the lone man into the scrub oak by the Moon Place.

Mister Davis stomped on a gopher hole in a rut by the salt lick. A deer raised his head and crashed into the privet. High behind him a hawk took a slow turn over Lover's Lane, and even higher an eagle hung over his eyrie and screeched at the rocks around from Profile Point.

Up the gully by the Tank, gnats and lavender butterflies flecked the spongy air over the rain swamp, and bees hummed in the corn flowers and willow blossoms. In Fairy House, hornets zoomed unattended into their tissue cones. Mister Davis kicked a red rock off the road and paused to puff at his pipe.

Along the road and all the way up to the Old Hotel and down to the Gate, the canyon cupped itself in long sweet wisps of grass that burst like plumage out of the mulch of flat colorless leaves and matted pine needles. Gray and russet crags were getting hot. Spiders began their flimsy travels; flies, in spontaneous generation, zzz'd onto warm landings in the Rat Houses.

In the Grotto on Rattlesnake Mountain the sun pulled at the dullness that slumped through lazy coils as female rattlers spread their young onto the rocks just up the mountain from where Mister Davis swung into his slanted walk toward home. Back to his dingy cabin near the gate, he prodded into thin smoke an ashy fire in his stove, mumbling and grimacing around the stem of his pipe. Summer inside his place was the same as winter—same temperature, same cloudy odor and unopened dim. From under his only door the first lizard of the season squirted past his stoop and into a scratchy Z along his yard.

Thirty-six curves up the Armchair road, the white frame Barton cabin sat easily on its haunches in Maple Fork, cooled in the growth of early June, shingles curled like leather, screens coppered brown behind peeling white studs. In its living room, yellow calsomine edged away from the walls, and in the kitchen, blue checkered oilcloth bubbled and cracked. It had been four summers since there had been funds for repairs, but Mother had kept the cabin tight with her delicate patches. In a few days it would shine like birch leaves. The white porcelain knob on its front screen door would be washed with Melo, the basin and pitchers would be scoured with Dutch Cleanser. Worn spots in the flat oriental rugs would be covered with smaller rag rugs, and scrim curtains would be stitched together with the minute tracings of a fine needle. The cabin's bleached roofbeams caught the first morning sun in the canyon.

Behind the cabin, Rattlesnake Mountain ran oak green over three bulges below its hot dry top and dumped thick foliage into the stream under the bridge where Mister Davis kneeled to scoop up a tin cup of cold water. As he drank, the water ran down from both sides of his mouth. He pulled a tan sleeve across the wet, spat into the skimpy dust, and threw the remains of his drink over his shoulder. It splattered on the white dangling blossoms of the chokecherries and dripped through the sunlight.

One turn down the road from Mister Davis, the notched

gate hung on cowhide straps that had not been moved in eight and a half months. It rested, no lower, no higher than the year before, indifferent to the beginning of the summer of 1935 that had already turned the canyon on like fingers at a wick.

"Everybody in!" Father slipped under the steering wheel and turned the key in the dashboard of the Hupmobile, now hot as an oven. On the soft velvet pile seat next to him in front were Mother, then Lena with Davy on her lap. Across the quilts stacked almost to the ceiling in back lay James, Katie, and Wid.

"Can we open the windshield?" Katie begged before the car had bounced down the divided driveway to the street.

"Depends on how dusty the road is," Father answered, running his right hand across the heads of the three behind him as he looked back.

Katie loved to watch his hard hands work, the hands he always called "way too little—you need big hands to be a really good athlete." She could tell just when he'd crank the windshield out and then smile in the rear view mirror when he knew the wind was whipping her ringlets out. She knew he knew the feeling even though what there was left of his hair was under his broad brimmed Scout Master's hat.

Father eyed Katie as the car started down Crystal and along Highland Drive to Sugar House. Her face looked so alive and happy to him that it nearly kept him from his driving. He never had to guess how things were with his only daughter. Her light eyes were like his, only sometimes inscrutably intense, and her face was as mobile as the poplar leaves moving past the windows. He found her looking, as she often did, so far off that he thought she must be lost. As he caught her eyes in the mirror, she flashed back to the moment, bringing it the immediacy that always caught him by delighted surprise. "Where do you go, Bug?" he asked her quietly.

She gave him the look that drew him to wherever she

was, to her girlishness under the tomboy, and her wondering. "To find me a pony," she answered.

Wid and James each had an arm out of the back windows maneuvering their propellers to catch the strongest breeze. Whittled last summer, the blades were a blurred humming and the boys' arms were giving in the wind.

"They look swell," Davy said longingly, turning from side to side on Lena's lap next to the window in front. "Why can't I just stick mine out for a minute? Just in the windshield even?"

"Because Father has to see, Davy, and that could cause an accident. You'll have a chance to try it before we get there, don't worry. Let's watch for Suicide Rock." Mother settled his wandering leg so that Father could shift into second with the chrome knob that moved the bent gearshift on the floor.

The car moved up Twenty-first South past the State Penitentiary where prisoners waved from behind barred windows above the stone wall that reminded Katie of the one around the Temple Grounds. Only redder. And maybe higher. Katie liked to wave to the faces in the shadow behind the bars. Even in outline they seemed uprooted and sad, like the frantic chipmunks and squirrels she and her brothers caught with carrots and crusts in boxes behind the fir tree at the cabin. They always freed the animals within hours despite their longing to tame them. If it was torture to hear them crash on the sides of the box as they raced against their walls, it was unbearable to see their eyes go shiny with searching and turn into dark swollen blobs of glazed terror.

Past four more big blocks and the car was headed into Parley's Canyon, Highway 40, the only route between Denver and the coast, one of the spokes that made Salt Lake City the hub of intermountain traffic. The cement of the road lay in squares with cracks between to allow for expansion in winter, and on the hot summer day the spaces spread to send rhythmic thuds into the tires and turn traveling into a lull

9

of wind and meter. Katie struggled to stay awake to see the stream. It would first appear below Suicide Rock, the high red obelisk that tilted away from the highway where the Indian maiden still plunged through the legend with her forbidden lover, into the shallows of the creek.

"Katie, did she really jump from there? How did she even get up there?" Davy asked, twisting till his mouth fell open trying to see the top of the rock.

"Easy," Katie answered. She saw braves on pintos, their heads bowed beneath tall feathers, felt a horse sweat under her, his bare back heaving and spreading her legs across him. She could have saved the maiden and her lover too. She would find Tony this summer and lasso him and get him back to Uncle Wooster's field. After she found her cat Shadow. She'd talk to Mister Davis. He'd know where they both were.

Between sandstone and white rocks that jutted out from scrub oak hillsides, the Hupmobile wound up the two lane highway with its lights on to preserve the battery. Father was in the automobile business and knew all the tricks of driving. The only thing he really knew better was how to control a ball.

He had learned to throw when he was a boy running along the railroad track tossing a dinner sack to his father, who was the most sober engineer on the Union Pacific run between Ogden and Evanston. Later his mother saw to it that he learned to throw, carry, hit, and handle any kind of ball. It started with baseball. "Mother would get us up at 4:30—that's in the morning!" he'd tell the children. "She'd say, 'Roust out, you lazy birds! How do you ever expect to be done with chores in time for the ball game! Now, of course, if you'd rather just turn over and die, I'd be the last to refuse to bury you—in cold water and pickle juice!' And we all got up—every day. And we did our chores with her *egging* us on. 'Hey!' she'd say from the back door, 'do you expect you're ever going to get around four bases without being tagged if you move that slow getting eggs?' Or maybe, 'Candland, you'll never make a decent pitch if you don't get more milk than that out of ten cows. Pokey hands!"

At Ogden High Candland Barton used his pokey hands to make any ball he touched do what he wanted it to. "Where'd you get that black sweater with the big orange O on it?" James liked to ask his father, waiting for the answer he loved.

"That's not an O," Father would say. "It's a zero — my batting average, remember!" Every time James would laugh, "O, Father!" and begin to shadow box under and around the big arms that without much boxing would grab him up and over his shoulders to wheel him around the room sing-songing, "I've got a sack of flourrrr. I've got a sack of flourrrrrrrr," just before swinging him onto any nearby cushion.

Candland Barton had gone to the University of Utah on a football scholarship and had stayed solvent by ironing the stiff four-inch collars of his roommates after practice every night. When he was a junior he enrolled in a Spanish class. "Fate," he always said.

Assigned the seat next to him was tiny Hope Ruskin, art major, member of the *Chronicle* staff. "So you're Hope Ruskin, the writer," Candland had grinned as she answered the first day's roll call. "Do you think you'll say it better in Spanish?"

"And you're Candland Barton, the bone crusher," Hope had responded. "Do you think you'll do even more damage in translation?"

"Maybe. Depending on my interpreter."

This had been a favorite story to tell the children, and it ended with Mother bringing out the pocket dictionary of Spanish whose edges were inscribed with Candland's definitive printing: "Ruskin-Barton, Inc."

"I'll never know how my father let him have me," Hope told the children, "especially after he rolled a mustard pickle across the table cloth and into Papa's lap the first time he came home for dinner. It must have been his wealth and position that made the impression."

"That's right," Father acknowledged. "Wealth of pickle and position of most direct route. That was the first time I saw your father really laugh. And it was the biggest relief of my life. He wasn't exactly jelly to approach about anything, let alone if it involved his precious little Hopie!"

"But you managed it, didn't you?" Mother said as if they were suddenly in the room alone.

Candland was a partner in a Depression-stunted motor company and drove a company car. So far he'd never had one of his own.

"We're just about to the first hot spot," Father announced. "It should be around that next curve. Right past the cement plant out on the flat."

"Just in time, too. Look at our tea kettle!" Mother said. The whole front end of the car rose in vapors.

"Oh boy! I speak to pour the first pan!" chortled Davy, bouncing his bottom against Lena's bony knees.

"Davy, just relax. You'll be maybe third or fourth," patted Mother. "You know it's too scalding hot on the first pour."

The square black car crunched off the highway and onto a grassy meadow between the road and the stream, where it stopped and spilled running legs from four doors. Wid snatched the long handled pan from its string around the front stand-up headlight and headed for the rushing creek. Father hoisted one side of the hood up onto the center to let the motor cool and was using a fat ball of rags to protect his hand while unscrewing the radiator cap in front. Giving it a gingerly twist, he pulled back, then twisted again, making faces in the sizzle. Finally the cap gushed into the air riding on the yellow geyser that shot higher than the roof.

Everyone went back to the geyser, waiting for it to die down, as it breathed acrid steam and gurgled into itself. When the bubbles pulsed below the rusty opening, Father signaled Wid to pour. With a long arm—and tongue and mouth that worked with it—Wid emptied the pan. When the last drop was in, James snatched the dipper and scooted for a refill. Katie did the third and Davy maneuvered the fourth pour standing on the sharp bumper, Father holding him by the back of his belt.

"Wow! Just listen to that! She's drinking now. She's about full!" Davy leaned closer to hear. "Sounds just like when eggs get beat in the whipping bowl, Mother."

The cold stream soothed the hollow rise of sound in the radiator, the car settled, and the family climbed into their second positions inside. The next stop would be the gate. And Mister Davis would be there. He always was.

This time Davy was in the middle of the back seat where Katie had been. He knew that after the gate stop he'd get a window, so his restlessness faded into a mumbled monologue. "I want to shake with Mister Davis. And show him my yo-yo. Bet he's never seen a yo-yo. Who'd ever have a yo-yo up the canyon in the winter? 'Cept maybe when he goes to Sugar House. Lotsa people have yo-yos in Sugar House. That's where I got mine—at Schramm-Johnson's." Davy droned on, as uninclined to press for responses as the family was to give them.

Katie was next to a back window, holding out her windmill and thinking about Mister Davis on her own. Every summer he occupied more of her thinking. She couldn't remember when he wasn't there waiting at the gate, a tin soldier, no age at all. He was tan all over, as if he were painted—his face, his hat, his clothes, his hands, his boots. He matched the road, exactly—like a toad that was made to not be seen.

Looking at his back, which was a lot of the way they saw him, the cousins said he was perfectly flat from his neck to his calves—no bottom. He seemed to have been ironed and then tilted uphill to look as if he were leaning from a platform. He could walk faster than Uncle Wooster's pony could trot and was often where no one expected him to be. And no one could calculate his being anywhere. That is, except for his regular trips up the road.

Every morning at eight he hiked the four miles to the top of the canyon, checking each cabin, vacant or full. He'd stoop to empty and reset the traps at the rat houses, the three unoccupied places just below the forty-three regular cabins. Then he'd look at every cooler in the stream all the way up and see that silt hadn't worked into the crocks that held the butter and cheese. He'd peer through the screens of the cabins and bend here and there to check under the porches—for what, no one ever knew or asked.

The road was his intimate province. Over his red-veined cheeks, his marble eyes roamed it the whole time he walked. He tossed off errant rocks, stomped flat the piles sifted up by gophers, memorized snake trails and tracks in the dust so that he could report in detail to the contingent of cousins exactly where, how deep and what variety the trail. Most of all, he was guardian of the road and keeper of the gate. No one passed without his knowing.

Mister Davis had come in the summer of 1929 to his two room cabin by the gate of Armchair Canyon, hired by Uncle Wooster from a Chicago sanitarium for railroad men. Uncle Wooster, whose 270 pounds were coddled everywhere into the biggest chairs and up to the most succulent tables, had something to do with a railroad and from his travels he brought home stories, presents and strays. Mister Davis was sort of all three. He was tubercular, the canyon people learned later, and needed the therapy of a high dry climate. His World War I army claims had allowed only dismal institutional living, and his wife of eight years, with his small daughter, had left him to puzzle his fate alone. So when Uncle Wooster had heard his tale while touring the facilities of the sanitarium, he had applied his usual extemporaneous cure and hired him on the spot. Bill Davis was to be year-round "ranger" in the Canyon.

His cabin had been there across the stream east of the gate but deserted for years. Restored, it took on the brown stain of occupancy and spun smoke through every night of every season. Each property owner paid ten dollars a year with his road assessment to take care of Mister Davis, who took with undentable seriousness his job of "keeping an eye on things" twenty-four hours a day, every day of the year.

What else anyone knew about Mister Davis was never told to the cousins. What they knew they found out on their own. One dark late afternoon in December Wid and James had been on their way home from the new library in the small business district called Sugar House, about a mile from Crystal Avenue where the Bartons lived. Although it was only five o'clock, the street lights were already on and the boys' breath turned white against the early dusk. They slid to a slick stop to let the freight train snort past the lumber yard, cross Highland Drive, and slither into the cold beyond Fairmont Park. They couldn't hear over the rumble and, besides, they were both busy peering through the cars watching for tramps, so James jumped when Wid jabbed his arm and hissed, "Hey! Look!"

James followed Wid's finger to the other side of the street to see a tan phantom slip off a fast moving car and slant off toward the blurred lights of Sugar House.

"It's him! It's Mister Davis!" blurted James.

"Yeah. Not in the canyon. Down here. I thought he was never supposed to come to the city," said Wid. "What do you suppose he's doing? Let's follow him."

James fell into quick step with his brother and they walked back past the library staying on their side of the street but watching over the traffic to see where Mister Davis might be going. He went first to the post office that was next to the library and came out carrying a floppy, flat package. They watched him wait for the one light, cross Twenty-first South and suddenly disappear into the black door that they didn't need to look at to know. It led to the dim of the Sugar Bowl, a blight on Mormon propriety and long standing bulge on the imaginations of the brothers and Katie to whom drinking was as unnatural and foreboding as the fire and pestilence importuned in their weekly Sunday School classes.

"What do you think he's gonna do in there?" whispered James. "Drink?"

"What else," said Wid officially, taking off his mittens and blowing on his slim hands.

"How long do you think he'll be?"

"Don't know. Wanna wait and see?"

For just over an hour the two boys took turns standing in front of Schramm-Johnson's Drug and drifting in through the revolving doors to warm up pricing footballs and soda water in the yellow haze of coal heat and hanging bulbs.

"Wid! He's out!" James shouted and kept running with the circling doors. Wid caught up half way down the block toward the railroad tracks.

"Look. He's over there, leaning on the furniture window." James pointed.

Mister Davis was a khaki monolith from his feet to his shoulders angled against the glass that outlined him like a lump of canyon mud. His pipe was unlit, his face a shadow of stubble. He pushed off into a weaving of buckled army boots and square army overcoat. Twice he raised his broad brimmed army hat by its creases and pressed it onto his forehead. The night freight was sliding through the dark toward the canyon. Mister Davis let maybe ten cars go by and then in one movement swept onto a car with his arm hugging a support, and was gone.

"I guess he's on his way back," James said almost to himself.

"Yeah. To what? How'd you like to be heading up Parley's right now—all alone?" Wid stuffed his hands into his sheepskin pockets.

"Do you think drinking helps?"

"I don't know. Wonder what was in the package? Let's go home."

Wid and James had waited till summer to tell about Mister Davis and the Sugar Bowl. At dinner in the cabin Wid asked, "Does he drink all the time Mother?"

16

"Probably more in the winter than in the summer. Loneliness is the one thing that can't go alone forever. It goes hunting company wherever it can," Mother said cutting evenly through the warm crisp crust to the soft center of the loaf she had laid on the bread board. "Just be grateful that you don't have to sleep hearing your own breathing. And be sure you always remember to ask why, not just what, when you're wondering about the things people do."

"Well, what about the post office and getting a package?" asked James. "I thought he didn't have 'a soul in the world'!" James' voice went soulful.

"That's what I understand," smiled Mother at his imitation of her, "but anybody can write for something, you know, even if it's just to see his name written by somebody else's hand. Who knows what can be ordered by mail? Some of the best and some of the worst things that ever jump into your brain come out of a mailbox."

The Hupmobile rounded the last curve before Armchair Canyon and Father leaned into the turn over the bridge. Everyone in the car leaned with him, fully awake for the first view of the gate. The road was already dusty and the bridge over the creek echoed under the tires. The faded sign "Armchair Canyon" hung above the ruts, and angled to its post was the gate. Made of quaking aspen poles, the peeled triangle rested its bottom on a squat pillar to which was affixed a leather strip with a padlock to hold the gate.

No one in the car even spoke to unlock it. Not on this time through. Mister Davis had to be in charge.

It didn't take any waiting. Before the car had billowed to a full stop, Bill Davis stood in the middle of the gate, his right arm raised, his left one massaging the smoking pipe in his teeth.

"Hello!" called Father. "How was your winter?"

"'Bout the same," Mister Davis offered, as he strolled toward Father's side of the car and bent down to look over every inch of people and load inside. "Never too much different. Lotsa snow this year. Still part of a slide up above Hickmans." He raised himself and stood with one hand on Father's window sill, a foot on the running board, with his eyes pulling his head to follow the pointings of his pipe in the other hand. "One by Rabbit's Head about gone, though. You can drive through all right. Don't know about the Ol' Hotel. And Larsen's is smashed flat. Whole roof a block down the road. Saw a mountain lion. He run when he spotted me. Up past Moon's. Run clear up to Profile Point before ya could say Jack Rob'son. Some bear tracks up by Eden in the Pines. Animals musta come way down to find food. Deer lick's worn right smooth. Musta been a hunderd deer poundin' those trails over into Lost Canyon. See maybe ten every time up the road. Henderson tried to live up there, ya know. Finished off the stone on his place, but he only lasted till Christmas. Too cold. Too deep to hike even to that first place after a couple of real storms. Your place looks good. Porch stacked up by spring, but all the doors held and no shutters fell off. Emptied the traps under the house a couple of times. Little stuff. Squirrel once. You're lucky no rats get in there."

"Did you see Shadow, Mister Davis?" exploded Katie from the back window. "Remember the cat we told you about when we left last year? The black one with the white streak on her face? The one we couldn't find when we had to go?"

Mister Davis turned to stare with his ice blue eyes at Katie. His lips almost smiled, looked as if they were trying but couldn't get past the flat edges that now puckered at his pipe. "Cat? You say cat?" he said leaning toward Katie. His pipe stayed horizontal, and to keep it that way his mouth stretched over his words and his pink tongue worked around the stem between his teeth.

"Yes," Katie persisted. "She was awful smart. And strong. And I've been thinking about her all winter expecting that you'd see her somewhere and maybe feed her something...or something." Katie trailed off, almost forgetting what she was saying in her discomfort at watching Mister Davis push one cheek closer to her to let his good ear hear

18

what she was telling him.

"Cat? Oh yeah. That big black slick-lookin' cat. Sure I saw her. Fact, she was a lot a different places, comin' out of here and there all winter. Fact, I watched her kill a rattler. Big one. Maybe from here to the bridge." Mister Davis used his pipe and drew a line in the air that would have been the longest snake anyone could ever have imagined—even longer than the ones he described all summer. "That dang cat was up there by Leigh's last fall, just 'fore the first real cold. This snake was crawlin' out of that granite shale and I wuz gonna go after him, but that cat come bouncin' out of the maples and tore into 'im. She planted her teeth right smack behind his head and just yanked and shook. Snake was flyin' all over like a whip." Mister Davis waggled his head to show the shaking. It came so close to Katie's face that she squinted and winced at having the attack take place almost on her shoulder.

"Then that black cat flopped the thing down and kinda looked at it there twitchin'. Then she picked it up by its neck and dragged it off into the bushes," continued Mister Davis.

"She took it with her?" queried Wid, who had slid toward the window from his seat on the other side of the car. "What'd she want with it?" he asked, shivering with not wanting the answer he knew he'd get from Mister Davis.

"She probly picked him clean. You know about rattle-snake meat. Best there is. Why last time I had some..."

"Mister Davis, could you maybe open the gate for us?" Mother interrupted in her most genteel and commanding way. "We have a lot of food that has to stay cold till we can get it into the stream." Katie knew exactly when her mother was going to bring anything unpleasant to a halt. Talking about snakes was bad enough; talking about eating them would sand Mother right down to nerve endings. Worst of all, exposure to such a Mister Davis story would alert her— as if she needed alerting—to more of what there was to avoid if a girl were to grow up to be any kind of a lady at all.

Mister Davis took to her low-voiced suggestion the way

everyone else did—with sudden and respectful deference. He walked his walk to the gate and creaked it open. Father drove through and stopped near the creek at the second hot spot to pamper the fuming that had almost quieted in the radiator. But this was the place for more than that. Here was the site of the first summer ritual.

Mister Davis locked the padlock and sauntered off to his cabin across the stream. The children tumbled out of the car, and while Father poured water on it they lined up on the canyon side of the gnarled gate. Wid administered the oath, declaring himself as he swore in the others.

"Everybody knows about this," he said as he took his pocket knife out of his boot-pants pocket. "First get your knives."

The three others dived for the bulges in their pants and came out holding their own knives in their fists.

"Bruv," Wid pronounced officially, "you've put a lot of notches in there, and Katie, so have you. But Davy, this is only your second time. You're old enough now to understand better what it all means." He looked at Davy, who was standing so straight his chin pulled his ears out over his collar bone. "What we do is promise we'll never go past the gate now that we're once on this side of it. No matter what, even if somebody drags us through, we don't go. That means we're here for good—for the whole summer. There's no 'city' left in us. And all the other cousins will do the same. That's how you stay in the club. So here goes with this year's notches." He walked through the line-up and to the gate. The others turned around and ceremoniously opened their knives, Davy needing help from James to pull the blade out of his.

"Never past the gate," intoned Wid holding up the point of the knife. Then he dug a careful trough into the hard bar of the gate next to dozens of others carved over too many years for him to know and moved away for James to do the same. Katie took her turn and felt more solemn than when she buried a kitten as she pressed her blade into the gray of the log and watched her notch fall to the ground. The knife was cool in her hand and she could smell the chokecherry blossoms and the black soil of the bank behind her. The creek seemed to roar in her ears and her mouth was dry. "Never past the gate," she said to her toes, and knew she would love this summer better than any she'd ever had.

Davy made his vow. "Never gassed the pate," he blurted. James looked at Katie and they were gone. In a flash so was Wid. They were consumed by the hysteria usually reserved for church or concerts. They stumbled around with their heads rolling and finally fell in the long grass by the side of the road to double up in delicious agony.

"Let's go!" called Father as he and Mother and Lena came from the front of the car. "Summer's here!"

"And so are we!" Mother added singing in falsetto, "and so are we, and so are we!" to the tune of "Finiculi Finicula," as she skipped down the dusty road to where she took the hands of a dejected Davy and swung him around to dance with her back to the car.

"What'd I say that was so funny?" he kept trying to ask. "How come they're laughing so hard?"

"I don't know," said Mother, smiling and hugging him. "But greater than the wise are those who can laugh, especially at themselves. Whatever you said, it must have been mighty jolly. It looks like you've made three crazy kids crazier than ever."

"Mother," Davy tried as he climbed back on Lena's lap. "Will I ever be as big as Wid and James?"

"Of course." Mother's smile drew inward. "You'll be as big."

"When?"

"About tomorrow, I guess."

"And when's tomorrow?"

"Tomorrow."

"Why isn't this tomorrow?"

"Yesterday it was."

"Then tomorrow will it really be tomorrow?"

"No. I'm 'fraid not. Tomorrow's a funny thing. To-morrow, tomorrow will be today. The only way tomorrow ever comes is in you. You soak up the tomorrows and call it growing." Mother's voice went hazy. "And I watch every day becoming yesterday—and call it...Whatever do you call it?" Mother looked wistfully past Davy up the Canyon. "But I guess either way, as long as we're both liking the sun to come up—on whatever day it is—that's the lucky thing."

Hope Ruskin Barton pulled a subdued but comforted Davy under her arm and snuggled him between her and Lena. The canyon had never been more lovely to her in all of her forty-one years of coming to its winding road for unwinding. As Wid and James and Katie giggled in the back in the last spasms of wan control, she reached to pat each of them somewhere and marvel at the sense of continuity that laughing in the canyon spun through her.

The Hupmobile dug into the June dust and curled with the road against the mountain. Katie watched the green tunnel open in front and then close in back as the car rounded its turns. It was even all right not to be on the running board. It was better—though she would never had admitted it—especially to Wid and James. It was better to let the canyon come by itself, not grabbing at it or having to close her eyes to squint in its wind. This way, lying on her stomach on the quilts in the back seat, she could breathe it in. "Before I know it we'll be having serviceberries and cream with Father for lunch." She winced to think of the tart first bite that would unzip her scalp, and she opened her mouth to taste the dusty breath of the canyon.

CHAPTER TWO

From the gate to Maple Fork and the cabin was exactly two miles on the speedometer. This early in June the road puffed a little under the wheels of the Hupmobile, but the dust was nothing compared to what it would be by July.

The hills were green, so dense that the stream could only be felt and heard just off the road. Mother had Father honk before each steep turn to alert any down-hill car that might be coming so that both could pull to the side and squeeze by.

Past the first curve Katie noticed the others stretch as she did to see if Mister Davis might be waiting in his cabin to watch them pass. Taboo for any of her exploring, his house was somewhere back in the thickets of willows, its taggle of smoke slim as a periscope. After it was engulfed by the birch and maple on the turn, the children could concentrate on the other landmarks.

"There's the deer lick! Boy, look at the trail up! Bet there've been a thousand deer down this year all right."

"Look at the fish pond at Henderson's. Still deep as ever. I speak first try!"

"There's Rabbit's Head!"

"There's the rock slide! Remember when we lost our knives coming down there!"

"There's the tree with the roots, still hanging on over the cliff by Moon's!"

Only Wid would dare mention the Moon Place. It was tucked back in a stand of birch and pines beyond the high dark bank that rose from the stream by the road. The black tar paper tip of its roof could be seen without walking up the narrow path to the porch. Katie wondered if Wid and James had ever been past the giant pine that grew into the path about twenty feet from the road. Daniel Moon lived there— when he was up. The whole place looked like him—sprawling, raw, dark, mean. At least that's what Katie thought he looked like. She wanted to really see him, not just from a distance. The few times he stayed in the canyon, everyone knew he was around. Fire pits would be filled with garbage. Milk buckets would have "awful stuff" floating in them. Hideouts, no matter how hidden, would be ransacked, trails would have rocks thrown on them, coolers would be turned over. She knew Wid and James had seen him enough, but they seldom talked about him as a person and barely acknowledged his place back in there. If he had any family, if anyone ever claimed an adolescent Daniel Moon, Katie had never heard about it. No family ever appeared. And neither did he much. But he was a presence, an omnipresence, that gave purpose to the building of secret huts and the stashing away of arrows and flippers.

"Here's the steepest place! Can you make it without shifting, Father?"

"Hey! There's the Armchair—right through there! Boy! Look at all the snow around it!"

"Do you think we can make it up there on the twenty-fourth? Think of the glacier we can slide!"

"There's the spring! The pipe's running. Uncle Wooster-with-the-Long-Beard must have cleaned it out."

"And there's our hill!"

Father pulled to the side of the road. "Who wants to be

the first to take the dairy things to the stream?" he asked.

"Me!" stocky twelve-year-old Wid quickly volunteered, knowing that although it was his job anyhow, it was now made an honor by Father's asking. Wid took his seniority with the same aplomb he exhibited in training snakes or operating on rats. His ease belied his skill, but it was a strange combination of deftness and unconcern that made him general of the Ruskin cousins who occupied the central cabins in Armchair Canyon.

Katie, James and Davy held on to their wanting to get out of the car too and watched Wid lift the heavy wooden box from the floor in front and disappear into the bushes and down the bank to the stream at the foot of their hill.

"Boy, it's deep this year!" he puffed coming back. I had to put the box on some rocks so the water wouldn't come over the tops of the bottles. We'll have to work on it some more later."

As he climbed in next to Katie he said, "Gee, the moss village is pretty much washed away. You'll have to start over on it again."

"What do you mean you'll? Aren't you planning to work on it?" she asked him as he ran his left hand through his tangled brown hair. The idea became more incredible in the asking. "Where are you going to be?"

Wid sighed, not uncomfortably, "There'll be other things this year."

Katie didn't dare ask what. She had never played with Wid quite like she had with James. He was over two years older than James, who was in her same grade. But Wid had always let her be around for most things, and she'd learned a lot from just watching. He let her whittle beside him—shaping arrows from wild rose bushes and whistles from kinnikinnick. She could watch him do anything with his knife except skin things. Even though James said Wid was the best skinner in the canyon—of rats, snakes, squirrels—it was all she could do just to see the skins after they were salted and stretched to be belts.

She went almost everywhere with Wid and James. When they and their cousins, Smithy, Phillip, Little Wooster and Charles went to empty traps at the rat houses, they expected that she and her girl cousins, Isabel and Jody Sue, would go along. They'd all explore the three deserted places on the way down the road. While the boys checked the traps, the girls would go through the houses, doing the regular routines like jumping to catch hold of a long pipe that ran just below the rafters of the First Rat House, then traveling its length hand over hand, legs whipping, knowing they'd get the first poppable blisters of the season there.

Every empty house had its special lures. The year before, eleven-year-old Isabel had discovered in an old dresser in the Second Rat House a partially full jar of Mrs. Plimpton's Freckle Cream. "Apply to affected areas three times a day. For best results...." The rest of the label was stained with water and "mouse tracks."

Isabel, who was Wid's age and stretching out of her chubbiness and into facial concerns, had said, "Let's take this to the tank in the gully and use it every day. And you two watch how it works."

"Do you think it's okay to use it?" asked her younger sister Jody Sue, unlike her usually uncautious self, which had more to do with her scorn for her sister's vanity than it did her concern about the taking.

"Why not?" Isabel exploded. "Certainly nobody's going to use it here!"

"That's for sure," Katie encouraged. "Not the rats at least."

Later that day the three hiked the twisty trail to the old tank above Katie's cabin. At one time the high-sided wooden rectangle had been used for water storage, but they'd always known it to be empty and had used it as one of their club-houses.

They climbed the ladder of pipes that hugged its east side, hitched onto the plank roof, and dropped through a black space into its cavernous hollow, letting their eyes adjust to the dark. As they sat leaning against one wall, they ate the vienna sausage sandwiches and carrot strips Lena had packed for their lunch.

Katie loved eating in the tank. It was having lunch in a very secret place, munching with care, talking low if at all, keeping an eye out for the intruder that might be lurking in the brush, crouching behind the maple clump, lying flat beside the stream bed—somewhere outside the stained heavy boards of the tank.

When they were through, the three, without a word or signal, stood up and took turns jumping to grab the edge of the opening and hoisting themselves to the roof. By then Isabel had carefully spread three separate layers of freckle cream over the areas of her plague, to the discerning disdain of Jody Sue and Katie. As they neared the edge and prepared to go down, Isabel stiffened.

"Did you hear that?" she whispered.

"What?" breathed the other two.

"That rattle! Listen!" Isabel mouthed.

The three were statues against the deep blue sky.

Not a sound.

"You're hearing things," said Jody Sue, adding under her breath, "as usual." Then she said boldly, "Let's go," heading again for the diving board plank that would spring them to the ground.

As Jody Sue started onto the plank, Isabel breathed a loud "Wait!"

She was staring at the rocks in the stream bed to the right of the plank. There, uncoiled but still except for its slowly swinging head, was the biggest rattler any of them had ever seen. The only thing that could have been scarier would have been Daniel Moon.

"Get back here, Jody Sue," Katie hissed.

Jody Sue edged back to the top of the tank and the three watched in horror as the snake sprawled its full length over the rocks below them.

"Where'd it come from?" asked Isabel. "There aren't

supposed to be snakes this far down by the spring."

"Sometimes there are," answered Katie. "Mother says they can be anywhere when it's this hot."

"What'll we do?" each asked the other, knowing that all they could do was wait until it went away.

They couldn't stop watching. And they couldn't believe it when, eons later, the snake began to coil and arch its head directly toward them and the plank.

"It's after us! Way up here. It's just waiting for us!" said Isabel, thunderstruck. "It'll just sit there and wait till we starve to death and have to go down."

"We could go off the other side," said Jody Sue, knowing there was no way to drop from that height unsupported without breaking something.

"Let's say our prayers," Katie suddenly said. The other two agreed so thoroughly they didn't even turn to look at her as she continued. "That snake's probably there 'cause we took the freckle cream. Let's say our prayers and promise to take it back, and see what happens."

"Good idea," agreed Jody Sue. "We never should've."

"Who'll say it?" asked Isabel.

"You, you're the oldest," Katie said without hesitation. The three kneeled at the edge of the tank, their eyes closed so tight their foreheads ruffled. Their arms were folded across their flat chests, their heads bowed, Isabel and Jody Sue with their Dutch cuts flopping over their cheeks, Katie's ringlets falling past her ribbon.

"Heavenly Father," began Isabel barely aloud, "Please excuse us for taking the freckle cream. We know it was very wrong. And we'll never do anything like that again. Promise. We'll do what's right at all times. We'll do Thy will. And please, Father in Heaven, make the snake go away. We'll be so good. So good!" Isabel's high voice went wispy. "Please Heavenly Father. In the name of Thy son Jesus Christ, Amen."

"Amen," said the other two in unison.

Gradually they raised their heads and peered toward the rocks. There was no snake. No sign of a snake.

"Where'd he go?" asked Jody Sue.

"Where do you think?" Katie answered.

The three walked the plank that didn't stir, jumped to the tree, and ran down the bumpy path to return the freckle cream.

That had happened the year before, the same summer that the boys had gone to the grotto. If she'd known about where they were going, Katie would have been with Wid and James. The only regular thing they didn't let her in on— that she knew about—was exploring by Mister Davis's. And that was because Mother had said at least three times, "Now Katie, I never want you to go to Mister Davis's place, not even with the others. And alone—not ever." But Katie still would have gone anywhere if the boys had let her.

And now, ready to pour out of the car at the foot of the hill in a new summer, she hated having her expectations tinged with the possibility of change. It irritated her to think Wid had suggested moving anywhere alone. But as she waited, her alarm at thinking Wid would be too big to make a moss village disappeared as he nudged her and James at the same time and said, "Hey, let's run up the hill! Can we, Father?"

"How about me too?" asked Davy scrambling off Lena's lap and getting out. "I can run faster 'n anybody."

The four took the steep hill, with its ruts and high center, as easily as the Hupmobile had. All wore the same outfits—a short-sleeved shirt with an open collar, starched even for the canyon, and a pair of "boot-pants" with sides like elephant ears that buttoned tight from knee to ankle to tuck into boots laced on hooks. This year Wid's boots were new, a gift from Grandma; the rest were half-soled and fitted to whoever had moved into their size. Davy had four pair waiting between him and Katie.

Mother always said, "You never want to go into the bushes in low shoes." So every morning four pair of boots would be lined up on the warming oven of the stove toasting their soles for the cold feet that would scramble into them before breakfast.

The boots knew exactly what route to take up the hill. Zig-zagging from one good push-off to another, the children leaned low and bounced ahead of the car to the white-sided cabin watching for them with its snub nose porch and wings spread-eagling in the maples against the red mountain.

"I speak to unlock!" Davy shouted as they panted off the road and onto the narrow trail to the front door.

"The swings are still up and so's the log cabin!" Whee-oo-ing, James veered as if he were falling from the porch and into a small clearing above. In one motion he snatched the fat knotted rope that hung from the elm and darted to the low roof of last year's building project, a five-by-seven-foot dirt-floored house of logs covered with the gray slick one by eights that had been the sides of the old "place out on the trail."

"I'm swinging from the boards that came from 'the place out on the trail,'" he intoned as he set himself for his swing, chuckling at introducing Mother's euphemistic terminology. He was tempted to say from the "outhouse" just to hear Mother say, "Oh, James, that's so plebeian!" Mother believed in delicacy, and no one was ever to mention anything about such a destination except in emergencies very late at night, and then only by whispering, "I need to go out on the trail."

Mother's vocabulary was a lot like her body—soft, plump and white. The whole family had come to use words gentle on her sensitivities: Hot dogs were wienies. A smell was a strange perfume. People weren't rich, they were fairly well-to-do. "Katie," she always reminded her explosive daughter, "horses sweat, men perspire—and ladies feel the heat." And no one ever died, they "left us." Not one person outside the family or circle of her girlhood friends did Mother ever call by a first name. The next-door neighbors of thirty years were still Brother and Sister Salinger. How it was Mother who was invariably called by everyone in the family to kill any rattlesnake that dared the premises would have been a mystery if they hadn't all seen her do it. She would charge out of the cabin holding a shovel taller than herself and follow the "crawler" anywhere to "do away with it." The only thing more daring was her sometimes reciting the verse the children had to grow into understanding. "Give us your racy verse, Flossie," Father would tease so that she'd chant:

"Go to Father," she said
When he asked her to wed,
And she knew that he knew
That her father was dead,

And she knew that he knew
What a life he had led,
So she knew that he knew
What she meant when she said,
    "Go to Father."

It had been a semantical labyrinth for Father and the boys to report their progress in tearing down the old place out on the trail and building a new one.

"Wid," Father would say, "carry these old boards out by the woodpile and leave the best ones to build a roof on the log cabin. But ask Mother if she wants any of them to use as supports under the washstand."

So Wid would ask Mother, "Mother, do you want any boards?"

"What boards, dear?"

"Ones from the place out on the trail."

"The new one or the old one?"

"Boards?"

"No, place out on the trail."

"Old boards from the old place."

"Where did they come from? I mean what part of the old place?"

"The sides I think, but we're using them mostly for a roof for the log cabin."

"I think I'd like to use just the roof unless you have some new ones."

"I'll ask Father."

"Where is he?"

"Out on the trail."

"Building?"

"No, still tearing down."

"Well, I'll just yoo hoo if I want something."

"Boards?"

"No, Father."

The log cabin had its roof pounced on as part of their swing-building summer. The cousins had all been either Tarzan or Jane, depending on their willingness to take flight, and one of the best series of leaps, swings, and grabs started from there.

James scrambled now up the ends of the logs to the roof, pounded his chest, shrilled "Tar-Man-gan-ie!" and swept onto the top knot of the rope.

Churning at the highest point of his swing, he let go to fly toward another rope hanging just out of arm's reach. Turning in mid-air, coming down with hands out and knees spread, he grabbed the next waiting rope from enough of an angle to give it momentum. Back once, forward again, and he was swooping out on the swinging rope fifty feet from the log cabin into a tree that bowed and quivered as he landed on its forked limbs. "Tar-Man-gan-ie!" he boomed. Wid and Katie and Davy lined up on the roof for their turns. Katie's hands could feel the rope, and she wanted to be were James was.

"Come get a load, you loafers," Father called from the car. "Let's get her opened up."

Opening the cabin under Mother's supervision was an all-day project.

"Just be patient," Father kept saying. "Mother knows about these things."

"If only Father were in charge of this, we'd be done by

now," Katie sighed to James as they tacked down the rugs on the long porch. They'd been cleaning and carrying since eleven o'clock, and it was now five, and there was no end anywhere in sight.

"I want to get up to Larsen's and see what the snow-slide did," she said. "If Mister Davis says the roof's clear down the road, the rest of it must be flat as a pancake."

"Flatter," said James. "Remember the Bluebird? There were piles of split furniture and stuff sticking up through the snow like warts."

"When do you think we'll be done with all this? Mother's jobs never end. And Isabel and Jody Sue are probably up there now. And Charles and maybe Phillip too. Maybe Father will let us take off for just a few minutes and finish when we come back."

"Ho, you know better. You get your work done first, remember? Like Grandma Barton taught him, 'Work hard so you can play hard.'" James sing-songed his reminder. "We might as well just start tacking faster." And he popped a handful of tacks into his mouth to be spit out one at a time as he'd seen the real carpenter do on Smithy's hut.

Mother worked in the kitchen with Lena, who stood like a shoestring potato, stiff and brittle, sloping in at both extremities. She wore paisley wrap-arounds and had straight black hair around the face of an eagle. As terse as she was quick, she could iron a starched shirt in seven minutes. Now twenty-four, she had come from Heber at seventeen to live with the Bartons. During the Depression most of the families in the canyon had a girl staying with them to help out, usually one wanting even as little as a dollar a week to get to the city to become something else. Not many girls stayed more than a season, just until they found a school or job or husband. Lena's seven years with the Bartons was a record.

Lena and Mother emptied the cupboards closed in by yellow and red checkered curtains on drawstrings, dumping dust out of the giant crocks that would store flour and sugar, moving the wood boxes, sweeping the stove and its ovens. There was no sink because there was no running water except for the tap on the back wash porch, and it was not fit for drinking. The dishpans were on the oilcloth shelf filled with water heated in the cast aluminum kettle on the stove, their oily suds constantly renewed from the red and white box of granulated White King.

Father and Wid had taken down the shutters that had boarded all the screened windows for winter and had stacked them under the cabin, which was built on stilts in front to let it sit high against the mountain for the sun and the view. With mops made from old towels and garments, they mopped all the floors that the others had swept, and everyone had a turn at beating the rugs hung over the outside railing by the front door. The thin orientals that had been worn down by the traffic at Grandma's old house on Ninth East dangled above the path to the downstairs. The one who was beating selected a place below to stand and swing mightily with the wicker beater. The dust rose with gun powder news to cabins clear around the mountain that the Bartons were moving in.

James and Katie had made up the beds after the coil springs had been dusted and mattress protectors laid over them. The bedding from the car was sorted like a dowry, each quilt and blanket belonging to a special bed. The sheet blankets smelled of just having been washed by hand on the board at home and hung in the sun in the back yard to dry.

"Pull that corner straight," Katie kept prompting James. "You know how mother feels about mitering corners."

"James, you have lackadaisical tendencies," Grandma often said to him, rubbing his curly hair and hugging him while he hugged her. As a little boy he'd rush in from roller skating or climbing the apple tree, hunt Mother or Grandma down and issue his quick command: "I came in for some lovings." Then, after the tightest hug possible on either side, he'd leave saying, "Thank you, that's better now."

Because of his maneuverings, Mother found it hard to use the "little willow" to settle James' infractions of anything.

34

When the others didn't mind or talked "smartie," the little willow came out of the broom closet to "tingle their legs" into remembering how polite and thoughtful children should behave. Alert to the ways of getting along, they recognized and acquiesced to Mother's willow. But, despite her admonishment that "a man who lacks responsibility is utterly useless," James could always work around punishment as he did around work. "My magazine route took so long today! Sorry I didn't get through in time to help with the lawn. Boy, I wanted to, but you should see how much I collected!"

On this opening day James had managed to make four trips to the car while Wid and Katie had made six. But he had taken Davy for a quick look at the traps under the house, and they had checked out last year's golf course to see if any of the holes were still playable. There they had shaved the long grass with shovels and flattened two ten-foot fairways where they drove the nicked balls Uncle David had given them with their hiking sticks turned upside down to make clubs.

Now, having tacked one side of the rug while Katie had tacked three, James suggested, "Hey, you know what? I'll bet Father would really like it if we checked out the pipeline. Why don't we get Wid and take a quick run along it to look for leaks?"

"Yeah, it's bound to need some attention," agreed Katie, managing not to smile, knowing exactly where the pipeline led and exactly how long it would take them to run its length and look over the rubber inner tube wrappings that plugged the multiple breaks in the rusty, corroded line.

"You think you need to take a look, huh?" Father said, not smiling either, just keeping his eye on the guy wire he was tightening to hold one of the tin chimneys straight. "That might not be a bad idea. How many do you think it will take?"

"Probably three of us," Wid volunteered, dropping from the roof at the back of the house. "Do you think you can get along without me for a minute?"

"Maybe for a minute. Tell them hello across the path."

The three dashed around the house on their softest soles, not wanting Davy to slow them down or Mother to stop them entirely. It took six minutes to follow the pipeline around the mountain to Fairy House where it sank under the road, then another two to trace it to its source, the fat barrel filled by the creek just below Martha's.

"Not too many leaks this year," Wid pronounced. "Not too many at all."

"Now that we're this close it seems like we ought to just sort of take a look at what's happened to Larsen's, don't you think?" suggested James nonchalantly.

"Oh, yeah!" Wid pretended to marvel. This *is* fairly close to there, isn't it?" Only a couple of curves away."

"I speak first in," Katie called as they started their run up the stream to intersect the road.

They whisked to the turn into Royal Park, entered its grassy road with its trickle stream, took a quick detour to rise through the air—three pumps worth—on the board of the rope swing, cut back to the main road, walked a chubby aspen that had fallen beside the road, dashed into the parking place of Armchair Lodge to see if there was a fish in the pond, plunged out through the bushes by Morgan Dell, and broke into a full run at the foot of the curve that adjoined Larsen's.

Sure enough. The place was smeared into its foundations, some of it still buried under snow and small parts of trees that had been smashed and carried by the slide.

"Boy, look at that!" James said as they stared from the flattened cabin to the swath of barren mountainside above it.

"You can't believe something like that could really happen! I mean, how could anything be that powerful!" Wid agreed, always fascinated with the workings of things.

Katie had started examining the debris. "Look, a sewing machine—and the treadle for it's clear over here. And pots and pans—everything, everywhere!"

Still standing and looking, Wid said slowly, "It makes you kinda sick, doesn't it. All their stuff just ruined. Boy, what would we do if that ever happened to our place?"

36

"Yeah. Even if you rebuilt it you could never make any of it the same," Katie mused, pausing for a minute to picture the emptiness. "What would you do?"

James had worked his way to the far side of the heap, bent like the others from the waist to be sure to see what was under him. "Hey, look at this!" He drew out of the snow a big disc. "A record. Lots of 'em." He struggled to free a metal rack that still held most of its records packed firmly together with snow.

"They're probably ruined, don't you figure?" James asked, already hefting the rack toward Wid.

"Sure," agreed Katie. "They'd have to be. All that wetness plus the weight."

"They'd ruin any needle they touched. Nobody'd want them the way they are," said James reaching to share his load with Wid.

"That's for sure. What do you think ought to become of them?" Wid asked, knowing James would have an answer he wasn't ready to generate.

"Well, I was just thinking. Remember the way those cardboard plate liners used to sail off the garage?"

"I'll say," said Katie. "They'd take off like they had motors. Remember how they'd dip and then soar way up?"

"And these'd be twice as good. They're so heavy they'd sail a mile!" grinned Wid. "But where would we sail them from?"

"L. G.," answered James as if he'd been planning it for a week. "It's right on our way home. We can just cut over there from Hickman's and it won't even be uphill."

"And then we can get right down to the path and be home in nothing flat," Wid laughed, "so fast that Father'll really be surprised."

James doled out records to each of the others to carry and they sped down the road to the path through Hickman's, and from there across the mountain, over the white rocks to two boulders, one backing the other to leave a flat smooth surface to walk out on. How the two rocks ever came to be called L. G. no one really knew. "I think it stands for Lilly and Gish," Mother had told them, "but it could also mean Let's Go," which seemed more likely to the cousins since they had never heard of Lilly and Gish, who, in their opinion, hardly deserved the distinction of having one of the best rocks in the canyon named for them.

"OK, here she goes!" James announced, taking a record between his thumb and fingers, turning his shoulder to the canyon below and flipping his arm from across his stomach. The record mounted the sky like a hawk, slow, arching, then dived for a few yards, looked as if it would fall, but caught some current and rose again, far down the canyon to fly clear past Uncle Wooster's and finally land somewhere by the stream a mile below them.

"Gee! Did you see that!" chortled Wid. "Wow! With this breeze they ought to get to the platform. I wish we could hear what happens when they land!" He picked a heavy record off the top of his stack and sent it zipping over the tops of the trees.

"I'm going to try mine from this side," said Katie when it was her turn. And she whisked a record from below her knees out into the sky that was almost purple over Eagle Rock Mountain rising across the canyon.

The three tried every throw they knew and some they contrived on the spot—overhand, underhand, standing backwards, sidewards. Each record took a different course. The children were in an ecstacy of illicit ingenuity. When the last flight had soared out of sight, they looked at each other and laughed till their sides burned. No one said anything. Wid was the first to find control in turning away, then Katie, then James. Together they plunged down the rocks to the road, shouted a running "Yoo hoo" to Leigh's, Grandma's and Uncle Phillip's cabins, and tore across the path home.

"Well, Father, we made it in *record* time," said James not daring to look at the others, knowing they were biting their lips just as he was, trying to look serious and ready for work.

"Great," said Father. "I guess the pipeline's in good shape

for all the attention it got."

"I'll say," said Wid. "Only a couple of places need rubber. We'll get those tomorrow."

"I'll cut the strips from the inner tube tonight if you want," offered Katie.

"Sweet as a win, all of you," said Father. "What have you been up to?"

"Us?" asked James, wrinkling his brow. "Us?"

"Oh no, never. Not you," smiled Father. "Now get back to your jobs." He gave each a glancing paddle and aimed Wid toward the shovel leaning against the box that housed the prickly fir tree by the front porch. "The whole yard has rocks all over it. Shovel them into the wheelbarrow and square the edges of the path."

Just then Davy came tearing around the corner of the house. "Where'd you all go?" he huffed. "You went somewhere without me again, didn't you?"

"We just went to check the pipeline for Father," reported Wid. "Come on. You can work with me on these rocks. Just start picking 'em up and I'll give you a ride in the wheelbarrow when we go to dump them."

Davy brightened and began tossing rocks without rising to see where they were landing. "You guys don't know what a fast one I am. But you'll see!"

By dark the house looked cozy and ready for living. Lena had heated creamed corn and Mother had made buttermilk biscuits and peach cobbler for supper. The family sat across from each other at the long table in the dining room, a screened-in arm of the cabin that let the sun hit the table all day and the stars be seen at night. They all had on their worn sweaters saved for the canyon, Father his bulky red one with the big U on the pocket and the rolled collar. Mother was in her smock, a billowy blue calf-length house dress, and a belted purple sweater mended and mended at the elbows in her minute stitching.

"Are you ready for the blessing?" Father asked everyone as the boys helped Mother and Katie sit first and then drew their wooden benches up to the table and bowed their heads. "Wid, will you tonight?"

Wid began with only a nod to say he would. "Father in Heaven, please bless this food that it will nourish and strengthen our bodies. We're grateful for it and for all the other blessings that we enjoy. Please help us to always be good and to deserve all that we have. We're thankful for each other and for this place to come to. In the name of Jesus, Amen."

"Wid, we're awful lucky." Father was serious for only a minute. Then he said, "Who wants a piece of chocolate cake? Wouldn't that be a splendiferous way to start this meal?"

"Wouldn't it, though," smiled Mother. "Just the thing for appetites and growing!" She reached over to touch Father's thick shoulder. "You'd have chocolate in your soup if you could, you boobie. Your sweet tooth is going to be the ruination of everybody—especially their expectations."

"What better than to expect?" he teased. "And what sweeter?"

After dinner Katie helped Lena with the dishes in the tight, warm kitchen while Father laid a fire in the living room stove. That stove had made the Mormon trek across the plains in 1847 together with the stilt rocker and the pump organ. It was tall and slender with a shining grillwork fence around the shelf above its scroll legs. On top of its isinglass door was more grillwork, and its chimney rose to an elbow, then up through the ceiling with a handle in it to damp the heat. Under it was a zinc sheet to protect the black tongue-in-groove floor that now shone like a dark mirror with being mopped. The brass poster bed in the corner was for Mother and Father, but Wid and James stretched out on their stomachs there now to play checkers by the fire till bedtime at nine.

Lena and Katie brought in oatmeal cookies and chocolate pudding with yellow cream and coconut over it served

40

in the frilled and flowered dishes that came in the Quaker Oats box.

"Katie, how about playing 'Danny Boy' to sort of start the season right?" Father asked, sitting back in the oak rocker with the high back.

Katie loved him to ask. She knew and would always know only three pieces, "Dee Ooo Lee Ay," which she had learned for Grandma, "Liebestraum" in a simplified version, which was Mother's song, and "Danny Boy" which was Father's. She went to the old black organ by the wall and sat gingerly on its round stool, twirling herself four times to be high enough to reach the keys and still be able to push the pumps. Before she touched the keyboard she depressed here and there a stop labled in German, as if she knew what each would accomplish. All the time she pumped the angled square pedals to start the wind through the organ. Finally she began the intriguing arrangement that made her feel primly accomplished, one that demanded that her left hand cross over her right to make chords above while the melody rippled simple and smooth under her right fingers.

The notes floated to the exposed rafters of the big room, past the pictures of patriots and pioneers, over the coal oil hand painted chandelier that blinked with the fire. They settled on the bookcase above the Victrola, over the tacked rug, onto the corner table and the window held open by a yardstick. They spread to the water bucket in the dining room, across the bear skin on the floor in front of the fire, over Davy and "The Honey Bear" book on the little red chair beside it, to Wid and James on the bed. As "Danny Boy" drifted off the flag hanging from the highest beam, down finally to Mother in her rocker with socks stacked in her lap for mending and to Father with a year-old Reader's Digest folded in his, Katie played with her heart yanking at her throat. The canyon days were here. She could feel the fire at her back snapping in the stove. Father must have added some stringy wood from last year. The shadows of the flames ricocheted off the wall and the rough roof and licked toward her in the rhythm of the music and her pumping. "I'm making the fire move with my feet and hands," she thought. "I'll pump it anywhere I want it to go. It's my fire. See, it works any way I want it to." She sped up her thrusts on the pedals. "There it goes," she mouthed, "with 'Danny Boy,' right up and down the whole canyon." The fire flooded her. It was beginning. Summer was just beginning. In a little bit she and the boys would undress by the fire and go in their slippers and warm bathrobes down the dark path to their downstairs room by Lena's. In the cold they would kneel for their prayers. The boys would wrestle in their bed till they fell asleep. In her bed, Katie would look out the screen and watch the ridge above the Crow's Nest give itself to the sky. She would recite under her hushed breath "Star light, Star bright, First star I see tonight. Wish I may, Wish I might, Have the wish I wish tonight." And then it would be morning, the first morning of a new season, and she'd never be able to remember what she had wished.

That night Katie's recitation drifted not to a wish but into the words that she knew her skimpy singing voice would never dare let out loud: "Oh Danny Boy, the pipes are calling. Across the glenn and down the mountain side..."

Around the mountain, across the path, Jody Sue and Isabel would be moved up with their family; Uncle Wooster would be bringing Goldie to the field for Little Wooster and Charles to saddle; Leigh's family with Phillip and Arthur would be clearing the horseshoe pit; Grandma would be coming up into her place in a few days when she got back from the Snake River with Uncle David. Down the road, Smithy and his folks would be opening their immaculate green cabin; farther down the hill Nephi would maybe put the tether ball up again—the old tennis ball wrapped in material and strung by a rope to the top of the sawed-off aspen; maybe Cousin Ann would be planning a taffy pull in Brookbee with the pine trees growing up through the floor and ceiling. Daniel Moon might even be up—Daniel Moon whose huge legs couldn't move fast enough to keep up with his destruc-

tion and whose bulbous hands couldn't throw a rock far
enough to hit even Davy—Daniel Moon, the Enemy, who
ruined everything he discovered. And down by the gate,
Mister Davis would be tamping his ashes, full of knowing
where everything and everybody was.

Katie drifted with the words of the song:
"And if you come, and maybe I am dying
or even dead, as dead I well may be,
Then you will search and find where I am lying
and kneel and say an avé there for me.
And I will hear, though soft you tread above me
And all my grave will warmer, sweeter be
And you will bend and whisper that you love me
And I will rest in peace until you come to me."

The sky came through the screen and lifted Katie softly
into its deep cave.

CHAPTER THREE

Within three days the whole canyon was organized. The cousins had assayed the possibilities of building: lumber from Larsens' could be used, nails pounded out of the boards could be straightened, sites on both sides of the canyon could be utilized to allow for handy escape no matter where the Enemy might show up. This year would be a good time to take to the trees—and go underground. In the hollow up from the Barton's, three aspen grew in a perfect triangle—just right for a two-story hut, the roof of which would be ideal for signaling across the canyon to the platforms high in the pines above Grandma's. In a flash somebody could climb to either and send a scout flag warning about danger. They'd just be sure to do all their building after Mister Davis had made his trip past the cabins every day.

Also, Uncle Wooster had come up with his best surprise yet—the disembodied cab of a truck. He had deposited it between his cabin and the stream to be used in any way the cousins might contrive. Uncle Wooster had a fine eye for surprises that a less imaginative man would fail to see possibility in.

A man of motors, he liked anything that ran. Sometimes he drove up in front of the house on Crystal Avenue in a bus. So big that he flowed over the driver's seat, he'd open the door and call "All abo—ard! Scamper on you kids! Take your places one and all. Just sit right down and follow this beacon right here." And he'd swirl his hand over his slick bald head and roar the motor. Loaded with everyone the Barton children could find, the bus would pull away with arms and heads out of half the windows to see miners in Bingham scooping for copper, a new contraption called a ski lift at Alta, or a university team playing in the stadium. In the canyon that was more his home than the one on Douglas Street, he kept horses for his own family and for anyone else who wanted a ride. "The thing about when Uncle Wooster comes up the canyon is that he never just comes," James told Katie. "There's always something with him—like new horseshoes for the pit last week or the gas that we got to siphon into the generator...or who knows what."

Uncle Wooster had a lean-to shack near the parking place by his cabin that was locked tight as a fist unless he was in there fussing with the belts and wheels that turned when he put gas in the tank. Then three cabins had lights and electricity—his, Uncle Phillip's and Grandma's. Everybody else burned coal oil lamps, ironed with flat irons heated on the stoves, and swept rugs or used roller brooms. But his wife, Aunt Lucina, entertained by Chinese lanterns and cooked on coils and even had a Frigidaire. Nothing was too fancy for her, or ever satisfactory. And the cousins went for weeks seeing parties come and go and watching the smooth brown bottles disappear from the stream under the bridge.

There were three generations of Woosters in the canyon: Uncle Wooster-with-the-Long-Beard, who was Uncle to Uncle Wooster; then Uncle Wooster, who with slender, brusque Aunt Lucine had one son of their own, Little Wooster. He wore chaps every day—real leather ones with an eight-inch fringe—and a cowboy hat, except when he was indoors. He smiled most of the time but always looked

46

puzzled. At twelve, his face was round and soft under two rises on a square, high forehead. His smile drew his cheeks up and gathered them around his light brown eyes, and the puckering formed three thin ravines above his arched nose. His hands were small, pawlike, and could pull a cinch so tight that even Goldie's wily bloating gave way when he strained at her saddle. But his sturdy chest and trunk dwindled into legs that looked and worked like triangular stilts. He had been born with club feet that now clumped and scuffed as he labored to go where the others went.

Uncle Wooster had brought him two measures of compensation: an adopted brother, Charles, to keep him company, and horses to take him where he wanted to go. Charles, though, chafed at any staying with Little Wooster, and a horse was too much for most of the uncut trails the cousins chased over, so Little Wooster spent a lot of time waiting. Wid, who was his age, was his best friend and stayed as much as he could manage. "You just go on, Wid," Little Wooster told him every time, "but be sure you get back quick. I gotta show you my new knots." And Wid, when he left, ran his hardest, wondering why his face burned.

How Charles felt about going or staying no one knew. Katie would have given anything to dare ask him about that, but even more about the orphanage. She pictured whippings and the dark goings-on of Oliver Twist whenever they passed the bulky red brick building behind its giant pines on Twenty-first South. Uncle Wooster, on another of his explorations, had found Charles there in a line in the front parlor and had picked him out for his lack of sameness to anyone he'd ever seen.

To Katie he was intriguing. His smile reminded her of a turtle—always there, always the same. Sometimes his lips parted and showed teeth, but they never changed shape, and only deepened his soberness. He had black curly hair and dark eyes that slanted slightly to make him look like an Indian—or, then again, like a turtle. Maybe it was because his eyes were that way—sort of squinting as if he were measuring some private distance—that made him deadly accurate with a bow and arrow or horseshoes. He was the same age as James but taller and much more wiry. He moved in and out of the cousins' doings like a badger, bouncing off their activities or hovering just far enough off to keep them on target.

No one knew how Aunt Lucine felt about the adoption, only that Charles said things like, "It's as hard to get her to like you as it is to get anything but old stuff to wear." Then his lips would move away from his teeth and it was hard to tell if he expected a laugh or sympathy. Everyone knew everything he wore was brand new.

Sometimes Charles disappeared for an afternoon and everyone suspected him of going down the road to the Moon cabin, maybe even to consort with Daniel Moon. Whether or not he did was pure speculation, but the idea that Charles would chance such an affiliation made him both awed and disdained. No one asked where he went; neither did they exile Charles from their regular projects. It was better to have him where he could be watched than somewhere conniving for their ruination.

Casualness persisted in their constant alert for the Enemy, but wherever they went, the cousins were on the lookout, always reporting with informed aplomb.

"I noticed bushes moving down by Rockwood's when I crossed the path this afternoon," James would say.

"And I know there were noises in the trees by the tank when we went up there yesterday," Wid informed.

"That's nothing," Smithy would state. "There were tracks all across our back yard this morning—great big ones—and they didn't belong to any animal!"

Little Wooster never looked straight ahead even going to dinner. "You hear that?" he'd ask Charles, stopping, and cocking his eyes and head toward something. Charles always said, "Hah!" but invariably looked when Little Wooster wasn't watching.

Like the huts and the undergrounds, the swings had been built as a handy escape from the always imminent danger, and not even a hike was ever simply a hike: It was a reconnoitering. Pocket knives, too, were for making flippers and arrows or whistles to use as weapons and alarms.

When the cousins began to dig the underground, they gathered the picks, shovels, and axes from all their cabins and chose a square in the thimbleberry patch below Uncle Wooster's. "If we dig it here, Little Wooster will be able to help us," Wid announced, stepping off a square eight by eight. Isabel, Jody Sue, Katie and Phillip, who was a year younger than Katie but old enough to be eligible for the club, began the clearing. First the shrubbery had to be hacked out with the axe, then the roots loosened. Then Wid, James, Smithy, and Charles began work in pairs behind Little Wooster who was put in charge of the pick to loosen the ground for the shovelers.

However, they had learned to watch him. Two summers before, Wid had been too close when Little Wooster threw the long point over his shoulder. It had caught Wid across the head. Luckily It had been a slanting blow, but it had opened a gash across Wid's scalp that oozed orange red. He'd had to be taken down to the city to have it stitched up. The whole way, he said, he had kept his eyes closed so he wouldn't break the pact of going past the gate.

The rest of that day no one could persuade Little Wooster to work with them again. Until Wid came back up late in the afternoon laughing and telling what a great experience he'd had, Little Wooster had just sat on the edge of the shallow hole staring at the pick beside him, the end with Wid's blood on stuck deep into the ground.

"I shouldn't a hit ya," he kept saying. Wid sat beside him and tried to pull the pick out of the ground.

"Boy, you sure are strong, Little Wooster. I can't budge that thing. Pull it out, will you?"

Little Wooster stood up and yanked the pick loose. "What d'ya want it out for, Wid? It hurt ya, ya know."

"Yeah. But it was my fault. I was so dumb—working right up there too close behind you. I sure should've known better." He pulled the pick toward him. "I sure hope it didn't hurt the pick!" He rubbed the pointed end of it. "Hey, it might've. Look, it's bleeding!"

He turned laughing to Little Wooster who looked perplexed for a minute and then started to laugh too as Wid punched him on the arm and said, "Just take it easy on the tools, OK? Quit eating so many Wheaties! We gotta do something to control your strength!"

Now each cousin took turns saying, "You're great with that pick, Little Wooster." And Little Wooster would grin, look back, and take another Paul Bunyan swing at the ground. The others came behind him, pushing their shovels into the softened earth with the arches of their boots and throwing the dirt and rocks over their right shoulders. They'd uncover a layer about a foot deep, following each other around, then begin another.

The ones who had done the clearing then had the job of shaving branches to weave together for a covering. When the underground was deep enough—about four feet—it would be canopied with the woven willows, branches of leaves, and finally dirt to make a camouflaged roof that was not nearly so sturdy as it was impeccably manicured to fool the Enemy into never noticing it was there.

Usually the entrance to an underground was through some splendidly designed trap door in the roof that almost always was too soon responsible for a cave-in of the topping, never engineered to hold up through the comings and goings of nine wriggling escapees from an Enemy more terrible because of his lack of definition.

"Let's make a better entrance this time—one that'll hold for all summer—and be easy to get in and out of," pleaded Smithy, to the agreement of all.

"How, though?" wondered Wid. "We can't go up the hill further—the dirt will all just run down into the underground."

"And we can't go further out 'cause of the stream," noted James.

"How about a tunnel?" asked Isabel.

"To where?" questioned Jody Sue.

"I don't know—just somewhere away from the pit."

"Well, like we said, it can't go up there or there or over there," Wid said, pointing three ways.

"How about up there, then," persisted Isabel, who always had ideas.

"We'll just bump into the truck cab up there," Wid said.

"But it's almost level. It'd make a swell tunnel," said James, backing away and stooping to survey the terrain.

"Yeah," said Katie, wanting to agree, "but what about the truck cab?"

"Hey!" exploded Wid, "I know. We could go under the cab and come up inside it. Boy! That would be slick!"

"Yeah," joined James. "Come up inside under the floor. We could hinge the floor boards and nobody — nobody — would ever discover our entrance!"

"Sure!" said Little Wooster blinking slowly. "Sure!" And he started off with the others to walk the straightest distance to the cab.

They executed the tunnel idea with the dispatch of ants. James and Wid cut out and reconnected the floor boards with hinges off the door to the log cabin, which by now didn't need a door anyhow, while the others dug the tunnel about half the depth of the main room. "It's best if we go in on our stomachs. That way we won't take a chance of bumping the ceiling and ruining it."

The tunnel was smoothed, its sides squared to precision, and each cousin took a turn slithering along it to drop hands and head first into the main room, two feet down. By the time nine of them had tried it, the tunnel was soft and fast, its end a rounded plunge to the firm floor of the big square. Even Little Wooster could scoot on his elbows along the hollow and drop beaming into the crowd.

Before any roof went on, the place was furnished. A rug from Isabel's far bedroom, a mattress from the unused cot in the Bartons' downstairs porch, a frying pan from Phillip's, an oil lamp that Aunt Lucine had discarded, a pillow and blanket from Smithy's hut. Smithy was eleven, thin and inventive but often sick. His father, who was very old—"at least fifty" according to Wid—had decided the summer before that his only child should have a hut of his own to invite his cousins to. So his father, Uncle Thatcher, had hired it built, resplendent with new lumber, square corners, and unblemished antiseptic furnishings. Everyone had visited there once, run fingers over the smooth surfaces, said "Gee — that's swell" and had never gone back. Smithy had wandered in and out often when he knew his father was noticing but soon found ways to slip away to grubby building with the cousins.

The final refinement of the underground before roofing was the fire pit. If Indians and Eskimos could make smoke rise through a hole above a center, surely they could too. The cousins dug their pit right through the carpet and laid a careful fire. "Works great, doesn't it," they'd say through squinched eyes, thinking of devious ways to protect their noses. If anyone started coughing there came a noble and always acceptable excuse to leave like "I think I hear Mother calling."

So the roof went on. It was stretched, pinned down, its willows covered with layer after layer of foliage and dirt, then patted, raked, distressed with rocks and the leavings of the dig to look as if no human foot—let alone hand—had ever been near it. Even thimbleberry stalks were replanted in the surrounding soil to throw the Enemy off the scent—or sight.

"For sure!" chortled Davy, invited to secret inspection. "You couldn't see it from the road if you tried!" And boy did I try! I been over there lookin' for a hour!"

For the next few days no excursion went past Uncle Wooster's without someone peeling off, tearing across the bridge, diving through the door of the cab, raising the trap door, and disappearing into the black of the tunnel. The others appeared not to notice the absence of a comrade and would ask an unimportant question as he or she rejoined the ranks en route to somewhere, everyone smugly acknowledging in silent composure the success of this underground as the best hideout yet.

To have an underground this safe was better even than having a fort. But it still had to be slept in. Every secret place had to be tried at night.

The night they decided to see if they could, the Barton children thought they'd wait until after dinner to make their proposition to Mother. "I wish we could wait till Father gets up from the city. He's awful different about things like this than Mother," said Wid.

"Sure, but it's got to be tonight, and if you do it right she'll listen. Besides, I've got an idea." James wandered toward the back door and disappeared.

"What's he up to?" asked Katie. "Mother's on the porch painting the rockers."

"Let's go back and watch. He's got something up his sleeve," said Wid, and they both headed through the kitchen and dining room and out onto the long screened porch where Mother was finishing the last leg of a now Chinese red chair, chatting with Lena about Grandma's coming up the next day.

"Boy, those chairs sure look swell," Wid said, walking around two of them giving them detailed inspection.

"I'll say!" agreed Katie examining them from every angle that Wid had neglected.

"How's your underground coming?" Mother asked, pursing her lips in rhythmic concentration on her brush.

"Swell, just swell," they both said in such concert that Mother looked up and smiled.

"Good. It's not going to cave in this time, is it?"

"Oh, no," chirped Wid. "In fact, it's by far the safest we've ever built. Not a chance. We braced everything so well. We even used reinforcements in the roof."

"Reinforcements? In the roof? You haven't covered it over have you? After what happened to the last one? And you're not lighting anything in there are you—candles or lamps or anything?"

Wid and Katie slipped each other looks, and Katie swallowed no saliva waiting to hear Wid's reply.

"Oh, you know how you brace the sides of the pit, with two by four's—sort of *reinforce* them," he suggested, turning his head toward and away from Mother at the same time to look convincing. "And no, no there hasn't been anything lit around the underground that you'd ever call dangerous—nothing at all."

Katie put the back of her hand over her mouth at the last comment. She had learned to revere her brothers' ability to tell the truth by not mentioning a thing or two.

Just then a voice dropped from the sky and all of them raised their eyes to the roof to see where it came from. "Hello, Mother, this is your favorite second son speaking. I'm delivering a special message from on high." Only the top of James was visible, upside down, leaning over the roof to peer through the screen. That side of the house was thirty feet above the ground and the roof sloped at a forty-five degree angle to let the snow slide off in the winter.

Mother took a deep breath. "What are you holding on to, Mister High?"

"My sense of humor—like you always told me to." James looked funny all right, his mouth upside down, working like a puppet's, his eyes curved downward, his blond curly hair hanging down like the plume of Mother's fancy pen, his hands showing white knuckles clutching the edges of the shingles.

"James Barton, I want you to go carefully back up that roof and then march straight down here. I want to talk to you." Mother had her calm, firm voice on.

"I want to talk to you too, Mother. That's why I'm here. A little bird told me that the underground is finished. And we all know that the only way to initiate it is to sleep in it overnight. So I thought I'd just ask you from here."

"Why from there?"

"'Cause I figured nothing would look dangerous after this—especially sleeping out in the underground."

"James, you may be right," Mother's tone was full of conciliation. "Just get down here and we'll see."

They all knew Mother knew there was no way that James' plan wouldn't work. The more unlikely his contrivances, the more chance they had for success.

"All right," she conceded when James sauntered onto the porch. "But take plenty of quilts. And remember it's going to be mighty dark in the dark." She gave them the black flashlight with the rubbery handle and bulgy head.

In the underground it was dank and stuffy. They decided not to light the fire or lamp, not admitting deference to Mother but aware that that was a good excuse not to choke up. They spread their quilts to go under and over them and slept in all their clothes but their boots. Isabel, Katie, Jody Sue, and Phillip were in one line, Smithy, Wid, Little Wooster, James, and Charles in another. The ground was hard to begin with, and within ten minutes any one of them would have sworn not a rock had been cleared from the floor in their digging. But what kind of sissy, what kind of scaredy cat would mention anything about lumps or the thick darkness that settled like fog when the flashlight went out? And who would ever voice the certainty that each fluttered with— that there were sounds outside the underground that were like no sounds but a human foot testing the branches overhead and walking off toward the stream to wait? Wid pushed his toe past his quilt to feel the end of Little Wooster, who lay as still as he was, and just as quiet. Katie felt him move and was glad.

CHAPTER FOUR

After that, except for a game of cards by lamplight now and then, the underground went unoccupied and almost unnoticed. By the end of June, Phillip had come up with the idea of building bugs.

"What you do is take a big plank, like the ones along Larsens' old flooring. You saw it off the right length and put some seats on it, one for the driver and one for the brakeman."

"Seats? Out of what?" asked Katie, ready.

"Out of smaller boards. You just slope them by planing the edge and then nail a board from the top of the back down to the plank for support. Then you put on wheels and—go down the canyon," explained Phillip who knew about things like this even though he was young. He tinkered while James and Charles played.

"But how do you steer?" asked Charles.

Phillip had seen bugs with washing machine motors that ran on roller skates. "You get a two by four, pretty long, and bolt it to the front of the plank with a spike or something and hook some rope to it. Then all you have to do is pull on the rope and you'll go where you want to. You can even make a steering wheel!"

"And how about stopping?" questioned Smithy warily.

"You hammer some boards on the sides of the plank, half up, half down, so when the one on brakes pulls the top of the handle, the bottom digs in the road and stops you."

"Will it really work? I mean, it seems like you'd get up so much speed..."

"Sure," Phillip interrupted Smithy. "You even hammer tin strips around the bottom of the brake sticks—to really dig in."

"But what about Mister Davis? Can you just see what he'd do if we dug up his precious road?" Isabel warned.

"Ah, how's he gonna know," said James. "He'll just think it's another one of his giant snakes making tracks."

"Well, we'll sure have to stay out of his way," Isabel said with a *tsk, tsk,* in every word. "In fact, I don't know about the idea."

"She's sure changed since the freckle cream," thought Katie.

Jody Sue and Katie were both very sure they wanted to build and run a bug. Charles was non-commital. "How about if you and Smithy and I go in together?" James proposed. He and Charles took fierce turns beating each other at horseshoes and gravitated to a kind of bristling competition in anything from hiking to fire building.

Charles studied the tops of the maple clump by the field and then shook his head. "Nah. I got some other plans," he said thoughtfully and walked toward the bridge that cut across the stream to his place. That meant James and Smithy would make a bug, and Jody Sue and Katie were sure they could put one together that would run as well or better than any of the boys'.

When Isabel saw that Jody Sue and Katie would be partners, she said she'd rather work on her sewing with Aunt Hope, who was always delighted to have a girl to teach to sew since Katie far from craved it. "Katie has two dispositions," Father said, "normal—and sewing." So Katie gallantly let Isabel take her place with her mother's needle while she made a bug with Jody Sue. On other days, though, Katie chose to make doll furniture with Isabel and bathe and coddle her dolls into it.

"I swear that Katie's a dilly," Grandma observed more than once. "One day she's measuring muscles and chinning with Jody Sue and the next she's bathing a doll to death with Isabel. Lucky for her those sisters don't take to playing together much."

Katie and Jody Sue started gathering materials for their bug. The only trouble was that there were no wheels anywhere in the canyon and they didn't have any money to send with their fathers to buy some in the city. But how could you run a bug without wheels?

One day Katie and Jody Sue decided they had to have some, right then. Their bug, they felt, was the handsomest one of all, sitting there by the field, its plank sanded smooth and painted vermilion, its seats soft and tailored in striped red and white ticking, its two by four shackled miraculously to its body with a huge bolt discovered in the tool shed behind Uncle Phillip's. Even the curtain rod axles were hammered on, held securely by nails bent over them in solid column from center to end.

"I know," said Jody Sue, "let's get some of the boys to trade off with us so we can use their wheels sometimes and then give them back."

"Ho! They'd never do that. Half of them don't have any themselves," replied a discouraged Katie. Then she lit up. "Hey, you know what we should do? Why not saw down a pine tree and then cut off four slices of the trunk — and have wheels!"

"Sure! Perfect! We could work on one of those big ones between our place and the lean-to by Eagle Rock. It'd be just the ticket!" agreed Jody Sue. They ran to borrow the axes hanging behind the doors of each of their cabins, and Grandpa's wire logging saw from the back porch of Katie's house.

Two hours later they slumped beneath the still-standing pine to eat their lunch.

"Golly, who'd ever have thought it would be so hard

to chop down a pine tree?" sighed Katie.

"I'll say," agreed Jody Sue. "Look at that notch—it's not even halfway through the trunk, and we've been chopping all morning!"

"How much longer do you think it'll take us? Maybe an hour?" suggested Katie in strained hopefulness.

"Maybe," ventured Jody Sue, not daring to say what she really thought.

"Well, let's go. How about using the saw for a while, you on that side and me on this." The two ten-year-olds wrenched the big saw back and forth against the notch, straining it till it twanged in its binding, hardly taking out a bite.

"Maybe the axe? Do you think? Since we're so far in?" proposed Katie with a heave of her shoulders.

For another half hour the two took turns with their heavy axes, flinging them with all the might of their so consciously developed muscles at the notch which seemed to keep manufacturing wood chips without ever getting any bigger.

"Let's go down to the stream for a drink. I'm so thirsty I could spit cement," said Jody Sue, giving her axe a toss but totally unwilling to admit despair.

"Better take our tools," said Katie reluctantly aware of Mother's admonitions about taking care of things. The two gathered the saw and axes and began leaping down through the bushes with the bounce of deer. Above them something screeched like a giant ripping a house in half. "Look! It's falling!" They stood staring at the huge tree toppling directly at them. "Yi!" gasped Jody Sue, grabbing at her cousin as she started running.

But Katie was already off.

The tree came down with a swish that pulled the sky with it, its tip crashing between Jody Sue and Katie, crushing the bushes into a rushing quiver. The two gazed at each other over the trembling limbs, unable to do anything else. "Maybe we better come back tomorrow for the rest of it," Katie finally managed. Jody Sue nodded. They took the rest of the hill in slow, deliberate steps, feeling for every foothold.

The next morning Katie was on Jody Sue's porch ready to go back. "You know what? It's lucky we brought the saw and axe home. Mother'll be asking for them. Father's going to cut wood tomorrow since it's Saturday. We'll have to use your axe."

Their search began at 9:00 A.M. By 11:00 they were still hunting in a bewilderment that was matched only by their need to have the job over with.

"Nobody loses a tree!" they kept saying. "Not even in here! We know this place like our own yard. How could you lose a tree?"

"Especially one that just fell!"

In another two hours they had convinced themselves that someone else must have carried it off, most likely someone with the same idea they had. That the tree must have weighed a ton didn't seem to be an issue. "Daniel Moon maybe."

"Or Mister Davis."

Right after lunch they decided to forget it. Katie had to go help pit apricots for jam and Jody Sue had to practice the piano. And slices of pine tree might not have been too good on a bug anyhow. Would you leave the bark on to keep it strong or chip it off to make it smooth? Either way the wheels would have been too heavy for the curtain rods. They would have gone right through them by the first curve.

From then on the only answer was a gradual dismantling of every wagon and wheelbarrow everywhere. Some of the partners found wheels, but not enough to go around. Katie began to plead with Father to bring up the green doll buggy that Grandma had given her for Christmas. "I'll be awful careful when I take the wheels off, Father. Honest. And when we go back down, I'll just take them off our bug and put them back on the buggy. What harm could there be in that?"

"Did you ever think there just might be a bit of wear and tear on those wheels—Katie-bug? Maybe a little friction going up and down that nice smooth road?" laughed Father.

But then one night he brought up six used wheels that

he'd got somewhere—solid metal ones that didn't match except that all their tires were missing and their rims were flat. "You kids can divide these up. Good luck to each and every one." And he rolled them one at a time down the path from the front door to the three oldest children coming up the path.

"Boy, how can we divide up six wheels?" wondered James. "Nothing I can think of runs on an odd number."

"Except a tricycle," snickered Katie.

"Hey, yeah! That's an idea," Wid concluded. "Why not a three-wheeled bug?"

"How? And whose bugs?" asked Katie, suspicious of any plan where the boys did the dividing.

"Well, Phillip and I have the four his father took off their wagon, and the wheelbarrow one didn't work even as a spare—way too big. But we're set. So James and Smithy can have three of these for theirs, and you and Jody Sue can have the other three for yours. You can just split the plank in the middle of the back and put one wheel there and two on the front. Slick, huh?"

It was anything but slick. The curtain rods they used for axles were prone to bend or break after a few turns of the wheels, and even when they hammered the ends of the rods flat to block the wheels on, they wore through and let the wheels fly off to roll like lost nickels down the road ahead of the bug that grated to a rickety stop. And at best the third wheel in the middle of the plank gave the rockiest ride any brakeman could ever stand as it bounced down the hump in the middle of the road. Even the padding of old drapes and bedding that they tacked to the seats in elaborate upholstering did little to take the jostles out of the trip. Turns at being driver became the most sought-after change that a raw-seated brakeman could aspire to.

"Let's go all the way to the gate today," Katie said one morning after they'd been running their bugs down the straight stretch from Phillip's to the ravine just past Uncle Wooster's. They'd been very careful never to have a bug in sight when Mister Davis came up or down the road. These days when he passed they made elaborate efforts to be somewhere in his path, but their conversations were conclusively short so that he'd leave quicker than usual and they could go back to work. Sometimes it was tricky to manage. Mister Davis always had a story brewing, so about one day a week the whole crew would meet him either below where their cabins started or above and spend a couple of hours marveling at his seeings and doings to get it out of his system. Katie continued to ask him about Shadow and Tony, planning a canyon-wide search as soon as there was time, but the urgency of finding out more about them had waned in the furor of this summer's projects.

"What if Mister Davis sees us? Him and his precious road!" reminded Phillip. "How do we dare go past the straight part where we can see if he's coming?"

"We'll just watch till he goes up the road and then start. He takes at least till after noon up there. He'll never know the difference," said James.

Everyone knew the scheme was not possible. How would they get their bugs back up even if they did make it down without his seeing them? There was no way except to pull them right up the road. They couldn't go off in the bushes or up a trail or anything. But it was time. The wheels now stayed on all the way down the straight part, and with tool boxes and spare parts carried behind the brakeman's seat, they could repair as they went.

Their bug being faster with its four wheels, Wid and Phillip started first, right after Mister Davis had had time to get up the road out of earshot. Behind them rattled James and Smithy. "We're off!" squealed Katie and Jody Sue as the bug ahead got to the path two cabins below the starting place.

They gave their bug a running push and jumped on when they couldn't keep up any more. "Boy, she's purring along!" shouted Jody Sue from the driver's seat. "She's never gone better!"

"Stay as far off the hump as you can!" yelled Katie, "to

save the back wheel!"

It wasn't the wheel she was most worried about. With her feet hitched up on the foot rest under Jody Sue's seat, it was all she could do to hang on to the brakes on each side and not slide off her seat when they rounded the first curve.

By the time they reached the foot of Maple Fork hill they were going faster than they ever had. The road was still dusty from the passing of the other two bugs and in the noise from the tinny wheels on rocks, the two girls felt as if they'd been engulfed in a whirlwind. "Wow!" giggled Katie, "Wow!" grinning so hard her cheeks ached. She could see only the back of Jody Sue's head but knew by her shoulders she was laughing too as she yanked the ropes to control the chattering turns.

They flashed by Uncle Wooster-with-the-Long-Beard's place and Katie saw him standing by his hoe looking with his watery eyes at what he thought he saw going down the road. One more curve and they were to the steepest part. Katie ground the brakes into the soft dirt to absolutely no effect. The bug spun around the turns so fast one front wheel tipped practically flat under its axle, but they kept going. Past Rabbit's Head. Into the long straight tunnel of green by the Second Rat House. Smithy's head could be seen far down the road bouncing behind James. The next turn was a sharp one.

"Watch out for this turn!" Katie shouted to Jody Sue, who already was anticipating it by inching her grip on the ropes closer to her knees and leaning far forward.

Just as they were about to round the turn, a car loomed in front of them. Without a sign or noise, Jody Sue jerked on the right hand rope and the bug shot up the bank and around the car at an angle which, with any less momentum, would have dumped them into the car's windows.

All the girls saw were two startled faces in the front seat as they flashed by and continued without so much as a slight reduction in speed. Only now they were laughing so hard they hurt, and Jody Sue knew she'd collapse, so she guided

64

the speeding plank with its jiggling two by four onto a flat passing place where they dragged their feet and puffed to a stop. There was no way to do anything but peel off their seats onto the ground and laugh till tears rolled into their mouths and ears. Finally Jody Sue managed, "Did you see their faces?" And they swooned again in choking spasms.

When they had recovered, they checked their wheels, straightened them as well as they could, and took off again to catch the others. In two turns they found James and Smithy struggling with a broken axle, and after waiting for them, the four found Wid and Phillip only one curve further on with their brake pulled off. All were ecstatic to have made it that far without trouble, and all had had similar experiences encountering the lone car so fast that not one had recognized either the car or its occupants. And the cousins knew everybody who ever came up and down—unless somebody was having a party.

"It's Friday," said Jody Sue. "They must be friends of Aunt Lucine's."

"Boy, there just isn't ever a car up this time of day," Wid noted. There was usually little traffic except for the fathers in the canyon going back and forth morning and night.

"And I'll bet they'll never try it again!" chortled James, and they all started laughing. "Imagine what that poor lady driving thought: 'Maybe one. Maybe even two. But three?' I'll bet she's going to be watching for bugs every corner she turns—even in her sleep!"

The gate was a long way down. It took most of the afternoon by the time they'd stopped "about ninety times" to make repairs. But they did it. They swerved into the passing place in front of the gate and pulled out their sacks of smashed tuna sandwiches and carrots to flop on the soft earth by the creek bed and talk it over.

"So great! So really great!" Wid said, waving his head. "I never thought it would take so long, though. Mother's going to be worried."

By now the shadows from the clumps of cottonwoods

were covering the grass by Mister Davis's bridge and it began to seem like a long trek back to the cabins.

"As long as it's this late, why don't we ditch the bugs in the willows and wait around till somebody comes by to give us a ride. We could just hitch the ropes to the bumper and let the car pull the bugs up," suggested James.

So they maneuvered the bugs out of sight in the grassy meadow by the gate and began a game of mumble peg. On about the fifth turn, as Katie was aiming for the circle with the knife point on her knee and her two fingers on the top of its handle, Smithy hissed, "Look out! It's Mister Davis!"

The cousins went on with their game as he sauntered toward them.

"Well, what're you kids doin' clear down here?"

"Just waiting for a ride up," said Wid.

"Who with, your father? Mr. Barton never comes till lots later'n this."

"No. Not necessarily. Just anybody who comes along. We know most of 'em. They always give us rides."

"How'd you come down? You kids don't us'lly hike this way."

"That's right. We just thought it might be a good day to see how the gate was doing," James chimed in, aiming his pocket knife for the slice of the circle that was thinnest.

"Haven't seen so much uv ya lately," Mister Davis said, lighting his pipe and puffing his cheeks and lips.

"No? Well, we've been around. Guess we've just missed each other. Anything new?" asked Wid, not really looking as if he needed an answer.

"Well, I know the pony's in Lost Canyon all right. Saw hoof marks on the deer trail clear up by the ridge. Little ones. No horse made 'em."

"We've been planning a search," James said. "Probably in the next day or two."

"How 'bout you, Miss?" he said, looking at Katie. "Ya ever find yer cat?"

"No. She hasn't been around. I'd sure like to though."

Katie wished it were some other time so she could really question Mister Davis some more about Shadow. She did venture, "Golly, I'd do anything to get her back."

"Well, I just happen t' have some stuff in my place that's awful good to tempt animals into comin' around. If ya want to, ya could come over there and I'd give ya some."

Katie looked at her cousins and brothers, and she knew there was no way she could get whatever it was from Mister Davis without a report going to Mother. And right now she didn't want to encourage him to be anywhere around for any longer than he had to be, so she resisted asking if he couldn't bring it out to them.

"Well, wha' da ya think?" he persisted when she hesitated. "It's the best stuff you'll ever find for a lure."

"What is it anyhow?" interceded James. "Just food— or something else?"

"Nah. Not just food. Animals don't go fer stuff that's got human smell on it. This here's some special stuff I fix up in m' back yard without ever touchin' it—mixture of special things no animal can stay away from."

"How come you don't have animals all over your place, then?" questioned Wid.

"Oh, I just mix it there and then store it where they can't smell it or get at it. But y'd be surprised how quick it works when I put it out some place. Animals come from all over. Must affect 'em like deer lick does deer."

Katie was more tantalized than she wanted her brothers to know. If there really were something that would get Shadow back, why not get some and try it? What harm could there be in that? But she could see the others fidgeting with their knives and weighting and unweighting their feet. They had to get rid of Mister Davis before a car came.

"Maybe some other time, Mister Davis," she said as James stuck his elbow in her arm. "Right now we've got this game to finish before a car comes along. But the next time down, OK?" James flipped his knife again and it stuck cleanly into the damp earth they'd cleared for their ring. The cousins

67

closed their circle with a turn of their heads to its center and even Mister Davis could not mistake the dismissal. He said, "OK, Miss. Next time. Y'll be real glad when ya see what I got. It's a sure thing, surest thing ya ever saw." He took a slow turn around the gate, checked the padlock, ran his hand along the bar, kicked dust off his boots at the far end post, and leaned up the hill to walk the distance to his bridge and disappear into the arbor of prickly shrubs that framed the path to his cabin.

"Whew," breathed Phillip. "That was close. Now if he'll just stay over there till we get a ride."

Katie started devising ways that she could slip away for just long enough to get to Mister Davis's for a sample of the lure. She couldn't imagine what it could be, but it must be really something the way he described it. And of course Mister Davis knew more about that sort of thing than anybody. How else could he live up here all year and still be alive? He had to know all kinds of secrets.

Just then a car came around the visible bend of Parley's and made the S turn into Armchair Canyon. "It's Sid Hickman," observed Wid. "I hope he's sober."

"It'd make a great ride if he isn't," grinned James, moving back toward the road to offer to open the gate.

The car idled through the gate and stopped so that Wid could stick his head down toward the window and ask, "Hi, Mr. Hickman. Could we hook a ride up?"

"How many?" Mr. Hickman asked, looking at cousins in every direction.

"Just six of us. We can hang three on a side, OK?" Wid persisted, waving the others toward the car.

"Sure, I guess so, but hang on tight."

"As if we'd do anything else with you at the wheel," James muttered gleefully under his breath to Katie.

"Thanks a lot, sir," said Wid. "There's just one other thing. We've got these bugs to pull up. If we could just hook them on behind…"

"Bugs?" said Mr. Hickman squinting his eyes and tilting

his head to look.

"Yeah, they're just some go-cart things we made. It'll just take a jiff to hook them on, and you'll never know the difference driving."

"Well, all right, just so you don't take long. I'm in a hurry."

"He's always in a hurry," whispered James. "And if he admits it, we're in for one heck of a ride!"

Wid and Phillip looped the rope of the four-wheeler over the bumper and tied it to itself. Then they latched the second bug around the hammered-on tool box of the first and did the same with the third bug that now strung two car lengths behind.

"Hold your breath," said Wid under his, "and just hope the wheels hang on till we get there. Maybe without our weight they'll have a chance." Then he climbed on the running board on the driver's side with Smithy and James while Katie and Jody Sue and Phillip stepped up on the other running board.

"Would you mind rolling down all your windows, sir?" requested Wid. "They can't hold on too well over there without."

Sid Hickman shrugged but slid to the other side of the car and rolled down the front and back windows so that the riders could put their arms in and find a grip for the turns they knew were coming.

"Wouldn't some of you like to ride inside?" he asked.

"Oh, no thanks," came the chorus. "This is just fine."

If they thought their ride those two miles down the canyon had been wild, it was flat compared to the ride up. Sid Hickman was what Mother would call a *smoothy*—barely going gray, with a cleft chin and very dark shadows where he shaved. He threw the car into low, jammed down on the gas pedal and never let up. The six on the outside clung to the car's upright supports with one of their arms and to the window sills with the other. There was no reaching for leaves or swinging of legs into the air. There was hardly any breathing. Only wide-eyed staring at what could possibly be next. Dust swelled up behind them so that even when they dared look they couldn't see the bugs. Anyhow they were sure they were lost. How could they possibly stay on with this speed demon ripping up the road? Trees, banks, shrubbery blurred past their squinted eyes, and finally cabins hazed into sight.

"Where do you want to get off?" Mr. Hickman called to Wid at the apex of a steep turn.

"Just anywhere sir," Wid shouted, "anywhere you'd like to stop!"

"You're a Barton, aren't you," Mr. Hickman leaned to shout. "How about at the foot of your hill?"

"Fine. Great. Anywhere," called Wid, scraping his fingernails on the ceiling of the car on a wide grinding curve.

Sid Hickman braked to a stop that threw his riders forward into leaps off the running boards. Before they had recovered, the car started off again.

"Hey! Wait! The bugs! We've got to get the bugs off!" yelled one after another, all charging after the car.

It stopped again with a slide in the dust, Sid Hickman poking his head out of the window. "Oh, yeah. Sorry, kids. Hurry, OK?"

Wid, Phillip and James ripped at the rope holding the first bug to Sid Hickman's bumper while the others surveyed what was left of Jody Sue and Katie's. There was a two by four with two wheels curled under like pigeon toes on threaded axles, and dragging behind it a plank with its tool chest and middle wheel missing. James and Smithy's bug was gone.

"Gosh! It could be anywhere," moaned Smithy. And I've gotta be home or I'll be in a real fix."

"Yeah," sighed James peering down the road. "How're we gonna find it before dark? It's probably on the road somewhere—where somebody'll smack it coming up."

"We better start back down," said Wid, pulling his bug to Phillip and handing him the rope. "You take this to your place and I'll go with James."

"No, Bruv, you and Katie better go up and tell Mother we're back. I'll just run down a ways and find it and then get a ride up with Father. He'll be coming any time."

"What'll we tell Mother? I better go with you."

"No, it can't be far. It was hooked on good. Probably didn't come loose for a long way—when the tool box pulled off. It'd be better if you...."

Just then Mother's voice came undulating over the trees and down the hill, full of the tremulo of sweeteners that sang into the "horn" from the Victrola. When she wanted any of them, she took the horn to the porch, put its narrow end to her mouth and turned it into a megaphone that could be heard from L.C. to the Crow's Nest. "Oh Wi-i-i-i-d. Oh Ja-a-a-mes. Oh Ka-a-atie," she called. "Come to di-i-i-ner-er-er-er."

"See, you gotta go. And you other guys too."

"But where'll we say you are?" Katie asked, reluctant to let James go anywhere interesting without her.

"Tell her something. You know. Just say I'm working on something for the bug. Tell her I'll be right there. Then when I show up with Father it'll all be OK."

"Look for our wheel too, OK?" Katie asked him.

"Sure." He started down the road at the jog-gallop that they used when they were in a hurry and had a long way to go. He could still see what he needed to, and by the shadows he knew he'd be able to make it clear back to the gate if he had to before Father came. He passed Cousin Ann's place and Uncle-Wooster-with-the-Long-Beard's.

"Say, son, where you off to so fast so late?" called Uncle Wooster-with-the-Long-Beard from the path by his iris bed.

James knew he couldn't hear if he did answer. Uncle Wooster-with-the-Long-Beard had been hit in the head by a horseshoe and was so deaf he always just beamed no matter what anyone said, a wet pink smile between his white beard and moustache that made his blue eyes glimmering slits. So James just waved and kept running.

Past the tip of Rattlesnake Mountain, on to the steepest

place, right next to Daniel Moon's, James froze. In the rocky place on the wide part of the curve was the bug. And stooped beside it was Daniel Moon.

Daniel Moon looked bigger than James had even remembered. Kneeling there in sloppy striped coveralls, his back to the road, he looked like a grown man, a fat one, with shoulders that sloped in back just like on the sides. His pudgy hands fiddled with the rope and the brakes and shoved the front seat till it split away from the nails and smashed on the plank. James couldn't see his face but he knew he'd be grinning that smirky grin that made his mouth look like a hole in a mud puddle where a rock had just been dropped, just a sinking between his two fat red cheeks. Nobody scared James like Daniel Moon. Not even the Skinner kids at home, who swore and threw bird stuff from the Roskelly's aviary all over anybody who dared take the shortcut home from Sugar House through their alley.

Daniel Moon seemed meaner. And bigger.

James watched as he stood up and raised a huge thick-soled boot over the back seat of the bug. As the foot came down, shattering the seat and flattening the back wheel, James tore at Daniel Moon.

"You leave that bug alone!" he blurted, lunging at Daniel Moon's arm to turn him around. "That's our bug and it's a good one and it's lost and I'm gonna take it home and you're not gonna ruin it ya big dope!"

Daniel Moon swirled around, his fat arm knocking James to the ground like a fly being wiped off a table.

James started to scramble to his feet muttering, "Ya big bully. Ya never do anything but ruin other people's stuff," and he knotted his fists in front of him the way he did with Wid when they used the bulky red boxing gloves Father had given them one Christmas. He bobbed and weaved and slid his feet keeping his chin tucked down in the crouch he'd practiced almost every night in the downstairs room with his brother.

"You pee wee!" scorned Daniel Moon in a voice higher

than James would ever have imagined it could be. He'd never heard him talk before. Daniel Moon always came and went with no one around, leaving huts smashed, traps set off, fish ponds riddled with rocks, bottles broken, and every cousin grim-jawed about what would happen to Daniel Moon if they ever caught him. "You putrid little pee wee!" He towered above James like a raring horse. "What're you doing on my property anyhow? This thing belongs to me now—not you, you pee wee."

"No it does not! It's mine. I made it and we lost it coming up the canyon behind a car. And it's mine, ya hear," growled James, skittering back and forth in front of Daniel Moon. "And I'm gonna take it home right now."

"You think! Just try, you pee wee." Daniel Moon inched toward James, flicking his fat fingers in the boy's face and bending his round head forward and down so close that James felt the splatter of the "p" and "w."

"I will, don't you worry. I will. I'll take what belongs to me and you better not try and stop me." James slid one foot toward the bug.

"You will, huh?" Daniel Moon swung his arm like a heavy bat and caught James across the cheek. He sprawled backwards over the bug and heard the back seat go down under him.

James jerked his knees up to his stomach, rolled to them on the far side of the bug and began to get up, but Daniel Moon took one straddling step over the wreckage and kicked him in the buttocks. This time James went down face first in the rocks and Daniel Moon stood over him, pinning him with a foot that felt like Castle Crags sitting on the small of his back.

"Listen you kid, you pee wee. You get outa here and don't ever let me see you around here anywhere again or I'll do a lot worse 'n this to ya." He lifted his foot and nudged James over to his back with his steel toe. "Now git. And git fast, ya hear, pee wee?"

James heard. He got up and edged around the bulk that

loomed above him, and started walking toward the road.

"Git, pee wee," Daniel Moon gave him another kick that sent him lurching forward. 'Ya better speed it, pee wee, or you'll never git at all!"

James moved faster but he didn't run. "No big ape is gonna make me run like a chicken," he thought. "Just you wait, Daniel Moon, just you wait till I get my brother."

James went into the lower level in front of the Barton cabin. He didn't have to call Wid. He was waiting on the swings watching for him.

"Where's the bug? Did you find it?" he said running down to meet James.

"Yeah. I found it. And a lot more."

When James told Wid about Daniel Moon, Wid wanted to go right back down and get him. "We could, you know, Bruv. The two of us could tear him to pieces." Wid was almost crying. "We'll get him all right. And the bug too."

"That might not work. It's pretty well ruined. He smashed practically all of it. We'll just have to make a new one. But, boy, let's get Daniel Moon!"

Wid brought the dented mop bucket full of water for James to wash up in and traded his dirty shirt for one out of the downstairs drawers. "You won't need to tell anybody about it. Not even Katie. She's helping with the dishes. She'd just fly off the handle and do something dumb."

"Yeah, like take Daniel Moon on by herself." The brothers chuckled and James tried out his bones, knowing that he hurt in a lot of places but not anywhere that felt like it could be helped. He knew that he'd end up telling Katie— but not till he was far away from the aching he was starting to feel — and the shivering that swept through him as he thought of Daniel Moon's little eyes.

CHAPTER FIVE

It was Saturday. That meant sawing wood and cutting and washing hair. Father, in his army pants, "trousseau trousers" as he always called them, and army boots with buckled puttees around his calves, led the children early to the wood pile behind the log cabin.

"Who's first rider?" he asked, pulling a crisp aspen or birch from the pile chopped earlier in the summer.

"Me! Me!" offered Davy, putting his arm around the log and helping Father drop it onto the built-in sawhorses. Then he climbed up on the log to ride it like a pony while Father, with one foot on the log for balance, began his sweeping strokes through the stringy skin and into the acrid center of the wood. A sawdust waterfall sifted from the cut into a rising mound of soft yellow that Katie could hardly wait to spread and finger as she watched Father saw in front of Davy.

Wid and James picked up the pieces almost as they fell and took turns whacking them into fourths with the axe on the chopping block far enough out from the sawing to be sure the flying sections would not hit anyone.

"Trade!" said Katie, and she moved to Davy's place in front, knowing that on the next trade she'd get to use the axe while James sat.

"You kids have a good week?" Father asked. He usually came up so late at night that he had dinner with only Mother after the children were all in bed. Katie knew, though, and probably the boys did too, that always just before he and Mother went to bed he came around and kissed them goodnight. He left at 6 o'clock every weekday morning so they never saw him then either. But even though he was gone so much it never seemed like it. When he was away, Mother officiated in their lives with such ease and presence that there was no room for insecurity. Often her directions included a sense of Father's being in on everything.

"Father wonders how you're doing with your practicing," or "Father is planning to bring some surprises for you to sell in the store, Davy." Davy and two other cousins his age had built a store out of winter shutters and were open for business any hour that anyone had a penny and needed some blow gum or a sucker. Sometimes they sold Mother back her oatmeal cookies or roasted apricot pits, but most of their supplies came from Father and were left in the morning on the dining room table with a note in his square clear printing: "FOR DAVY AND HIS PARDNERS. MAKE MONEY, BUT BE FAIR. LOVE, FATHER."

When Father asked about the week, they all told everything they could think of. They loved to. Except some things, of course. Daniel Moon didn't get mentioned for almost another month.

Saturday had always been Father's day, not just in the summer. In the fall it meant football and Father refereeing. One Saturday night at the kitchen table Uncle Wooster said, "Candland, how could you call that clipping penalty against Utah in the third quarter? Why that back was way in the clear before Thompson ever landed!" The children knew in general what their father would say, but were always surprised when they heard it.

"Wooster," he laughed, "if that's the only mistake I made all afternoon, I'm tickled to death!"

Wid and James had been sitting with the players on the

bench where their father always let them watch the games. During the half they would sidle behind him into the dressing rooms and soak up the heady sweatiness and talk of the giant players. For years they had thrown passes to each other on the edges of the field—that is until one Saturday when James had run for a touchdown with Wid chasing him and everyone in the stadium had stood up and cheered. They never wanted to be on the field again after that. Katie went too. Once when her big brothers started off with her mother and father for the game she had complained, "Here I am four whole years old and I've never even seen a football game!"

She was almost sorry, though, when she did get to go, because sandwiched between one of her uncles and Mother, she always felt sleepy and restless in the endless time before they all stood at the west gate waiting for "the menfolk" to come for them, Father's cleats rattling the pavement, his black cap pushed up so that his broad thinning forehead shone in the arc light that hung over the fence in the late shadows.

"That was so good," she'd say excitedly to Father as he swept her up every time on his arm that fit her thighs like a swing seat.

He took turns taking the children one at a time on out-of-town trips to officiate games. Once Wid got lost in the station in Boulder, Colorado, and Father had to pull the cord and stop the train while Wid raced down the tracks and caught up. And Katie had had her ringlets spun by a Negro lady Father had asked to work on them—a lady who had a job doing something else on the train—and they'd come out upside down somehow and a "real sight" for Mother as Katie and Father disembarked at the station at home.

But the trips were rare and remembered—the crashing and heaving in the tunnel between cars, the green plush of the stiff seats and the little hammock for clothes above the berth which Father told Katie was her place to sleep, and the crisp-soft French toast in the diner—with maple syrup not made from melted brown sugar. It was all mixed up with

Father and football and Saturdays.

On the night when Uncle Wooster had questioned Father's decision, Wid had asked Father about it while the children were all upstairs lined up waiting to brush their teeth in the big white pedestal bowl in the bathroom. "How come you think Uncle Wooster could see that play from clear up in the bleachers better than you could right down there next to the players?"

"Is that what it sounded like I said?"

"Well, yes. You admitted you made a mistake."

"Did I? Well, maybe I did. That wouldn't be the worst thing that could happen. The worst would be not admitting it if I did. There's nothing much harder on a man than not being able to be wrong. Then he has to be a slave to making every fool thing he does look good. Nope. Give me any day the chance to say I missed one and then let me move on to do better the next time."

"But if you called the penalty right, you should have told Uncle Wooster. You were a lot closer than he was."

"You never win anything trying to argue with a man who's seen something different than you have. Best thing's just to know that no two people are ever going to change on what they think they saw, but they're never going to really quarrel over it if one of them just plain listens to the other."

"But *did* you see Thompson clip that runner?"

"I sure thought I did. Of course. That's why I blew my whistle. But if being a referee teaches you one thing it's that you've got to decide—quick, sort of on instinct—and then stick by your decision. You won't always be right, but the only good official is the one who knows he's right most of the time and is willing to gamble on his own promptings. On that field you can't afford to pay attention to anything but your own sense. Not to the crowd, not to the players, not even to the other officials. You have that whistle in your teeth to blow when your brain tells it to. And it's funny how you do, sometimes without even knowing you've done it. The old head works for you while you're running all over the place trying to follow the play. You've learned the rules and they just pop up and tell you when to blow, no matter what."

"Is that why they let you referee Utah games? I heard Uncle David say once you were the only one that ever got assigned to your own school."

"I don't know. They're probably just hard up in this neck of the woods." And Father gave Wid's shoulder a hard pat that changed into a rub up onto his neck and into his mat of hair. "You better get those teeth brushed before Mother comes up wondering what's happened."

Now, on this Saturday in the summer when the sawing and chopping were over and the stack of wood was knee high by the block, the children lined up holding one piece of kindling straight up in each hand, arms outstretched, and Father loaded them to their noses with the sharp-edged wood. Barely seeing the path over their sticks, they carried them to the kitchen where Mother had the wood boxes cleaned and wiped out for filling and pushing back under the curtain.

Then Father carried the round corner table out of the living room to the back of the house, sat each boy on it in turn, and cut their hair with the clippers that he squeezed and aimed up the necks and cheeks tilted to his touch.

In the early days, if it hadn't been for the talk, the process would have been unbearable. Even though Father squeezed the clippers as rapidly as he could, they moved over their trail faster than they clipped, and the pulling was fearful. But he learned to temper his speed, and the boys, a towel around their shoulders and Father's fingers on their jaws, squinted through the ordeal knowing how many times the clippers would have to scuttle up their necks until relief would come in the scissors touch-up. At the end, Father would snap the long slim barber scissors over the tops of their curly heads, snipping here and there over the comb with more flourish than finesse.

"Boy, would I like to have my curls cut off like that," wished Katie every time. Instead, she bent over one shallow enamel wash basin after another as Mother lathered, scrubbed, rinsed, and then poured lemon juice over the tangle of her light brown hair. Then it had to be towel dried, fluffed, and receive Mother's "tonic." That was a rumbling of Mother's fingertips that drummed like hoof beats against her scalp. "For a loose scalp and healthy hair," Mother said each time her fingers galloped across Katie's head.

And that was not all. Katie then had to sit on the high stool from the kitchen and try to think of something else while Mother "worked from the bottom up" with the fat handled ivory comb to unsnarl her curls. Once smoothed, the hair was wrapped one strand at a time around Mother's forefinger with the oval brush and bobby pinned as a tube until it dried. "Such nice hair," Mother always said on about the twelfth ringlet. "Thick, but no rat's nest. Just be glad that it's not half as curly and heavy as mine was. Oh how I used to try not to cry getting snarls out!" Katie did too, but she'd have died rather than have one of her brothers see such a "girly" thing.

On Saturday afternoon Father took everyone for a hike, usually to the Crow's Nest or Castle Crags or Lover's Lane. When they got back, they had the only big night meal of the week—beets and greens steaming, fresh string beans, and stewed chicken with milk gravy over potatoes mashed to perfect fluff. Mother instructed, "If you use the masher thoroughly before you add any moisture, Katie, your potatoes will be smooth as Uncle Wooster's head." Katie loved to whip the black handled masher up and down in the big kettle and hear its rhythms clunk on the sides, knowing Father would say, "Katie, these are probably the most smoothed out potatoes I've ever had the ecstasy of eating!"

On Tuesday and Saturday after dinner everyone had a bath. Father lifted the oval tin tub off the wall by its handles and put it on the kitchen floor where he and Mother poured kettles and dishpans of water into it from the stove. Each time a different child got to be first, new water being added to warm what was left for the next one. The first had only about four inches of clear water, the second about six inches, and the fourth had not-so-clear but above the knees of still hot luxury. They all came out shining and ready on Saturday night for clean wooly pajamas and an evening of staying up till ten in the living room.

The Saturday night fire was Katie's favorite. At first all the chips from the day's chopping were used for kindling so that the flames raced up the chimney and the tall stove sounded as if suspenders were snapping inside. That night Katie watched as Father kept feeding in the chips until they were gone and it was time for the big pieces. As soon as the fat quarter logs went on, the fire changed, settled. Katie's spirits followed the darting and the crackling and resented the settling. It was as if part of her seeped out and up in the smoke that was visible only after the chips were burned. Why was there so much smoke in the logs? Why could the chips and kindling dance off without a trace, and change the whole fire when they were gone?

Mother put a record on the Victrola, winding the gold handle three times every few minutes to make the long needle weave its way across the thick grooves to the center where it wavered under its round clock-like holder and then swayed in hisses till lifted off. Once in a while Mother moved the lever on the flat by the turn table and made the record speed up or slow down. John Phillip Sousa and Caruso would wail into deep groans or whine higher and higher into mice sounds that sent Davy throwing his head in delight.

They played Spoof with cards and spoons, squealing and snatching when they had a matched foursome. Then there was Steal the Pile and Slap Jack. At the end Father and Mother took turns reading aloud, Father *The Light in the Clearing,* with the name of Mr. Peabody bringing smirks everytime between James and Wid, and a chapter from *Tom Sawyer,* with everyone agreeing that James and Tom would whitewash a fence exactly alike. Mother read some poems, "The Spider and The Fly," "Barefoot Boy With Cheek of Tan," "Captain, My Captain," and "Little Boy Blue," ending with "By the shores of Gitche, Gumee, by the shining Big-Sea-Water, Stood the wigwam of Nokomis, Daughter of the Moon Nokomis."

Katie listened from somewhere far off, letting the words come out of the fire that held her as she sat on the bear rug. "No two words come out alike," she thought, "like no two flames ever do. They just slip out and play with each other and go somewhere. And you try to remember them and all it is is a feeling. Like remembering how it felt on that curve when we passed those ladies in the car."

Davy had fallen asleep during the stories and had to be carried by Father to his cot on the screened porch which was moved in out of the cold every night when Mother and Father were ready to go to sleep. He was not wakened for family prayer, another Saturday event. Father or Mother said it, but even if it was short, Katie felt bones going through her knees, and when she opened her eyes to check, Wid and James were wriggling at the end of the bed, and James never missed opening at least one eye to tell her he was feeling his bones too.

The only thing she didn't know was that on that Saturday night more than James' knees hurt. Sitting in the tub had been an ordeal, and raising his arms to chop wood had made ripples of hurting run up his neck and into his head. Daniel Moon was with him however he moved, and the plan for getting even was festering in every ache.

CHAPTER SIX

"How about if we go to Sunday School on
our bugs this week?" Katie proposed to Wid at breakfast.
She and Jody Sue had put the high metal wheel from the
wheelbarrow on the back of their bug. Wid had offered it
since it could never be used as one of the four on his and
Phillip's. It hoisted the back end pretty high and was more
bouncy than she could believe with the seat of the brakeman
tilting toward the front. "We could take turns with Charles
and James," she volunteered.

Every Sunday some of the cousins started at the top of
the canyon and ran the three miles of cabins shouting through
the horn, "Sunday School, Phillip R. Ruskin's, eleven o'clock!"

Uncle Phillip, the oldest of Mother's brothers, was a
pillar of the Church. He brought to life his father's dry humor
and his mother's zest for "anything virtuous, lovely, or of
good report or praiseworthy." He loved boats and the fish
they took him to, and his invitations to boat or canoe on the
Snake River were never turned down. He took Grandma
traveling all the time. "There's only one trouble," he said,
swooping in with her after driving her to St. George "to get
some sun" three hundred miles away. "I never go fast enough
for her—even with that new Auburn. If she can't feel the wind

inside, she thinks we're not moving."

Uncle Phillip spoke in the Tabernacle on Temple Square at every General Conference of the Mormon Church and was sententious and awesome there; but in the company of his wife, Aunt Sarah, he never could be serious for very long. Once on a visit as a General Authority — a member of the Council of the Twelve Apostles — he was asked by a very young attender, "Are you *really* one of *those?* A Twelve Apostle, I mean?"

"Yes, young man," replied salty, statuesque Aunt Sarah for her shorter husband, "he certainly is."

"Golly," exclaimed the boy, "I thought they were all dead!"

"They are," replied Aunt Sarah. "They just won't lie down."

Uncle Phillip's cabin in Armchair Canyon was around the mountain from Hope and Candland's, just down the hill from Grandma's and up from Uncle Wooster's. During the summers he let his daughter Laura and her family, Jody Sue, Isabel, Florence, and two little brothers live there most of the time because he and Aunt Sarah were "on the Snake." But it was always called Phillip L. Ruskin's place, and was the site of Sunday School every Sunday of the summer.

Depending on the weather and the time of the summer, anywhere from fifty to seventy occupants of the cabins would assemble on the shadowy porch at Uncle Phillip's on chairs, stools, and benches brought from surrounding places. The cousins were in clean shirts and shined boots and never noticed what the others wore. In the wide doorway to the living room the dining room table was spread with a white damask cloth and on it were plates with slices of bread stacked neatly on them. A globular pitcher full of symbolic water stood by four barrel glasses.

One of the fathers conducted, Uncle Phillip if he was there, and his oldest son Leigh led the singing with a booming voice and ranging ruler while Laura played the twangy piano from the living room. Katie's favorite was "Our mountain home so dear, where crystal waters clear, flow ever free...." As the music swelled and rose, she felt her hair rising with it.

Then there was the breaking of the bread, the pouring of the water, and the blessing of the sacrament by one of the young men on his knees by the table. "That they may keep His commandments and have His spirit to be with them. Amen." The passing of the bread and then the water was by the deacons: Wid and Little Wooster and any other boys over twelve that came. Katie always made sure her tiny piece of bread was without a crust as she selected with her right hand and passed the plate on with her left.

This time she looked up from the plate to see Father get up from his chair and excuse himself past the knees of the row he was on. She leaned forward and could see Mister Davis standing outside the screen door signaling Father to come. Katie's throat went tight and her stomach knotted together. She looked to see if James had seen Father. No. He was trading pocket knives with Charles.

Father and Mister Davis disappeared beyond the house. Katie knew something was very wrong. Mister Davis never came around the cabins when people were there, and he never was seen on Sunday.

Katie was glued to the door so that when the glass came to her, Brother Edmunds had to tap her arm to tell her it was there. She jumped and took the glass and a sip that she let trickle down her throat thinking, "Oh, Heavenly Father, don't let it be something bad—like about the bugs." She didn't dare even nudge Jody Sue.

The sacrament was over and Cousin Ann was announcing which rooms the three classes would be held in right after singing practice. Again Leigh stood up, raised his shoulders a few times, opened the song book and said, "On this beautiful Sabbath morning we'll sing a song for all you young people. 'Shall the Youth of Zion Falter,' page 97."

The three hymn books around the rows were opened but not looked at by anyone as the congregation began by heart with Leigh's infectious vim. "Should the youth of Zion falter when defending truth and right? When the enemy assaileth, should we shirk or shun the fight? No!"

"No!" Katie shrilled, "No!" she sang, staring at the door, knowing there was a new Enemy assailing.

Father came back in just as they stood up to "separate for classes." He looked solemn. Katie knew it had nothing to do with the Sunday School class he was going to teach. The few times she'd ever seen him look like that before she'd tried hard to forget.

She filed into the living room with the others between ten and fifteen for a lesson from Father. Sitting between Jody Sue and Isabel on the piano bench, she waited for Father to start. He walked right past her without a look or a pat. "Something's really wrong," she thought. He set his books on the chair by the stove and asked James to say an opening prayer. James squirmed. He'd asked Father over and over not to call on him. "I just go like a stick," he said. "I can't even think, let alone say anything." But here, in front of everybody, he set his jaw, swallowed three times, and said the quickest prayer even Katie could remember.

"Father in Heaven, thank Thee for this nice day. Help us to have a good lesson. Help us to remember it. Name of Jesus, Amen."

"Thank you James." Father watched him walk back to sit on the floor by Charles. "Now about the lesson. I want to tell you a story. When I was playing football in high school, there was a fella named Oscar Dobbs. I'll never forget him. He was a skinny kid. No coordination at all. Couldn't throw or catch or even run much. But he loved sports. Loved to watch others do what he couldn't. He would have been a great cheerleader, he was so enthused about the games and everything that went on out on the field, but even that would have taken ways to move that he just couldn't master." Father walked slowly back and forth from the piano on one side of the living room to the stove on the other with his head cocked back and his eyes searching the past like a spotlight.

86

"So Oscar was sort of our mascot, you might say. Every team has somebody who carries the water to the players and gives them encouragement as they go in and out of the game. But Oscar was a lot more than that to us. He was our best stuff. When he'd rub our sweaty heads with a towel and say, 'Man, are you playing a game today!' he'd make us believe it. He'd come running out on the field when there was a time out, dragging his feet even when he was going his fastest, his arm that wasn't carrying the water bucket kind of flopping like a rag doll's and his head waving back and forth from one shoulder to the other like that was going to move him faster." Father flopped his left arm to illustrate. "He'd give everybody a drink out of the dipper and rub a towel over the backs of our necks smiling and saying, 'Come on, you guys. Nobody's ever gonna beat you!'

"Course we lost plenty, just like any team. But old Oscar never seemed to remember anything but our wins. And our best days. It's a funny thing what that did for us. He really was our spirit. We learned to forget the bad days like he did and go into every new play like it was going to open up a sure-fire score.

"I guess we came to depend on Oscar more than any of us realized. One day he missed practice—and Oscar *never* missed practice. He'd be the first one there, getting out the equipment, lining up our helmets and gear, setting up the bench—or a dozen other things that made everything easier for all of us. And he'd always seem like he was having the best time of anybody. And here we were the ones getting to play! Well, this one afternoon he didn't come. 'Where's Oscar?' every single person asked as they came into the locker room and then out onto the field. All of us just shrugged our shoulders and said we couldn't understand it.

"But everything was different that day. Oh, you'll probably say, of course it'd be different, what with all of us expecting such good service and all. But it was a lot more than that. The life in us was gone. We tried to practice. We ran plays, blocked, did some tackles, pushed each other around some. But nobody cared about any of it.

"Everybody just wondered to themselves where Oscar was. The trouble was we didn't know where to look. We'd taken Oscar so much for granted that none of us had ever bothered to know much about him anywhere but in athletics —where we were the stars. But when he didn't show up for a whole week and it was time for our big game on Friday afternoon, the coach organized us to try to find out where in the heck he was. By then we all knew—and admitted—how much we needed him to be there.

"He lived with an aunt who said he'd gone to school every day. She hadn't noticed anything different at all with him. His teachers said, though, that he'd been absent. But that was before the time of absentee lists and such, so they'd all assumed he'd had to stay home for something. The only thing anyone could think of to do was to wait till after the time he usually came home from school and be there to talk to him. That, unfortunately, was exactly when the whistle would be blowing for the game to start—without Oscar, without spirit."

Father's broad chest rose in a long sigh, he stopped walking, looked at his boots, stuffed his hands in his pockets, and slowly continued.

"We played so bad, so bad—every one of us—that Coach Nalgren couldn't even bawl us out. The whole team was beyond repair. We slipped, we were either slow or so fast we were off-sides, we fumbled, we let the other team open holes the size of the Empire State Building. The first half ended with us behind twenty-eight to nothing!

"In the dressing room we all just crumbled onto the benches and stared. Just before the whistle for the start of the second half the hall door opened and in came Oscar, scrawny, looking like his body was not connected at all to any of his arms or legs, panting so hard his breath came in little jerks. Everybody was too surprised to even ask where he'd been. We all just watched him go automatically to the equipment closet and start lining things up.

88

"'Finally, Coach Nalgren said, 'Oscar, you meathead. Where've you been all week? Don't you know what happens around here when you don't show up?'

"'No,' said Oscar raising his head and shaking it, looking bewildered and gray from his scalp to his jawbone. 'Does something happen?'

"'We get all messed up,' the coach told him. 'Who in the heck is going to straighten up the towels if you don't?'

"'But I didn't know anybody noticed. I mean, who cares about stupid old towels when you're playing ball?'

"'Everybody, that's who. Where have you been anyhow?'

"Well, Oscar looked like he couldn't believe anybody in the world would ever be wondering where he'd been. He said, 'Well, I got in a mess. I pass that old house over by the dump every day on my way to and from school. And this one day it looked deserted. These two old ladies 're usually out poking around in the dump for whatever they live on, and they weren't there. So I decided to check. And sure 'nuff, they were gone. I watched every day for a week. I even banged on their door to make sure, and they were gone.'

"'Oscar, there isn't time for all this. Just tell us where you were all week—and save the details for later,' the coach told him.

"But Oscar wasn't about to hurry. He kept telling how he'd finally decided that since no one was living in the old house any more he'd just have a look at what was there, to see if he could maybe help the two little old ladies somehow. But the place really was empty for good, everything gone except some grimy old plates that he thought nobody would want. So what do you think he did with those plates?"

At this point Wid and Katie and James were looking back and forth at each other and moving some in their seats.

"He said, 'I thought it wouldn't matter at all if I just took those plates, since nobody else would ever want them, and then I could use them for practicing my throw. You guys know what a terrible throw I am—anything would be worth tryin' to make it better. So I took the plates, old ugly ones, about twenty of 'em, I guess, and I went out to the dump and practiced throwin' 'em as far as I could across that mess. Best way I could think of to get rid of 'em.'"

By now James had started to wiggle his toes and cross and uncross his legs, and Katie and Wid were clamping their jaws and running their tongues around the inside of their teeth.

"'But what did that have to do with you not being in school or out to practice all week, Oscar?' one of the fellas asked him. And do you know what Oscar said?" Father paused, looking slowly from face to face around the room. "Wid, do you have any idea what Oscar might have said?"

"No. No, I haven't got any idea," stammered Wid.

"James. Do you have any idea?" Father's voice was not harsh; in fact, it was gentle and persuasive.

"No. 'Fraid I don't either," managed James shaking his head vigorously.

"How about you, Katie? You almost always have some idea."

But Katie didn't answer at all except with a definite shake of her head and shift of her bottom on the very hard piano bench.

"Well, let me read you just one of the Beatitudes, from the Book of Matthew in the New Testament. These are some of the best ideas Jesus had on how a person ought to act if he wants to be on His team—either as a player or water boy or anything." Father pulled at the silk string that marked his place in the black leather Bible and read, "Blessed are the pure in heart: for they shall see God." He raised his head and repeated, "Blessed are the pure in heart. What do you think 'pure in heart' might mean?" he asked Katie.

"Somebody that's pure, I guess," she offered, gnawing on her cheek.

"Could you maybe give me an example?" Father pushed, rocking his shoulders, holding his Bible in front of him like a football in one hand. "Like a...well do you know anybody who you might call pure in heart?"

"Grandma maybe? Sister Snow?" Katie saw Sister Snow drift in and out of meetings and homes, her wavy blue-white hair set like her smile, her arms always full of dutiful rolls to be taken or rolls to be eaten—always afloat on well-nurtured selflessness.

"Well, maybe. Grandma especially. But maybe we'd better get on with the story of Oscar. You remember he was telling us why he hadn't been at practice all week. Well, Oscar went on to say he threw all the plates and then went back to the house where the two old ladies had lived. And lo and behold, what should he find but both of them back—looking for their plates! It seems they'd gone off without them to live with a brother who was sick, and they hadn't noticed about forgetting the plates till they'd started to fix a meal to take to him and it had taken a week to get back to search for the plates. By the time Oscar was knocking on their door they were frantic. And so was he. He couldn't bring himself to tell them what had really happened to the plates, so he just acted like he was helping them hunt while he thought about what he could do. Finally he told them he'd get them some plates and for them not to worry." Father paused again and looked at Wid.

"Can you imagine at all what Oscar could have done to make it up to those two ladies?"

Again Wid was stumped. He rubbed his temple with his left hand and his thigh with his right. "I guess he had to think pretty fast," he suggested.

"I would think so," Father agreed, "knowing how much those old plates must have meant to them—how bad they'd have felt to think Oscar had taken them, old as they were, and ugly." Father ran his fingers through the back of his graying hair. "I guess there's nothing much harder on a person than counting on someone for something and having them not be what you thought."

Katie was massaging her ear with a harsh thumb and running a hand in and out of her pocket. "So what'd he do—Oscar?" she asked in a voice that came from below her collar.

91

Father looked at Katie for a second, his mouth mellowing almost into a smile. "Well, old Oscar did something that seems to me to be about the purest thing I've ever heard of. He gave up coming out for practice—the thing he liked better than anything in the world—and even missed school—which was a plenty hard thing to do since it meant getting behind in every class. He said, 'I figured the only way to get back the plates was to earn 'em back, so I did. I went down to where they're cleanin' out the canal—you know after they drain it for fall and they have to get all that yuck out of the bottom. And I asked if they didn't need somebody to do some scrapin'. And sure nuff, they did, so I worked there every day till I made three dollars—which was what the plates cost at Woolworth's, twenty of 'em—and then I bought 'em and took 'em back to the ladies and here I am.' We all asked him some questions, like why did he buy new plates if the old ones were old, and what did the ladies use all those days he was trying to get enough money to buy new ones, and how did he explain it to the ladies when he showed up with their plates. And all he said was, 'I just told everything like it was, and I figured I better get new plates to make up for takin' the old ones. Even if I could 'a gone and got all the old ones and mended 'em back together there would 'a had to be some kinda difference on accounta me and what I done. It wasn't just the plates. It was me had to be put back somehow.'"

Father peered down at the open book in his hand and read slower than before, "Blessed are the pure in heart for they shall see God." Then he squeezed the leather cover to close it and said, "Sometimes I think seeing God is a privilege that only certain people get—not everybody all the time. Not even somebody all the time. But most of us some of the time. When things are right we can see Him in the fire in this stove, or in the pine tree out there swaying against the sky, or in a little baby grabbing for your hand, or in somebody catching a ball on the run." He looked slowly all around the room and then said, "I guess the only time we're not eligible to see Him is when we've been careless enough to let go of what makes

92

us pure in heart. Nobody does it to us—we do it all by ourselves. We let go. And we usually know when it happens. Things just get out of kilter and we don't see anything right. Why here was Oscar, simple, pure as your first breath, and he knew when he wasn't right—and he knew what to do about it. He wouldn't have seen the good there was in even football, let alone us, if he hadn't cleared things up for himself first." Father had walked over to the double doors leading to the porch. He opened them to the sunny day and turned to the class, still sitting waiting for more. "Have a good day, everybody. I'll see you later." And he walked out to and across the porch, then out of the screen door that slammed itself when he was halfway down the path to the parking place.

"Boy, not even a closing prayer," James said under his breath, getting up and walking the same route with Wid and Katie on either side, leaving the others still stretching to decide what their bodies were ready for.

When the three were up the trail almost to Grandma's, they turned to each other in the kind of knowing that living together provides.

"How'd he find out about the records?" James wondered. "And why today? Gee, I'd forgotten all about even tossing them. How long ago was it?"

"About three or four weeks anyhow. You'd think it would've come up before now if it was going to," submitted Wid.

"It had to be Mister Davis. Good old Mister Davis. You saw him squinching in at the screen, didn't you? And Father going out to talk to him? I knew it had to be something bad. On Sunday and all," Katie said. "But I thought it'd be about the bugs."

"Well, what're we gonna do about it?" Wid began, all business. "Father doesn't give you a story like this one just because he wants to talk."

"What I always wonder is how he can always come up with one that just hits the spot, the very spot that something's gone wrong in? How come he always knows how to tell one of his stories and then just let go?" Katie mused.

"Oh, he only looks like he lets go," James nodded, "when he knows darn well he's got you. There you are, just wriggling on his pin, so caught you don't have any choice except to go right out and do something different so you can quit wriggling."

"How the heck are we gonna earn enough money to pay for all those records? Gee, there must've been a couple a dozen—and do you have any idea how much a single record costs?" Wid moaned.

The three made leveled hollows in the dirt with their boots and did a lot of work with their mouths, looking at the dark blue sky through the green bushes. They could hear the crowd sifting out of Sunday School and knew it would very quickly be time to go to the road and then run along the path to their place for Sunday dinner. Aunt Elizabeth would be there, and Grandma, tying long aprons around their sturdy middles to stir gravy for the pot roast and make yellow mustard that would prickle their tongues.

"Grandma!" James almost choked. "Of course! Grandma!"

"Yeah! We can work for her! And between us all we can make enough to do anything!" Katie agreed, remembering Grandma's generosity with cures for doll ailments and cap gun replacements when a trigger broke.

"And she won't even ask what it's for," Wid added. "Remember when I needed a new flint for the marble tournament last year?"

"And then when she made us our pads?" interjected James, "with elastics for our knuckles. There was the flint inside, rolled up, like an egg in a bird's nest, and Grandma never acting like she knew one thing."

Grandma always gave the perfect thing, just enough to surprise and never enough to sate. She was the right one, all right, to go to in this emergency.

"What'll you ask her?" James said to Katie, knowing she'd be the one to talk to Grandma. After all, Katie slept in Grandma's bed with her every night in the city, and they

94

talked about everything. Mother called Katie Grandma's shadow, and Grandma did seem to have Katie somewhere around most of the time she was home. Or she was doing something for her. When the coal room wasn't needed any more in the basement because the furnace was converted to gas, hadn't Grandma called the workmen to turn the room into a play house for Katie?—with swirly stucco on the walls and the floor painted light green and the coal shoot jarred out so a window could be put in and flimsy curtains hung over it. And hadn't the wood bin been made into a closet and the whole room filled with Katie's doll furniture and dolls—all fourteen of them that got bathed every day? And didn't Katie clean everything always and keep it spick as anything so Grandma could visit any time and be pleased that it was so "tidy" and tell Katie so, so that she'd keep on being "Granmunner's 'unny bunch?"

Yes, Katie was the one to approach Grandma.

"I'll just ask if we can have some jobs—like sorting her wood boxes or shining her stove or pumping her toilet—the one up the hill. She has plenty of things for us to do, don't worry." Katie didn't mention that she also intended to tell Grandma about the records so she could help estimate how much it would cost to replace them. There was no use working more than they needed to.

Later that afternoon Katie walked Grandma up the almost-no slope to her cabin from the grassy parking place where Father had let them out after dinner. Grandma's hand felt like soft chamois. Her hands and face were a brownish yellow. "Chameleon skin," Mother called it, "tawny till it hits the sun, then instantly brown. But ladies of my day and Grandma's don't like it to look suntanned—that's considered coarse—so we keep it covered." And indeed they did. Even with sleeping where she slept, Katie had never seen anything but Grandma's hands and face, except maybe very rarely the tops of her toes dipping like a gopher into her slippers. In Mother's house no one ever went barefoot, not even on the carpet.

"Grandma, I've got a proposition," Katie began.

"Well now, that's a surprise for a little girl who never proposes much—not much at all," smiled Grandma, squeezing Katie's hand three times in their secret signal. "I wonder what it could be."

Katie squeezed back three times.

"Well, Wid and James and I need to make some money —fast. It's what you might call an emergency," Katie said, trying to look indifferently at the squirrel that was squabbling in the high pine next to Grandma's porch.

"Fast money, eh? Sounds pretty frisky. What could a little sit-at-home like you be needing with some money?" Before Katie could think of a good way to ease into the answer, Grandma continued, "You know it is most interesting that you should bring that up right now. It just so happens that I had a dandy job in mind for you that I was just going to suggest on this very visit. Now isn't that what you'd call a coincidence?"

Katie knew all about Grandma's coincidences. They were always so coincidental. She opened the door and Grandma stepped into her cabin. She moved ahead of Katie to one of the wicker rockers, swished it around to face out over the green gully below where the two streams merged, and motioned Katie to sit with her. Grandma comforted her delft blue shawl around her ample shoulders and then plumped herself into the chintz cushion in a grand arrival. Grandma was Katie's idea of what Queen Victoria must have been like —only happy. She never left her room without making her bed and herself "presentable," which meant having her black ash hair tightly in its bob, her stout sufficiency quartered in "stays" from bosom to thigh, and a dress of fine weave and intricate tailoring setting off the flow of even canyon activities in a majesty that defied defiling by coal scuttle or chamber pot.

"This job is one I've wanted done for a long time actually," Grandma said, turning to Katie and pulling her rocker closer. "But don't you think we need something a little cool to freshen us up for this kind of business talk? How does a slice of watermelon sound—as a sort of tider?"

Katie knew Grandma knew just exactly how a slice of watermelon would sound. Watermelon was one of the things that Grandma always had on hand that was never part of regular eating at the Barton's. Grandma had treats every minute, like peanut brittle that she poured on the slab of marble, or macaroons from ZCMI and oranges from the Sugar Merc or little round filets from the Modern Sausage—all places that delivered to her any time of day.

Without further encouragement, Katie sped to the stream and brought back the dark green melon covered with tiny black rounds that had collected and needed to be washed off in Grandma's blue enamel sink. That the water ran—and into a sink—and that there was even hot water from the slender tank warmed on the roof—all of it was luxury to Katie. When a new group of Grandma's ladies were not yet up for the week and Grandma was alone in her cabin, Katie got to stay with her. They had a cozy dinner on the linoleum topped table in the dining room under the huge pine and then played Honeymoon or Draw Bridge at the blue card table that was always set up in the living room.

Grandma would say, "This game is thorough. It can teach you to concentrate like nothing else." She'd run her fingers across the top of the fan of her hand. "By the time the third trick's been taken, you ought to know where every card is—and how to pull it out at precisely..." and she would whisk a card from the dummy to her left and snap it on the center, "... the moment it will do the most good—or harm." She would gather the four cards in her trick with the edge of her palm and fingertips in the same clean snatch that Katie used for jacks.

But Katie's mind scooted out from over her cards to the way the veins ran like blue worms over Grandma's knuckles. Above them was the brooch made of purplish blue sapphire that was always at her neck, and in her hair the combs with pearls across them that held back her "strays" behind each ear. It was too hard to care whether the Jack of Diamonds was high or to consider the ample possibilities if that King of Spades just played by Grandma was a singleton.

"Oh, Katie, you little silly!" Grandma would chide when Katie played a trump on her own ace. "You can't stand to be hedged in by counting anything, can you—not even trumps." And then Grandma would hug her and say, "Pshaw! I wonder how you'd do at give-away."

Through all their games they munched pink peppermints or grapefruit sections salted and sugared "to cut the acid and bring out the sweet—just like a little spanking does for a child," Grandma would say. No one ever got by with nonsense around Grandma. Even though she knew how to please, she expected to be pleased in return. She often told the children she lived with: "What Job proved with all his boils and losing everything he had—his cattle, his children, his wife, his position—what he proved was that he could say 'I know that my Redeemer lives' because he found out there isn't a way in the world that you can control what happens to you—you can only control what you do about what happens to you. Don't blame the Lord—or circumstances. Things happen. Life happens. All you can take care of is your response to it; so learn to take care of that response." Katie never tried harder than when Grandma was within earshot. At those times she even managed to keep her temper pretty well and not fly off the handle at a needle that wouldn't work fast enough, or at a column of figures on her arithmetic homework that took forever to add up, or at Davy when he left her play stove plugged in all day.

"About this job," Grandma now said to Katie cutting juicy pink triangles out of her melon. "You know Bloomerville."

"Sure."

Bloomerville was the clearing between the two streams under Grandma's house that was hidden from both the road and the cabin by a covering of foliage so thick that it was almost impassable. Katie knew how to slip like a rabbit under the dogwood and sumac and snuggle into a niche with a granite rock for backing and be secluded for hours. It was her favorite place in all the canyon. It surprised her to know Grandma ever thought about it.

"I want to have that whole area cleaned out so I can see the two streams. Seems a shame to have all that activity going on down there and not be able to see it as well as hear it."

Katie's heart sank. She felt just as full of leaks and just as swallowed by what she heard as the last birch bark canoe she'd made and set in the stream. Bloomerville was like a cave or private lair where nobody could find her and she could think about fairies or practice mumble peg or read or have a pony of her own. And now Grandma, of all people, wanted to take all the secret away and let it be there for everybody's looking.

Katie's head raced. How could she squelch Grandma's idea of seeing the streams and still keep a job that would let her and Wid and James get back some pure heart by replacing the records? What if she lost the chance? How could she explain to Wid and James? And even if she could, Bloomerville would be finished. Everybody would know. Even the stinging nettle on the side toward the road could be cut down to get in there, or people could learn to pinch a stem hard, upward, not downward, and not get stung while they held it aside and slipped through like she did. Fairies would never come any more. They'd be afraid. The candles on their wings would blow out with too much human breath. So if that were the case, why not say "all right" and clear it out? There'd be another secret place. Maybe not one so soft or quiet or handy, But so? She kept telling herself the canyon was filled with secret places. Bloomerville wasn't so much.

Katie spit a black seed onto her plate, and it bounced like a tiddly wink over her rind and onto the toe of her boot. She stared at it for a minute, fascinated by the way it stuck even to the brown polish. She wiggled her toe. It stayed. She wiggled again, determined to finish her project before taking on another. This time the black seed slid off to the rug and

Katie pushed forward on her chair to be able to cover it with her sole. Then she looked up at Grandma and said, "Course. That would be really nice for you to be able to see what the streams are like when they get together. They do funny things to each other."

"Do they Katie? How do you know?"

"Oh, I've watched them sometimes—when I've been on hikes and stuff."

"What kind of things do they do?"

"They talk. One creek is old. It's come all the way down from the spring up by the Divide, past all the cabins and under a thousand bridges. And the other one is just a baby, just started up there above Castle Crags in your gully. It thrashes around when it bumps into the big one and hates not being on its own anymore. After that it just becomes part of something else. It can't find its own sides, and none of its rocks come with it."

"That sounds like pretty sad talk to me," said Grandma, leaning to put a hand on Katie's ringlets that were still smooth and shiny at four o'clock in the afternoon. If Katie had noticed, she would have known that it had been a not-right day, not if there had not been a single thing worth getting mussed up over.

"When do we start, Grandma? I hope it's soon 'cause we have a really important thing on." Katie turned her rocker around with little shoves on the floor until she faced the living room. She could see Grandma still looking out over the green ravine where the streams crashed into each other to sound like rain in a torrent. Katie loved to think of Grandma the way Mother talked about her. She wasn't sure what she knew by herself and what had been told her. But she did know that Grandma somehow managed like a blue spruce in the wind, and always had managed.

Sleeping that night on the cot in the corner of the living room at Grandma's cabin, Katie heard her breathing across the room in her downy deep bed but could not see her over the heap of quilts on her feet. She liked to deliberately hold back one breath in five to match Grandma's slower time. It was the one thing she could stand to wait for. Every time, though, Katie had to keep pushing the pillow under her cheek so that she could see over it until the very last minute and feel that she was sleeping with Grandma. But the pillows she slept on here at Grandma's were too puffy and she couldn't see. She had to count on the fire to send her off. Watching it, she made its dancing on the ceiling match the rhythm of Grandma's breathing too. All three rose and fell together, as companionable as smoke, flame, and tinder. The last thing Katie noticed was the flames going faster than either she or Grandma could possibly breathe.

Katie walked home from Grandma's slowly on Monday morning, down the road, across the path, hardly even watchful for a rustle in the bushes.

She was in no hurry to tell Wid and James that they could start on the project under Grandma's house. "There's plenty of places for a secret place," she thought, "like down there by the old cooler. Or behind the wood pile. Or below the platform by the moss village. Or on the way to the Bluebird." She kept trying. The whole canyon was one big secret place, all hers. But by the time she was within throwing distance of Smithy's tin roof, she knew something. Ten is too late to start on that kind of place. You have to grow up with that kind. It has to be discovered when you don't know about much, so it all feels made to fit. And then you grow into it till it's tight and snug and fills all your crevices. But it can't stay that way long. It stays the same, but you don't. And sometime when you go to slip inside it and feel the way you always have, it's no good. You've grown, and it hurts not to fit anymore. Some places you find out about growing past on your own, and even that's no fun. But when something else makes you say goodbye to your place, it's about the hardest thing there is. Because you can never go back.

"Gosh," Katie said to herself, "how do you keep from being eleven—in October?"

CHAPTER SEVEN

The 24th of July in Utah is bigger than the 4th by a long shot. July 24, 1847, the Mormon pioneers first looked over the valley of the Great Salt Lake. Brigham Young, sick in his ox-drawn covered wagon, but able to rise from his bed long enough to see where he was, is said to have said, "This is the place, drive on." Every year a great parade floods down Main Street on the morning of the 24th, and celebrants feast, fling and send fireworks into the night in every part of Mormondom. Because of living summers in the canyon, the Bartons had never seen a parade, but they anticipated the holiday like no other in the year. In the canyon they had their own kind of festivities.

The day started at 7:00 A.M. with the big hike to the Armchair. "Hurry and get that breakfast down," Father admonished. "And no leaving a drop of oatmeal. He who leaves oatmeal 'oat' to be left home!"

"Oh, Father!" the three oldest said in chorus, shaking their heads and grinning.

Already the two scout canteens were filled with spring water, the tin cups had been strung through belts, lunches were packed in cloth bags that could tie or be tucked into waist bands, long sleeves were rolled down for protection from thorns, hiking sticks were set by the front door, and bandanas were tied around necks ready for holding back hair or pulling protection over a nose in real dust. Or they might —the titillating thought prevailed—be used for a tourniquet.

All the cousins down to and, this year, including those Davy's age got to go. Father's only stipulation was that "everybody has to get there on two legs, not four. No piggy backs allowed." This was Davy's first year to go beyond the Divide. Until now Mother and some of the other ladies had gone that far—about half-way—eaten lunch with everyone and then brought the smaller ones home. Katie knew that she would never grow up to be a lady who would ever come home from half-way. But this year Davy and Matthew had been planning for days what they'd do on the hike. "It'll be a cinch," Davy told everyone, "being as I've been to the Divide at least four times. The Armchair's only twice as far, so I've as good as been there a couple of times already!"

Katie loved to get Davy ready for anything. He was patient with her wanting to comb his wavy hair over and over and tie a tie on him even for "every day." He'd stand with his hands in his pockets and his chin raised while she soothed, "Oh, Davy, what a fine outfit! You look ten times better than you did in your Little Lord Fauntleroy!" Then he'd start swinging his fists. Nobody, not even Katie, could mention the outfit Mother had dressed him in to have his picture taken when he was four. That day Wid and James had to leave the studio where the man had his head stuck in the drapes behind the camera so they wouldn't make him either laugh or cry. And then Mother had tinted the picture with her oil paints on cotton swabs so the suit looked all light blue besides ruffly. Since he had to look at it every time he went past the bookcase in the entrance hall at home, Davy had become the very best one in the family about taking his friends to the back door when they came. That way they could go straight to the basement stairs to throw the football up and down under the bangy furnace pipes and never be exposed to the hateful picture.

"Katie, I'm not wearing any tie on the hike, though," he warned as she advanced on him after breakfast.

"Oh, I know," she assured him, "I just want to show you how to tie your neckerchief."

She led his chubby fingers through the routine overs and unders and smiled at his perplexed fumblings. "That's right," she said, "there'll be plenty of us around for knot tying when you need it after you get bitten by a rattler, or your leg has to be cut off."

Davy was by this time in the summer as dark as a native —his brown eyes matching his brown curls, face and arms. When he appeared in any snapshot it looked as if he were standing in a shadow. All that was clear was a smile. Katie called him "Davy Treasure" and the boys called him "Babe" when they were teasing, which seemed to Davy to be most of the time. "My name is David Gill!" he would tell them, refusing to answer or come to any of the other names. "And some day I'm gonna be big enough to call you Bruv. Then you'll be sorry you ever called me those dumb old names."

"And what will you call me?" Katie smiled.

"Probly in time for nothin'," he threatened, with an old joke of Father's, not able even then to resist a white grin that brought Katie hugging and paddling him.

With each brother things were different for Katie. But James was important in ways that she couldn't explain. She and James talked about everything. James was less than a year older than Katie and they were in the same grade in school. When she had started Kindergarten he and Wid had walked her to school the first day because Mother was in the hospital having her appendix out. Katie had gone dutifully into the Kindergarten line and watched as Wid disappeared around the corner to the second grade and James lined up with the first grade boys to march in when the bell rang at Highland Park School. It was the first time she had ever gone anywhere with James that he hadn't kept her right beside him. In the classroom a few minutes later, she sat on the floor at Miss Ralphs' feet looking up at a monument of strangeness and around at a cavernous expanse of faces set in grim resolution.

"That's Miss Ralphs, all right," she thought. "The same one James had for a teacher. Only bigger."

Miss Ralphs began giving instructions and handing a gritty glob of clay to each child sitting cross-legged in the circle. As she bent over to drop the damp lump into Katie's hand, there was a typical affirmation of James' knowing everything. "Yep," she thought, "just like James said—you can see her lungs when she bends over."

Everything Miss Ralphs did was overlaid with a kind of predictability that hung it with drudgery for Katie, who felt as though she were doing it all for the thousandth time: how the clay had to be kneaded into firm workability and then worked and worked till whatever shape it took was a monster of boredom; how the cardboard post office in the corner was to be manned and operated with solar precision; how the big rug was rolled out for rest time and how she had to lie out straight and couldn't curl her knees up the way they were supposed to go because she might kick somebody; how Miss Ralphs always talked like she was more than one person, when Katie knew she was talking about everybody except herself.

By recess Katie thought it must be night time. When Miss Ralphs announced in her sickly voice that "*We* will all go outside now and play very nicely," Katie let loose her knees that had been held so tight her calves hurt, and was herded with the thirty others toward the playground. It was all she could do to pass up the girls' restroom where every child but her had "paid a visit" on a programmed tour of available conveniences. She had been so shaken by the sight of what lay bare within the doorless stalls that she had refused to take her turn on the pretense that she already had and needed only to wash her hands with the lilac fragrance that bubbled from a plunger above the fat basin. But she knew James would be waiting for her on the gravel diamond by the first grade fountain.

"How'd it go?" he asked, walking toward her, his knickers neat around his blue stockings, and tossing a softball that had protruding seams.

"Think fast! Here," and the ball zoomed directly at her chest. She snagged it, ran finger print fingers around its seams and whisked it back overhead to James without looking away from him.

"Well? What'd you do?" James persisted. "Did old Miss Ralphs pull her usuals?"

Katie saw James start to grin the way he always did when he was thinking about things that should be serious. He was the brother she tried not to sit by in church because they always got the giggles. Like when the song said "Yoo Hoo unto Jesus" and they had to leave, hunching up the searing aisle acting like they had the nosebleed.

"James..." Katie wanted to sound brave like she knew Wid and James would have been, but all she could do was bite the inside of her top lip and try to swallow and look at the gravel she was sorting with the toe of her high white shoe.

James walked to her and swung his arm around her shoulders to hang his hand over her collar bone. "You don't like it, huh?" he said. "Yeah, well, I can't say as I blame you, the way old Miss Ralphs has to smile out everything she says —and her having so much too much to say. Nope, can't say as I blame you."

Katie was clamping her bicuspids together till she looked like a chipmunk, and tears ran without a curve over her cheeks and onto the waterwave taffeta blouse that Mother had made her try on eleven times in the making.

"There's gotta be something we could do," James continued, his left arm around Katie, his right still twirling the ball up and catching it in an easy rhythm.

Katie ran the knuckles of her right forefinger across her nostrils and then remembered the hanky Mother had pinned to the belt of her jumper when she'd laid it out before going to the hospital to have her appendix out. The note from

Mother, lying on top of the dresser, had to be read by Father on the morning of starting school. On the outside of the fold it said:

> There was a young beautiful lady
> Whose name was all light and not shady
> For school she did start
> With a song in her heart,
> And everyone sang, "There's our Katie!"

Inside was:

> How I'll miss being here to kiss you off to your first big day at Highland Park! Oh, what a lucky school to be getting you! Have a lovely time learning, Dearie, in your beautiful new velour dress. And be a lady.
> I love you always,
> Mother

Katie didn't want to be a lady going to school. She wanted to run out, dodge, cut back, and catch the siren ball that James could throw her. Or be behind him on roller skates jiggling down the dented driveway at the ward. Or sitting high in her perch in the elm that nobody could get to without jumping from Salinger's garage to the limb made shiny by the hands that had snatched it in their swoops. She wanted to be sitting there on the perfect prong that cupped her bottom and leafed her head while she listened to the stories James made up—or make up her own about monster clouds that played Run–Sheepie–Run with the branches and always got away. Right now she wanted it to be summer so she could poof up like a cloud and be off into the blue, floating over the mountains up there, past the Crow's Nest, down onto Armchair road, and right into her secret hiding place where the long grass matted like fingers when she sat on it to burrow into its streamers. More than anything she didn't want to be crying. Anybody big enough to go to school where Wid and James did ought to be big enough to be a good sport.

"Katie, I've got it!" James caught the ball and moved his other arm to the back of Katie's neck to become a rudder in the walk he started her on.

"What are you thinking, James? Where are we going?" Katie had never had any desire to alter James' directions, sure as they were to end up in something more spectacular for being scary. Like when he had her loosen the screen inside their classroom in Primary while the teacher was rasping at someone on Tuesday afternoons at the Ward House where they went to church. Then she and James and Wid and certain franchised friends would scrunch in later when the building was empty and titter "John Dew the Magician" to an empty hall from behind the pulpit in the chapel or play "The Happy Farmer" with their bunched fingers on the cold black pedals of the pipe organ, or with their most rapid eyes see what other kinds of bathrooms looked like, and be ready to run for the window if Mr. Tomlinson, the janitor, came clinking in. James knew the quickest, wiliest ways to anything.

"I'll just take you in my class—with me. Miss Lindsay won't care. Wid told me she's great," he said now, engineering her toward the first grade door.

"What about Mother?" Katie wondered in her most solid voice.

"Why worry? Why should she even know? By the time she gets home from the hospital we'll be all set."

James could manage. He took Katie to his teacher and explained, "Miss Lindsay, Katie here's my sister, and we're sort of used to being together, and she's not liking it much being in Kindergarten by herself, so I was wondering if she could just come in here and sort of give it a try." James kept his arm around Katie's shoulder but let her inch backwards enough to feel she wasn't really there. "She's pretty good at things—and I could help her if she needs it. I noticed there was a vacant desk over there by the window," he finished, guiding a silent and still teary Katie past Miss Lindsay's skirt and across the room to a desk about half way down the last row.

Katie slipped under the slanted shelf and sat with her back touching but not her feet as the first graders crashed into the room and Miss Lindsay funneled them to their seats.

James whispered, "I'll have to sit over there. Just do everything she says and it'll all work out." He slid under three desks on his way to his own.

Miss Lindsay didn't seem to mind that Katie was there. Every now and then she looked at her when the class was droning out "cat" "mat" "sat" as she raised cardboards with words hand-printed in India ink on them—but she never asked her for the answers Katie was itching to give. During afternoon recess Katie played first base on the team chosen by James and hit a high ball that let her get to second while Euan Blanch slid home.

"That won't hurt anything—you hitting that double and getting Bryon out on a throw to second. Did you see Miss Lindsay watching? She's the teacher that checks the playground at recess and P.E. She's bound to figure you're ready for first grade if you can handle a ball."

James' confidence spilled over into the later afternoon when he casually requested, "Miss Lindsay, Katie would probably learn a lot more if she could sit on my side of the room. Mother'd really appreciate it if I could kind of keep an eye on how she's doing."

Miss Lindsay turned out to be a teacher who didn't use a smile. Hers just came, like color in invisible ink when it was dipped in water, shining there clear on a sheet that had been totally blank. It was amazing how often it came when James was manipulating a game or a page or an argument. Under that smile Katie traded places with Dale Pepper and spent her school years on James' side of everything.

Six years later, James was still getting Katie into things and out of things and talking over anything they didn't do together. Even gravitating to worlds of their own never changed that. On the hike they were easy with anyone.

The trek to the Armchair started at Barton's with Father

recruiting new forces as they passed every cabin. Along the path they picked up Smithy, on the other side of the canyon Charles and Little Wooster, who had saddled Goldie and was perched on her waiting to ride as far as there was a passable trail. Below Uncle Phillip's were Isabel and Jody Sue, and around the curve by Leigh's the group picked up Phillip and Matthew. Phillip was handsome, wiry, full of ideas, and was a secret pal to Jody Sue, his double cousin and best friend. Sometimes they let Katie play with them together and she felt honored because they knew each other in the city too, and carried an aura of confidentiality that summer affiliations seemed too simple for.

Matthew and Davy fell into matching strides several inches too long for their short legs as the line formed: Father in the middle, Goldie and Little Wooster just behind, the rest ranked across the width of the road. They hiked in step chanting, "I left, I left, I left my wife and forty-eight kids, I left, I left..." "Hustle!" Father said between words, "The first one to cave in is a piker of a hiker."

There were regular resting places, and no one would have suggested stopping anywhere else. At Royal Park they lay on their stomachs to drink from the clear smooth trickle that came directly from a spring. They cut through Morgan Dell and took a look at Marcus Evers' horses in the clearing that smelled of them and made Katie tingle with wanting to race with Marcus on the pinto that he sometimes let her ride bareback. Then they were onto the road where cars hardly ever traveled—the grassy centered, almost grown over road that buggies and wagons had rutted when they had traveled years before to the Old Hotel.

Lambert's cabin stuck out from the mountain like a peg, and underneath it, from its stilt supports, hung the best swing in the canyon. Take-off was more a dive than anything because pushing back would have meant cracking a head on the floor above. Each took a lunge into the chokecherry air kicking like a caught fish at the end of the groaning rope. Little Wooster stayed on Goldie, cheering every swing.

It was 9:00 A.M. and beginning to get hot—the dry, sparkling Utah hot that pervaded even the canyon by the middle of July. There had not been a single rain storm yet that summer, and even now, as they cut through the zig-zags that rose in a dry creek bed between Lamberts' and the Old Hotel where there was shade from aspen and maple and dense scrub oak, their long sleeved shirts stuck to their arms and backs, and their hair curled around their necks and foreheads. As always, the spring was there as a last rescue, a crystal sheet of isinglass that was the final drinking place on the hike. They all stretched out flat and let the cold water sting their teeth and throb clear into their ears. Little Wooster dismounted and tied Goldie to a maple clump so she would not get a gulp that would give her the heaves. He went down to the stream, joints bending and lowering like a camel, and took long slurping draughts with the others, all of them disdaining the tin cups in their belts.

"Next stop, The Old Hotel!" Father proclaimed as they stood and tucked in their shirts, all looking up the trail that dove into the bushes above.

"Tell us the ghost story of The Old Hotel, Father," Davy requested, taking giant knee-chest steps to keep close to Father's boots.

"You mean you'd want to hear a ghost story right out here in broad daylight?" asked Father. "Why it'd lose all its scare."

"Oh, no it wouldn't," protested Davy. "In fact, it'd be scarier 'cause we're right here where it all happened. I promise—I'd be plenty scared." He glanced around him at the tight brush and up at the trees whose tops collided with a deep blue sky, and felt far away from everything. "In fact, I'd probably be scared before you even started very much," he said under his breath, remembering how the story always affected him listening to it in the dark at parties.

"Sure, come on, Father," urged Wid.

Katie wanted him to tell it so much that she didn't dare press for it. Sometimes, she knew, the best things happened

112

all by themselves, suddenly, without being looked forward to or encouraged. Just by themselves. Especially things with Father.

But everyone else urged, and Father fell back to the end of the group so that they all could hear, and began the famous story. "It must have been about ten years ago, a long time after The Old Hotel was abandoned. You know, all of you, the road up here used to be traveled all the time when The Old Hotel was open for business. It was at the very top of the canyon, just at the foot of the Divide between Millcreek and our canyon. And it was sort of the thing to do to come up and stay overnight. People from all over the valley would drive their buggies up to have dinner on the porch and look out over the canyon at the sunset and then have a room to sleep in away from the city heat. But gradually fewer and fewer people found time to drive all that way, and The Old Hotel went out of business. I guess that's the only way any of us remember it—sitting up there on the hill kind of sad like a lady waiting for a train that never comes—all empty and deserted, a place for animals to make nests and for all of you to carve your initials to say you've been there.

"I carved mine four times already," Davy announced.

Father rubbed his hair and went on, "Well, one day two of your older cousins, Eric and Bradford, were talking with some of their cousins, and they bragged that The Old Hotel wasn't really a scary place at all—and that they'd just as soon sleep there as any place they could think of. Just because nobody had stayed there for a lot of years didn't mean that it was haunted or anything. It was just vacant, that's all. So, of course, the other cousins dared them to do it. They said if Eric and Bradford would take their sleeping bags and no flashlight or candle or even matches, and go up to The Old Hotel and stay inside it—anywhere inside it—through a whole night, then they'd win the bet. And you know how important it is to win a bet."

"Yeah, really important," Davy said earnestly.

"So Eric and Bradford got their sleeping bags and right

after dinner they headed up to The Old Hotel, right along this very trail. It was starting to get dark even before they were this far up, so they hurried because they wanted to be sure to get all settled before it was too dark to see. They raced up past here to the rickety old stairway leading up to the porch. Eric was the oldest, so he went up first, two steps at a time to show Bradford how not afraid he was. Going fast would prove a lot. So Bradford went fast too.

"They opened the squeaky door with the screen partly ripped off and walked across the porch, looking at all the initials and sayings that people had left in the railings and floor over all the years. Everybody they were related to seemed to be there, and the lettering stood out more clearly that it ever had in the daytime. The old boards in the floor creaked and squawked, but neither of the boys said anything about never noticing that before.

"They decided that the best place to sleep would be in the huge living room. Remember how it is? A lot like all of our cabins—in the middle of the house, only with a fireplace and exposed rafters. They tried to act nonchalant, like, of course, that would just be the logical place to stay, but actually they both had looked pretty carefully at all the possibilities and had both concluded that it wouldn't be too bad to be able to close another set of doors between them and the rest of the place.

"They stretched out their bags in one corner on two old cots with exposed springs, figuring that would get them off the floor—above rats or squirrels...or anything else. It was sort of different to be thinking about sleeping where something—any old thing—might be crawling or running around or going over them. When it came right down to it, there were quite a few things they hadn't really thought too much about before right then. But they kidded about how unscary it all was and talked about what a fine time they'd have telling everyone about their adventure." Father paused to catch his breath. They were hiking up a steep trail at their usual speedy clip, and trying to make himself heard over the whole line

114

of hikers was real exertion. "Maybe we'd better stop the story here," he said. "You all know what happens anyhow."

There was the wave of groans and "No! No! Keep going! We never know what happens!"

He went on with what he had never intended to stop. "Well, Eric and Bradford slipped into their bags and went to sleep very fast. They'd already decided that would be the best thing—to just slip off and let the night take care of itself before they had any trouble with it. A while later—neither of them had any idea of how much later—Bradford woke up and lay there in the dark listening—to what, he had no idea. Then he heard it—the scraping sound that must have waked him up. It was a scraping on the stairs out in front, not awfully loud, but loud enough that he could make out a progression of scrapes moving gradually up toward the door. He reached toward Eric's cot and shook the arm that he located outside the bag. 'Did you hear that?' he whispered. Eric, of course, hadn't heard anything—or he would have been awake, too. He was even kind of upset at being disturbed in the middle of the night. 'Hear what?' he asked and just turned over to go back to sleep.

"'That noise—that scraping out on the front steps,' Bradford told him. Eric opened his eyes and stared into the thick dark, a dark that was so dark that he couldn't make out Bradford's face that had to be no more than a foot away from his own. Now he could hear it. The scraping was almost to the top of the steps, almost level with the floor they were on.

"Neither of the boys dared say anything else—or move. They just listened, so hard their ears rang and their eyes bulged and swept from side to side. There was a pause. A long one. Then the scraping started again, slow and regular, one step at a time. Scrape. Scrape. Closer. Closer. Then another pause. A longer one. Now on the top of the stairs. But even when the scraping stopped, they both knew they could hear something. Something breathing. The room they couldn't see throbbed all around them. It beat in and out in time with the breathing.

"Then, all of a sudden, there was a ripping, like the whole front door was being smashed—or pulled off. They both pictured the short distance between that door and the double doors leading into the room they were in. All there was between was the bedroom wing and those doors. And now the thought of those doors being any protection seemed ridiculous. Whatever could do that to the front door could do the same to those inside doors. And there they'd be—just lying there, helpless, waiting for the same thing to happen to them.

"They felt frozen—all except right under their eyes, where the skin twitched. Where could they go? There was no other way to get out of the room. And they sure couldn't try getting past whatever was on its way across the porch. By now the scraping had started again. Scratchy, heavy, digging into all those initials in the floor, coming closer and closer to the living room. Closer. Closer. Bigger. Louder.

"Finally Eric whispered, 'The rafters!' and both boys slid out of their bags and felt around for the walls next to them. Running around the walls at two different heights was a wainscoating—you know, a two by four with a molding on it that divides the wall boards into sections. Well, they remembered how that was, and they felt around till they found the lower strip. Even though they couldn't see each other, they did everything at just about exactly the same time. Almost like they were giving signals.

"As soon as they touched the bottom two by four ledge they stepped onto it from their cots and pushed up to grab the upper level. They'd been doing this very thing to get into the rafters of their own cabin for years, so they knew how. And they were fast. They were the kind of fast you are when you absolutely have to be—the fastest there is. When they caught hold of that upper two by four, even though it was barely wide enough to let the tips of their fingers find a place, they hoisted themselves up and swung a leg over the beam that ran across the top of the room.

"They both hung on, lying lengthwise on the beam that

116

was only a two by eight standing on end—pretty skinny to lie on. Then they worked their way to what they thought must have been the middle of the room. They hadn't been there a second when there was the same crash at the double doors.

"They could hear the scraping now, so clear it felt like it went right along their backs and into their brains. Scrape. Scrape. They could feel it, too, like a giant wind hollowing out the room; something moving its bigness very slowly, very carefully. It moved all over. First to one side, then the other, working its way to the back corner where their sleeping bags still were, gaping open and smelling of them.

"The scraping stopped in the corner. There was a shuffling. Then a ripping. Like a knife cutting through layers of quilts and blankets. Eric and Bradford didn't dare take a breath. The two by eight sliced into their stomachs, and their arms hugged on so hard they had no circulation. But you can bet they hung on. Nothing could have pried them loose. Right below them they heard whatever it was begin to move again. The coils of the springs in one cot squeaked and they knew it had climbed onto it. Then there was a scraping around the wall to where Eric had been only a few minutes before. The whole room seem to heave with the weight of it. The Old Hotel swayed as the thing moved, so that Bradford and Eric felt like they were being rocked out of their perches."

Davy and Matthew had split ranks and were each sidling as close as possible to Father's boots, reaching for his big hands and eyeing the trail. Davy looked up at Father even though it made him stumble a little, and squinted his interest. "They didn't fall down or anything, did they?" he ventured.

"Well, no, Davy. As a matter of fact they stretched out on those beams for a long, long time. Whatever it was down below tried every way to get up to where they were—they could tell by the sounds—but finally the scraping started on the floor again and went out the doors, across the porch, and down the old stairs. But Eric and Bradford didn't dare move, not a muscle. They waited up there in the rafters till morning, and even then, it was hard to make themselves come down. They could see their sleeping bags—ripped to shreds, just like they'd have been if they'd been down there. But they figured they'd hear if the thing came back, so they eased down and then just tore home, lickety split.

"But as soon as they saw their family, the first thing somebody said to Eric was, 'What happened to your hair?' Because with all that scaring—and you'll probably never believe this—quess what?—his hair had turned totally white. Yep—white as Uncle Wooster-with-the-Long-Beard's."

"But, tell us what it was—whatever it was that was up there," begged Katie, wanting to hear as urgently as she had the first time she'd heard the story.

"Well, the whole canyon wanted to know that same thing, of course, so they organized a search party that went right back up to The Old Hotel and started hunting. And they found tracks all over the place—as big as dinner plates. Grandpa Ruskin said it was a bear so big it could have killed a boy with one swipe of his paw. It was an old one and maybe not so quick as it might have been—or agile—but it'd come way down for food. You know nobody but Mister Davis ever sees bear up here. But some of the men went hunting and tried to find him to shoot him. But it was no use. He was too smart for them. So you know what? I figured, 'Candland, get busy.' And I went all over and scouted him out and I killed him with my *bare* hands! And ever since he's been lying on the floor right next to the bed where I can step out in my *bare* feet and *barely* appreciate him."

"Oh, Father," Davy grinned. "You did not! You didn't ever kill a bear with your bare hands."

"Think not? Well, a man can't expect everybody to believe him all of the time. But I'll tell you what. If you really want to know the inside dope—listen here." Father leaned down to whisper into Davy's ear.

"Oh, Father," Davy said, in contemptuous knowing, "You know I can't ask the bear! He's dead."

"Well, if we see his live brother along the trail today,

118

maybe he could tell you," Father offered, and they were at The Old Hotel curve.

But The Old Hotel was everywhere, coasted down the mountain like spilled noodles against the force of a river of snow that still stuck up in patches through the remains of shingles and boards and screen. Even the rock fireplace was strewn through the trees.

"Let's not stop," Wid said, edging around the spill of the rubble. No one else even wanted to look. Some other time they might hike up and search for their initials in the pile, but right now The Old Hotel was a cemetery for itself, too new to be tolerated in any but the briefest encounter, and then only in the silence of recognition.

Just beyond The Old Hotel the shrubbery began to thin out. Within ten minutes, the group was above the timber line, hiking in the snapping saxifrage and bright orange Indian paintbrush. The heat felt hotter. "Now?" asked James of Father, pulling his shirt out over his pants like a bellows.

"It is kinda hot," admitted Father. "I guess Mother wouldn't mind—this far off the road." So they peeled off their wet shirts and tied them around their waists. Katie and Jody Sue were as happy as the boys to get rid of theirs, but Isabel fell quickly to the end of the line and dawdled with some rocks, waiting for the climb to start again.

"Hey, Isabel," what's the matter?" Katie called. "Don't tell me you're not hot!"

"Actually, no. It's one of our cooler hikes," Isabel answered, still looking raptly at the rocks.

Jody Sue walked toward her sister suspiciously. "You're just trying to make us all think what a lady you are," she accused. "I know you—always after the impression."

Isabel didn't answer. Katie sensed the tension that sometimes flared between the sisters, so she walked down to Isabel saying, "Come on, Isabel, you know how much easier it is to hike without a shirt on."

It surely had always been for her—feeling the breeze dry

her back as soon as moisture formed, being able to wind up for a rock throw without material to jerk at her arm. But Isabel was silent. At a closer glance Katie could see that she was as red as her neckerchief and not looking anywhere. Something was wrong, but Katie couldn't feel her way to it. "Oh, let's just go," she said to Jody Sue. "If she doesn't want to take her shirt off, so what?" and she started back up the mountain.

Then Jody Sue began to giggle and trotted ahead of Katie.

"What's the matter? What's so funny?" Katie asked, keeping in step with Jody Sue. Usually she knew what was so funny, and it bothered her to be missing it. But Jody Sue wouldn't tell anything except to say, "Just be glad you're not eleven."

At the Divide they peered over seven ridges on one side and eight on the other. Above them was only Pine Top, and below them the green rivers of Armchair and Millcreek canyons. Now they were hiking across the ridge on big rocks or stony trails through the sagebrush and sego lilies all the way to the Armchair.

Their mouths were dry as soda crackers and they all would have sampled their canteens, but it was too soon. It took an hour and a half to clear the ridges. Beyond each was another until the stone Armchair finally loomed gray and jagged. They clambered over the loose rock at its base and began to climb up its back, their stomachs grabbing with the idea that rattlers might be along any crack. On the tip of its left arm Father reached for the flag pole anchored in a pile of rocks. "Who has this year's flag?" he asked, grunting with trying to loosen the stake.

"I do," said Davy, proudly pulling an old undershirt out of the front of his pants where he had stuffed it early that morning.

Father took the flag and tied it to the pole with some twine from his pocket. It blew its crinkles out in the breeze, and everyone shouted, "Ray!" as Father reset the maple post.

120

They all found crevices in the rock and wriggled for a good
fit to occupy during lunch: smashed vienna sausage sandwiches, more milk-warm oranges, melted Hersheys, and a
judicious sip of a drink from one of the canteens. On the tall
back of the Armchair they were so high up that Katie's
insides bit each other if she looked down. They all threw
every rock they could find to test how far "down" was.

"Let's go," Father announced. "Last one down's your
father's uncle!" They scattered to the back of the huge rock
to begin the hike home. Coming down was the best of all.
Father took one of Matthew's and one of Davy's hands and
plunged off the ridge, over the tumbling rocks to the bushes
that hit his waist and their eyes. Behind them leaped the
others like fawns, half galloping, half jumping, their arms
raised high above them, their shirts back on for protection
from the wild rosebushes that spurred up through the soft
dense clumps of brush. They never stopped going, just ricocheted off the ground and bounded another span yelping and
laughing as the unexpected tossed them like ping-pong balls
down the mountain.

At the top of the Devil's Slide where the creek bed
started, they waited to run one at a time. Katie could remember the time Father had let her stay high up and had run
down ahead of her. She had started down like him, easy,
bouncy, but down was farther than she had estimated and
her weight began to get ahead of her. She couldn't stop running, but neither could she catch up with herself. Her arms
windmilled and her legs jack-hammered against the slope
that sucked her down. She would have sprawled flat, but
Father had caught her just in time, as always, surrounded her,
his chest against her fall. Now she knew how to come down
with the rest, like reined horses, their weight back, their legs
giving and letting go in the rhythm that was control.

Finally there was what was left of the glacier, only a
ribbon of sooty, grainy gray. All but Isabel took their shirts
off again to sit on and slide in twirls and swishes that had
only trees for brakes. Then they were in the Bluebird gully,

121

racing to the road along the squishy narrow swamp where butterflies collected and erupted as they streamed through. In the field at the bottom were Goldie and Little Wooster, both relaxed in the shade with full stomachs and easy waiting.

"Was it a good hike?" Little Wooster asked.

Wid trotted directly to him and offered him a hand to get up with. "It was OK," he said nodding, "but you probably had about as much fun here in the shade. Awful hot up there."

"Wanna ride with me, Wid?" Little Wooster asked grunting onto Goldie.

"Sure. Why not? As far as Morgan Dell anyhow. Boy, I sure do need a rest. You're lucky not to be tired for the bonfire tonight." He put his left foot in the stirrup Little Wooster kicked toward him and swung on behind the saddle. "Maybe at Morgan Dell we'll switch. Katie'd love to ride the rest of the way. You know her and horses."

Katie barely heard him and thought, "Yeah, and I know you and how much you want to play leap frog between Morgan Dell and home—on the straight stretch. How come it's me you pick on and not James or one of the others? How come it's always me for dishes and stuff?" Then she got thinking about riding, and no matter how hard she tried not to let it happen, it started to sound a lot better than she wanted it to.

It was four o'clock. By the time they got home it would be almost time for the bonfire. They were all dusty and smelling of heat and the sage they'd sprung in and out of, but the bounce was still in their legs and they played leap frog down the road, accenting every spring with a Tarzan call. Rounding the curve by Hickman's, Wid executed a flying bound over James that catapulted him into a run for his balance. Staggering to a stop, he began to bend over to become the frog that James would leap, when he saw Daniel Moon. Daniel Moon was alone as always, walking up the inside of the road. He had on his bib overalls, and his fat jaws rolled into his neck above an undershirt. His arms looked like half-inflated balloons and his stubby fingers were rubbing the hollow marsh reed that he sucked in and out of his wet mouth. His eyes were smaller than any other part of him, with so little of them showing that their color was undefinable. His hair was the yellow color of a milk snake and fell in strings across his forehead from the pompadour it had been greased into.

Wid's throat tightened and his groin hurt. He straightened and faced Daniel Moon who stood enough downhill that their eyes were almost even. James came tearing around the curve expecting Wid to be bent over for him to brace his hands on and straddle in a flying vault. When he saw Wid was upright instead and glowering at Daniel Moon, it was all James could do to cut his stride and slide around Wid to a dust-puffing halt. The three were statues, bronzed with surprise and fear. James' chest heaved and his mouth stayed open to accommodate his panting. "Now," he thought, "now, Daniel Moon, we'll see about that bug."

Just then Father and the others pounded around the corner. "Well, hello," Father said to Daniel Moon who still stared at Wid and James. "It's too bad you weren't around for the hike, Daniel. We've had a dandy." He strode toward him and put out his hand. Daniel Moon's hung like a bag of wet sand. Father kept walking toward him, and when he was close enough, he raised the extended hand to pat Daniel Moon's shoulder and, leaving it there, said, "I hope you're coming to the big bonfire tonight. Biggest of the year, you know."

Daniel Moon still didn't say anything. He just looked uncomfortable with Father's arm around him. He flecked away the reed in his fingers, took a deep breath, still looking from James to Wid, and hulked himself out of Father's reach. "Yeah, well, maybe," he mumbled and shuffled past the cluster of cousins that had gathered in deep breathing curiosity. Wid and James turned to watch him amble off, his gray striped behind looking like Princess Alice, the elephant in Liberty Park.

"What if he comes?" James blurted to Wid as soon as they could free themselves from the crowd. "Can you think of anything that'd ruin a bonfire more?"

"Yeah. And he's just the type that'd do it — just to be obnoxious."

"Why in the heck do you think Father would invite him? Their family never comes to anything—and the bonfire's just for the cousins. Maybe Sunday School—or a hike even—but a bonfire?" James could still feel the boot that had ended their last encounter.

"Well, all we can do is hope he doesn't come," Wid said, shaking his head and kicking up the dust with his toes as he walked.

"Or...," James said, his eyes narrowing with a plan. "Or, we could do some figuring about if he did come."

Wid didn't need to ask more. The idea was alive and adrift. It was time.

The bonfire was built between the horseshoe pit and the stream in the flat fenced meadow below Uncle Phillip's where Uncle Wooster's horses were kept. Dry, barkless birch and aspen were dragged in and their hewn trunks laid like a teepee over crumpled newspaper and chips. When it was lighted, the fire burst through the logs and caught their ends, and as the night wore on, the trees were jostled continually into each other so that the fire never changed. Its peak was a yellow orange and its skirts pulsing red and gray, so the wienies and marshmallows skewered onto sheer-pointed kinnickinnick could be dangled over either the blaze or the coals, depending on whether an eater preferred a black, crisp outer or a bubbly tan one. The wienies were a special treat. They were juicy, plump and had a tough skin that Mother always insisted on pulling away. "Nothing more indigestible," she'd pronounce as she ran a paring knife down the puffy pink and loosened the covering.

But the 24th was a day for indiscretions—like corn on

the cob—usually taboo for young tummies. But still Mother would say, "Never look over-anxious in your eating. There's nothing more impolite than seeming like a p-i-g-g-i-e."

Another holiday recklessness was the use of matches. The children were never allowed to strike matches except under the supervision of an adult. So, of course, they struck them whenever they could sneak some away. Katie sometimes pushed a whole handful into her pocket so she could strike them on a rock in private. She loved the sulphur smell and the licking of the yellow up the stick that curled almost into a ring if burned till only fingernails could hold on. Jody Sue could put a lighted match in her mouth, close her lips to douse it, and then blow a perfect ring with its smoke. Katie never could do it well, even with plenty of secret practice. But on the 24th they were allowed to light all the matches they wanted, to start firecrackers, or worms, or pinwheels tacked to the fence posts, or the dazzling ends of sparklers that could write initials or inscrutable sayings on the dark. Whenever a match or anything it had lighted went out, it was thrown into the creek—fast—so it would sizzle.

When they had eaten, Charles and James, the champs at horseshoes, took on all comers. Even Father and the uncles could never beat them. Katie watched a while and then slipped across the bridge to the red sandstone steps that led under the stanchions of Uncle Phillip's. From there she could see everything but still be alone to shoot her caps as slowly as she pleased. Her gun was something she'd never dreamed she could ever have—a repeater, a surprise from Grandma. The handle was flat and rounded. It just fit her hand and she could pull the trigger without budging anything but her first finger. The side opened up so that she could thread a whole roll of caps into the pegs that would feed the gray bubbles on the red tape up next to the muzzle where the hammer would splatter them into blue smoke. Even with a repeater, though, Katie liked to wait until all the smoke had dissipated before she fired again. That way she didn't clutter up the possibilities. Sometimes when they all had wars in the field she'd draw and shoot like the others in a rapid ta-ta-ta-tating; but, alone, the slow squeeze and pause was the best.

Katie was sitting there out of sight feeling her gun when she saw Daniel Moon. She had never seen him up close before. Now, seeing him not ten feet away sent Katie into a haze of figuring: how she could run up the trail behind her to Grandma's and then back down the road to the field, how she could shoot her gun so loud and long that everyone would come running, how she could escape like a chipmunk right past Daniel Moon and over the bridge to the safe bonfire.

But he didn't see her. He was too intent on maneuvering his way through the dogwood by the stream, watching the party as he moved toward the bridge. Mostly he was watching James, who was directly through the bushes pitching horseshoes. Charles and James had perfected a technique that let their fingers release the heavy shoe into an arc that floated like a slow-motion thrush until just before it dropped, when it would turn and open up to clank in a dusty thud around the peg. Father said James was a natural with any running or hitting or throwing. He flowed into whatever movement he needed with the ease and precision of a doe— effortless in everything he did. Now as he bent, scooped, pitched, he was making as light of the game as he did of adding columns in Miss Brown's arithmetic class. Daniel Moon stooped to pick something up. He stood holding it by his side peering through the brush. Then he dropped it and sauntered back to the path and over the bridge to the field.

"What in the world is he doing?" wondered Katie, standing up and following him. He looked like the biggest thing she'd ever seen, and she knew he couldn't really be that big since he was only fourteen or fifteen.

Daniel Moon joined the party with a skewed smile that made everyone uncomfortable. Father was the first to turn from where he was squatting over a wienie stick to greet him with, "Well, you made it! Great! Here have this one. It's done just right." He handed the stick to Daniel Moon and went

126

to get him a bun. Everyone else had moved to the table where Uncle Wooster was cutting the watermelon.

James missed his ringer by two feet. Wid picked up his knife and came from where he was playing mumble peg with Little Wooster and Phillip. He sidled up to the edge of the fire where Daniel Moon was leaning out of the smoke and holding his wienie to droop over the most vivid flame.

"Hi," he said looking at the fire. "You up for very long?"

Daniel Moon eyed him without turning his head and didn't answer.

Wid persisted. "I mean, how often do you come up the canyon anyhow? It seems like your place is mostly empty most of the time."

There was a long silence, both boys magnetized by the flames that were consuming the meat on the end of Daniel Moon's stick. Wid shifted his feet and tried again, aware that James had found a replacement for himself in the horseshoe game and was ambling over toward the fire. "Does your family stay up for long when you come—or just overnight sort of?" he asked the ashes at his feet more than Daniel Moon. Daniel Moon moved the stick from his right hand to his left and stuck his empty hand into the well of a front pocket that reached to his knees. But he didn't say a word.

James was now standing casually on the other side of Daniel Moon, back a little, where Wid could catch his eye without being noticed. Only the three were by the fire. Very smoothly James drew out of his front pocket a hand so full of something that it caught on the way out and had to be worked free. Wid kept talking. "Daniel, what do you do in the city? I mean, where do you go to school? What grade are you in? Who's your teacher? Or, I guess you have more than one, for sure—any one you like better than the others?" His questions left only small grainy spaces between themselves and obviously expected no answers.

Daniel Moon watched the yellow fingers of the fire char and shrivel his wiener until there was nothing left on the stick except thin black frays. Even then he made no move to draw away. It was as if the glow and motion of the fire melted him. The muscles in his face let go and its soggy surface sagged and pulled his mouth open. His cheeks were blazing and for the first time that Wid could remember his hair looked dry. Every now and then he ran the tip of his tongue from one corner of his mouth to the other, and the slices for his eyes were so thin they looked closed. If Wid held a question back for a moment, he could see no difference in Daniel Moon's appearance; but he knew his voice was somehow part of the lulling that was taking place.

"What's your favorite hike up here?" he asked. "We had a great one this morning. The Armchair. I guess you've been up there before—probably lots of times. We go every 24th. Sort of a tradition I guess you'd call it. Have you ever been over into Lost Canyon? We never have either. But I'd sure like to go sometime. Mister Davis says it's so quiet you can hear birds from the other side. That must be where the deer live all summer." Wid gave his monologue pace and inflection with no suggestion that he was in anything but a normal conversation.

James stooped to pick up a stick that had been dropped by the stone edging of the fire and came back up not five inches from Daniel Moon's billowy coveralls. Very slowly he brought his full hand even with Daniel's back pocket that jutted out from his folds, and eased something into the cavern. Daniel Moon's tongue made another trip across his mouth. Except for the fire, nothing else stirred.

Wid's questions began anew. "You ever skin a rattle snake? The last one we skinned was full of babies—I mean real little snakes. I always thought snakes laid eggs. That really surprised me. You know how to salt 'em and make belts? You have to be careful how you set 'em up in the sun or they'll dry too fast and curl. Nailing 'em down in a sort of shaded sun's the best. You ever open their poison pockets? The littler ones have the most venom. We stick the tips of our arrows in the poison and we're ready for anything. It's a good feeling to know you have a supply of poison arrows right there in your quiver. Any time anybody attacked you'd really be ready."

James had stooped to level his stick over the hot coals until the end began to glow and smoke rose up from it like a piece of string. Then he drew it toward his face to examine it, gave it a long blow to watch it light up, and stood up behind Daniel Moon. Wid could see him raise the stick and bend its limber center to let the tip curve into Daniel Moon's bulging back pocket. Wid talked faster. "It's a funny thing how that darn poison works. They say it won't really kill you unless it gets to your heart, but I'd sure hate to fool around with it."

A thin wisp of smoke edged up past the hem of Daniel Moon's pocket. For a second Wid felt very sorry for something. Daniel Moon looked sad there with the fire making maps on his face. Wid was stunned to think that it could ever be possible for Daniel to be sad. How could anybody so mean ever be sad? But he didn't have time for more thinking. Suddenly James flashed his thumb toward the horseshoe pit and Wid turned and left with him in a walk that said there was an urgent game afoot.

They had made it only to the middle of the field when the popping started. It was like a machine gun at the Ward show. Except not regular. Loud, ear-splitting cracks, louder for being unexpected, whacked at the night. Everyone turned as if coached to see the source. It was too early for fireworks. One of the uncles always started them after the watermelon. And no one was handling anything. There was not a firecracker or cap gun in sight. But the bangs kept coming.

Daniel Moon was facing away from the fire, his eyes propped open with surprise. He stood with his legs apart and his stick still clutched in one hand. With the other he began slapping himself all over. Every time there was another bang his feet shuffled forward like the carding blocks Mother used to get wool ready for quilting—stiff, staccato. He began turning around, his head yanked over his shoulder to see what was behind him. His back pocket smoked and jumped.

"Gee, Daniel," Wid cried, "you're on fire!" And he and James ran toward the boy that outweighed them both together.

"We've got to put you out!" exclaimed James. They each took an arm and escorted Daniel Moon like a flopping puppet to the stream. He gave no resistance, just danced string doll fashion on the ground.

"Boy, you're dangerous!" said Wid. "Nothing but the whole thing'll do!" And he and James swished Daniel Moon around so that his backside was to the creek.

"Sorry 'bout this," James apologized, and both boys gave Daniel Moon a heave. After a giant splash, he flopped and hissed like the best dead sparkler ever, gasping at the ice cold water that covered everything but his head.

"Wow, Wid, that was good thinking," James said loud enough for everyone to hear, as he reached for Wid's hand in an eloquent amen. "I hate to think what would have happened to Daniel if you hadn't been so quick. Why I actually think he was on fire!"

"He actually was," Wid nodded. "Most amazing thing I've ever seen. Spontaneous combustion—right there by the fire. Must've stood too close or something."

Daniel Moon dripped out of the stream, water emptying from seams and pockets, his head bent, his fists clenched. Father and Uncle Wooster had given him a hand out and stood on either side of him asking how he was and what in the world happened. For a minute he panted and glowered. When Father started toward him saying, "We'd better get you some dry clothes," Daniel Moon waved him off and clumped across the bridge to disappear down the trail where Katie had first seen him.

"Going home we better check the underground," she thought. Then there started a grinding in a far corner of her. It felt like when an animal was hurt—raw, sicky. "But he's so mean," she kept telling herself. "And he'll probably ruin the underground going by it." She tried to pull herself back to the bonfire and all the people. But there seemed so many of them—and only one of Daniel Moon. She wondered how

130

it felt to be the only one anywhere. Like kindergarten? Only with no James to go find?

CHAPTER EIGHT

"The 24th seems to be kinda full of accidents lately," observed Katie the next morning at breakfast. "Remember last year? When Jody Sue got her blue freckles?"

"Boy, I'll say," said Davy almost triumphantly "When Phillip shot her with the gun."

"He didn't exactly shoot her, you know," Wid said, reaching for the salt. "He just had a pistol loaded with blanks that he hid from the roadshow at the Ward."

"They sure make neat freckles, though," Davy said wistfully. "Boy, think what a swell freak you'd get to be with blue freckles!"

It was a sultry morning, and thunder clouds bulged along the far ridge. The air smelled of the dust the wind picked up as it rippled from Pine Top down to the road and up again to the Saddle.

"We better hurry if we're going to get anything done on the swing today," James said, easing through the kitchen and out the back way. In Grandma's gully they were building the best swing ever conceived. It took off between two towering pines, a thick rope knotted to a crossbar of two slender pines wrapped in a chain. It had a single bar for a seat that would be tucked under a swinger as he straddled the rope and pushed off from a platform on the mountainside to sail out forty feet over the gully. But before their day's work had begun on clearing the bank under the platform, rain nipped the wind. From high in the ravine the cousins could watch the tree tops gather and roll like part of the sea as the storm rumbled down the canyon toward them, smelling of the Great Salt Lake. Lightning cut through the tumbling sky, and thunder cracked into the crags just above them.

"Let's head for the maples!" James yelled.

They made it down the trail to Grandma's and then to the road in their quickest time, not wanting to miss any tangle the wind might set up in the maples.

Next to Uncle Phillip's parking place were the best wind trees in the canyon. Each cousin shinnied monkey style up a lithe trunk to its tenuous top, where weight alone would start the swaying. Without the wind, there would be no returning the saplings to start again, but with gusts like today's, there was no stopping the momentum. As soon as one blast had tossed trees and riders almost to the ground, laughing and shrieking, another would whip them back up and over to the other side, trying to reach each other's hands, daring to extend the dip by waving one arm and leg away from the wind.

The excitement of the wind in the maples came only two or three times in any summer, and this was the first time this season. They stayed until they were drenched and the wind had let up in the steady downpour of the rain.

On the way home across the path Wid called back to the others, "Did you see the men up on the hill? They were running like mad from the lightning. You could spot them from the trees. I'd say it's time to go see them working on the poles."

Before August arrived, the regular hikes had been taken, the moss villages had been made, all the available wood had been used up on already built huts, bugs, squirrel traps, and now the maples had been climbed in the wind. It was time for new exploring.

The power company had been petitioned the year before, and this summer, men were in the mountains with their tripods and dynamite bringing electricity to the canyon. James had wanted for weeks to see the dynamiting, and for once, Wid had wanted to foil a project. He told James he couldn't stand to think of having lights with switches in the cabin. He liked the old lanterns that got black with smoke. Katie agreed—only it was the square yellow flame that intrigued her as she wound the wick up and down.

The men had worked their way from Parley's Canyon around the lower foothills where only sagebrush and mountain mahogany interfered with their digging, and now they were blasting on the perimeters of Rattlesnake Mountain. Poles were planted every fifty or seventy-five feet. The men had been less than temperate in their admonitions to the cousins early in the summer when they had edged too close to their operation. "You kids stay out of our way or you're gonna get it like you never got it before!"

Father, too, and especially Mother, had warned about the dangers of being anywhere around when the dynamite went off. So far, the children's days had been full, and they had managed to resist the urge to see how far the rocks flew and how deep the hole was before the pole was hoisted into place. But now Wid had spotted their movements and there was no question about where the day would take them.

"Just us three this time since it's so close to this side of the canyon," Wid said; but Katie and James both knew there was more to it than that.

"How'll we arrange not to be seen?" Katie asked. Skepticism over one of James' or Wid's plans was not native to her but had become an uncomfortable necessity since they had had to earn the money from Grandma to pay Mr. Larsen for the records they had tossed. The adventure that seemed so recklessly reasonable as it happened had resulted in two weeks of afternoons spent digging and clearing in Bloomerville, and her secret place had become a bonfire pit for anyone who wanted to have a party.

"We'll figure out a vantage point—like the Indians did—from up above 'em. They'll never even know we're anywhere around," Wid pronounced.

"I know the perfect place to go for where they'll be today," James said. He pursed his lips and looked thoughtful.

"Where? They're right above our cabin almost," Katie said.

"Right. That's how come it'll work so easy." James started to talk his directions with his hands. "We'll start out like we're going up our gully to maybe the Old Mine or Echo Point. All the way we'll keep our eyes peeled for Lost Lake, just like on any other hike."

For years the cousins had been determined that somewhere in the canyon there was a lake. There had to be. Think what they could do with a lake when they found it! Once on the way to Happy Home they had run across what looked like the remains of a beaver dam, rotted logs on top of each other in a long line. There must have been a lake there at one time. And with the stream as big as it was, it surely had to have somewhere to pile up besides down in Parley's. Near Lover's Lane in the pines, too, there had been sure signs of a bowl for a lake. One of their hikes would turn one up, no question about it. Anyhow, the search would continue, this time as a guise for taking them where they wanted to go.

"If we go in that direction, we'll be miles from the men," Katie noted.

"Yeah, but only for a while," James said. "When we get high enough in the gully, we'll cut back around the mountain and end up way above them—where we can see everything they do and they won't be able to see anything we do."

There was silence for a minute before Katie voiced what all of them were thinking. "That will take us right past the grotto."

No one had forgotten for a single second what had happened in the grotto the year before. And Katie remembered that James had told her he'd never go there again. "What about going there?" she asked him.

"We can go either below or above it. There's no reason why we have to get really near it at all," James said; but they all knew that the grotto was just the center of a whole mountain full of rattlers that could be under or on top of any rock they came across. No one had ever hiked that mountain without seeing at least one.

"James is right," Wid said. "We can be careful. It won't be that hard to get across to where we can see everything. I'll take the axe to use in case we need it. Maybe we could chop down an aspen on our way home—for sawing."

James and Katie knew Wid would never carry a heavy axe on a hike just for getting wood. They looked at each other, but when Wid picked the axe off the back porch wall where it hung on four nails, they snatched their hiking sticks. They all had a last drink of water and were off, up the gully with its cool pungence, past the tank and spring above it, which by now was stagnant and slimy, run dry from the long summer. Immediately beyond the spring the mountain became almost solid rocks, with crisp saxifrage brittling in the sun. The rocks grated and the plants snapped as they walked over them. Katie imagined this must be like the earth would be in the last days, scorched until there was no green left.

Even though they were dripping wet and panting they hardly paused. This was a short hike really—only maybe an hour from home, not one to have to prepare for or even take a canteen on. As they neared the grotto, Wid stopped and James and Katie lined up to look. There were the red boulders circled as if some child had used them for blocks.

"Why don't the rest of you go high here—clear up over that knoll. There shouldn't be snakes up there. And besides it's wide open and you could see if anything was around," he directioned.

"What do you mean, 'the rest of us'?" asked James. "You're not going past the grotto, Bruv!"

"Yep. That's just what I am going to do—go *past* it. I've gotta see if what we saw last summer was really so. And I've got this for protection." Wid held up the axe.

Katie was cold. Her shirt was sticking to her shoulders and she knew the stockings inside her boots were soaked, but she felt as chilled as she did sleigh riding. She had always wanted to see the grotto, to go there and kill some snakes and bring them home to show her brothers. But now the thought of Wid's even going near made her mouth dry and her tongue work. She knew he would, though.

James did, too. He'd known for a year. "Come on then, Katie. Wid knows what he's doing. We'll meet him around the knoll." He knew that Wid would feel anything but deserted as he made his way alone down the rivers of rocks while he and Katie began the climb up the knoll.

As Wid neared the grotto, he lowered the axe that he had carried until just now on his shoulder. There were the same stacked chunks of sandstone making an almost complete circle. Their sliced sides absorbed the sun, striated and dull. "The rocks are only about knee high," he marveled, remembering them as at least twice that. "In August they're shedding their skins—right over their eyes," he could hear Mother saying. She never mentioned the word "snake." They were "they." "Watch where you step because they'll strike at anything." He saw his dusty boots flatten out footholds in the rocky hillside.

"Around the bottom," he thought. "Then I can see into the empty end of the circle—see everything in there and still keep my word about going past it." He found he could all right. Standing below it he could see the same clumps of gray green stillness, stacked sometimes on each other, here and there in motionless movement. "Go past now. You've seen. You've done what you came to do. Get back to the others," he kept telling himself. But he was transfixed. "They do look evil. Like nothing. Like living nothing. Why do they get to live anyhow? Why are they even here? All they do is bad. Anything that makes you scared like they make you scared has got to be bad."

Wid was sweating. Sweat ran down his wrist and into his palm holding the axe. "I won't run this time anyhow, snakes. If you just lie there in the sun, I won't bother you; but if you came out here after me, I'd never run. Not ever again." The idea sent goosebumps over his arms and scalp.

Gradually he began to move. Forgetting his boots and where they were landing, he inched around the grotto still watching the throbbing heaps in its enclosure. At the far end of it, he turned away and glanced down to see a slender tan line move toward his right boot. It was a young rattler in a straight course down the rocks. "Perfect to take back and show the little kids what to watch out for," he thought. He raised his axe only shoulder high, choking its handle as it rasped down into the rocks. The snake lay in two almost equal parts. "Fine. I'll chop off the rattles and give them to Davy only two little ones, though."

As Wid reached for the amputated rattles, his hand picked up the part with the head on. "Boy, what a little one. Almost cute," he thought. "Funny...just like with a baby rat or something. Being little makes anything look good." Suddenly the snake, or what was left of it, recoiled like a spring. It twitched and its head darted. Almost before he dropped it, two pin points of blood surfaced on the round of his left thumb. Staring at the specks that grew hardly any larger as he watched, he saw the half-snake slither off to die.

"I better get down. Those are fang marks!" he thought and started a sliding run away from the grotto, his head racing. But just as suddenly he braced to a stop. "That's the dumbest thing you could do," he told himself, remembering the first aid tips in his scout manual and Mother saying, "If you ever get bitten, stay still, put on a tourniquet, and get rid of the poison—fast." "And besides, Barton," he scolded himself, "you weren't ever going to run from the grotto again, remember?"

Wid sat slowly down on the rocks about twenty yards below the snake, in plain sight of the knoll. "James and Katie'll come. I'll just make a tourniquet," he thought, mouthing the words. But out of what? He could tear his shirt. Or use the handkerchief Mother always made them take in a pocket.

Better still, there was lacing up the front of his polo shirt. He yanked it out of its holes and tried to wind it around his wrist using his teeth to hold and his right hand to manipulate the lace. It tightened easily. His hand began to throb and the veins stood out en route to his fingers. "I should cut it open," he thought. He started to dig for his pocket knife. "No, that's Mother's job. I'll wait."

His head swirled some, but he forced himself to breathe evenly and think. In the near distance he heard the explosion of dynamite. The mountain shivered. He could hear the landing of soil and rocks. He could even smell the nippy scent of powder and newly exposed earth. "Wow. We're a lot closer than we thought we were. I hope James and Katie didn't go past that knoll. They wouldn't have. They could have seen where the digging was by the time they got that far. Don't think about that. They'll come. They'll know to. They'll come."

Wid turned to search the mountain above, but he waited for over an hour before he saw a figure moving toward him. It was someone alone, coming down through the bushes sidewards. He raised his right arm to signal where he was and closed his eyes.

When Wid opened his eyes again, he was lying against the bank of the path curled up like a snail. Someone was patting his shoulder and saying huskily, "Hey. Hey. Wake up!" All he could see as he opened and closed his heavy lids was stripes. He breathed deeply and tried again to focus. His brain registered the same thing—stripes. The hand on his shoulder was trying to ease him over. He closed his eyes and let it happen. He was turned gently to his back and his legs were straightened out. Something went under his head. A hand, he guessed, as it smoothed the ground and stayed under his neck to keep him level.

"Hey, you okay?" he heard dimly. This time the voice shot through him like the pain in his hand.

"Daniel Moon!" he breathed, "Daniel Moon!" He opened his eyes and looked into little pale blue eyes.

"I'm gonna take you home," Daniel Moon said. He

slipped his other arm under Wid's knees and gathered him up. Wid felt strange, taken care of, as if Mother had been there with her cures. He let his eyes close and his body give as Daniel moved along the rocks as smooth as a cat, turning, raising or lowering Wid's body to miss the underbrush, seeming not to notice the steep descent and his load, which he carried like kindling.

Luckily the cabin was almost directly below them, and Mother, who had seen Wid's arms and legs dangling as Daniel Moon walked silently down the trail with him, met them at the woodpile. She assessed the situation, went back to the house, and returned to the woodpile before Daniel had slumped Wid against a tree and disappeared.

"Stay still, Wid. Right there." She leaned him against the box around the tree. "You know how sorry I am, but you also know this has to be done, and you'll be a brick—that I know."

Davy and Lena stood back to watch. Wid gave mother his arm. It was longer than hers by almost the hand, and she had to inch up it as she steadied his thumb and tucked his arm between hers and her plump body. Adroitly she drew the sharpest knife in the house across his thumb—twice—to make an X over the two points where the fangs had gone in. Because of the tourniquet, blood hardly spurted. Without a wince, Mother put her mouth around the thumb and sucked at the wound, spitting and sucking several times. Wid looked pale but was so bewitched by Mother's skill that he didn't pull away. It seemed easier by far than having a sliver extracted with her alcohol needle.

"Hey! What's going on?" came a call from James in a scramble of rocks from up on the mountain. "Where's Wid? We were supposed to meet..." He saw Wid and started to say, "Boy, Bruv, you sure missed the excitement. What a blast!"

By then he was where he could see what was going on, and Katie came from behind him to stammer, "Wid! What in the world? What happened?"

"He got bit—by a rattler," Davy said, almost proudly.

"Just got a crazy little snake bite," Wid said passively. "And I do mean little. Boy, was I dumb!"

Finished, Mother smiled and patted Wid's cheek. "You did everything just right, Wid. I'm proud of you," she said. "Your father will be too. And so will Uncle David." Mother smoothed his hair back and said in the calm that signified crisis, "It looks like we'll need to take you down to Uncle David."

Uncle David was the family physician. He moved with purpose. No motion was wasted. His coat came off and his bag came out when he visited, and his therapy was regarded as scary but miraculous. The summer before, he had come to the canyon to innoculate all the cousins for typhoid and diptheria. Their arms had swollen and their heads had ached, but nothing had compared at all with the plunge of the needle into its stinging bed. None of them had ever had it happen before, and few of them felt the same about Uncle David for some months after.

Uncle David seldom came to the canyon, but in the other seasons he came with Aunt Clarice to call on his mother and sister every Wednesday night and Sunday morning at 1287 Crystal Avenue. The children expected nothing more certainly than Uncle David.

One Wednesday night he was late. He was never late. Some time after Katie was in bed, she heard him come and heard Mother ask in that same too calm voice for Grandma to come downstairs. The three went into the living room. Not wanting to miss his visit or the reason for it, Katie padded down the stairs and peeked through the French doors before going in. Uncle David's head was wrapped in bandages and he was sitting on a footstool in front of Grandma sobbing into her lap. "She's gone. She's gone," he kept saying as Grandma rubbed his shoulders and swayed back and forth shaking her head. "Oh David, my David," she comforted. "First your sister Alice and now your Clarice. Oh, Heavenly Father, bless the poor boy who did this!"

Katie learned later that a young boy had been driving

drunk, had run a red light and killed Aunt Clarice, who was making calls with Uncle David on their way to visit Grandma. Uncle David had not wanted someone else to tell his mother about it, so he had them bandage him up at the hospital and then insisted on going to tell her himself. From then on, when Uncle David came, Katie would let him do anything and not flinch.

Just the idea that Wid would be seeing Uncle David relieved Katie. His effect was even more sure than Mother's. Already she had her shoe bag packed. In it were a thermos of something hot, a banana and a cinnamon roll to provide for any being faint from hunger, and her good shoes that would be exchanged for her driving shoes on arrival at the clinic. No lady ever drove in shoes she expected to keep presentable.

Hope had been one of the few girls to drive in 1916 on the wide streets of Salt Lake City. With his surgeon's fingers, her father had stitched her the leather cushion she still used to put behind her back so that she could reach the pedals and still see over the dashboard. Even so, from the rear, the car looked as if it had no driver.

She told Wid, "I'll drive the car up as close as I can to the front path and Lena and I will be able to get you in. You're going to be just fine. It's good that Daniel got you home."

Wid wanted to ask about that, but somehow it didn't seem important enough to try to talk about. He just nodded and let himself drift again.

Mother put Wid in the car and headed down the canyon for the clinic. Out of the open window as they started away, Wid said to the line-up by the running board, "Boy, here I go past the gate for this year. Bruv, how come you never get sick—or anything? You must be accident proof. How about some quick lessons?"

"Yeah, anytime," James answered. "But you sure do keep things interesting. Maybe I'm not too anxious to put the stymie on it!"

Groaning in low gear, the black Auburn that belonged to Grandma but which Mother always drove and always had on hand in the canyon crept down the steep Maple Fork Hill to the road and out of sight.

Katie and James couldn't believe what Mother had said about Daniel Moon bringing Wid home. They had to confirm it with Lena. That he had been bitten by a rattler—a cut-in-half one—was hard enough to understand, but that it had been Daniel Moon who had been the one to bring him home was totally incredible. James remembered the night of the 24th when he and Wid had been talking in bed, Wid lying on his back, his arms at his sides. After a very long silence, he had said, "Bruv, you know what?"

"What?" James had asked.

"Daniel's lonesome as heck."

"He oughta be. What's he ever done to deserve anything else?"

"I don't know. I sure don't know much. Boy, I don't know much at all. Less and less all the time. But I keep finding myself wondering—which comes first the meanness or the lonesomeness?"

It had been so still for a minute that they could hear the forked maple outside the screen ruffle its leaves, and the chipmunks having their nightly party on the roof two stories up.

James had turned to face the outside wall, pounding his pillow into shape, and saying, "Yeah. Well, maybe we oughta check on a few things tomorrow."

But they never had. He and Wid had gone to try to find Daniel Moon the next day, but his place was deserted as usual, and they had figured they'd take care of that some other time. Now, only a few days later, Daniel Moon was the one to show up at their place.

"I just wonder if he did anything to Wid," Katie said, boiling with premonition, forgetting her ambivalence of the night at the bonfire.

"He didn't," James was quick to assure her.

"How do you know? Look what he did to you."

"That was different."

"How? you didn't do anything to him except try to get your own bug back."

"Yeah, but that was different. You learn a lot when you get going behind things."

"What do you mean—behind things?"

"I don't know. It's hard to say. You just end up somewhere else. You don't figure out how it happens, that's for sure. You don't even try to or it messes it up." James paused and almost started to say something, then paused again with his hands in his pockets and his head down. "I guess it's sort of like when you get over a cold—all of a sudden you just are. Quiet as moss growing. Without noticing even, something's different in you. Maybe you oughta ask Wid. He knows a lot more about it than I do. He's been there a while."

Katie was flooded with a warm deliverance. Somehow she didn't have to feel bad toward Daniel Moon anymore. "But why?" she asked herself. "Did carrying Wid home make that much difference? How could it? One minute Daniel Moon was the Enemy, the next...How did it work? Could just one good thing cancel out all the others?" She didn't want to think any more about it. All she knew was that now all there was was Mister Davis. And he didn't ruin things the same way Daniel Moon had. He just made her nervous. But in a way that drew her, like putting her tongue into a sore tooth and being gratified that it still hurt.

Katie said she thought she'd go down to the spring for a cold drink. "Can I come? I'm awful thirsty too," Davy asked.

"No, Hon, not this time." Katie forgot to pat him. She walked to the foot of the hill, then past the path to the platform and into the grassy dust by the spring. She put her hand under the icy clear stream that arched from the pipe into the wooden box that stored it. The pipe was a hollowed-out tree bound with thin metal strips, the oldest line in the canyon.

"Father in Heaven," Katie said into the splash on her hand, "please help Wid. He's awful good, probably about as good as there is. I'll do anything you want if it'll help him. I won't play cigarettes with Jody Sue and the reeds. I won't take off my ribbon when I leave Mother and put it on just before I come back. I won't go to the bathroom outside—even when no one's around. I promise. I'll do anything. I just wish it had happened to me. I deserve it a lot more than Wid ever did. I even wanted to go to the grotto. Just to act big." Katie pulled her hand out of the cold water and it ached clear to her elbow.

"Being numb is worse than hurting even," she thought. Tears seemed to start in her throat and come out her eyes. "And the only thing that helps is moving. If you hold still, the numbness just sets in and stays." She watched her fingers open and close into her palm hunting for feeling.

Wid was back within a few hours. He arrived with a bandage around his thumb as big as a hornet's nest. But he was walking just fine and was full of the tale of his adventure. "Boy, what a deal! The doctor Uncle David got to take care of it hadn't ever treated a snake bite before, so he had to look it up in a book to see what to do. He'd read along a little ways and then do what it said, and then read some more.

"You mean nobody else has ever been in there with a snake bite?" James asked, incredulous.

"What about all the people who must get bitten all the time?" Katie agreed. The children had always felt that such a phenomenon was just part of living in the mountains. They themselves had seen a lot of rattlers but had learned early from Mother most ways to take care of themselves when they did. Wid's accident had been a fluke. Mother was the one they called whenever they came across a rattler within her range. She would bounce out with her trusty shovel, march into bushes if necessary, barely visible, her short arms working like a jack hammer, and attack. They never worried about her, only wondered how long it would be before she came out carrying the shovel straight out from her waist with "it" ready for inspection and burial. It was never Father that they called. For all of his six-foot manliness, he laughed and shrugged that he hated snakes—that they in fact scared him—and that

146

they were Mother's province.

Hope Ruskin and Candland Barton seldom let themselves be designated by convention to be anything. Their areas of concern and effectiveness were determined by strength and circumstance. Who led, who followed, was as undelineated as smoke and flame. To each other they simply brought each other and went from there. *Who* killed the rattlesnakes seemed no question at all. Only that it was done.

If Wid had felt any chagrin in his folly, it faded now. The cousins had begun to gather to hear his story. They each inspected his bandage and marveled that he was still alive, let alone lively, as they heard the full accounting, told with the muted exuberation of one accustomed to playing the hero returned.

Wid sat on the bench outside the front door, the one they pounded nails into to make designs and initials. Davy sat between Wid and the tree where James was—as close as he could, watching Wid with wide open eyes that seemed to do his hearing.

"Well, first he got a needle this long and filled it with horse anti-serum—like the book said that he kept reading out of. Then he pumped it into my thumb till it blew up like a balloon. He cut it open some more first. He said Mother did a great job, though. She probably stopped it from going all through me. Oh—and they left the tourniquet on—only tightened it. And that made it blow up more, I guess. Then after a while they took off the tourniquet. But they kept me lying down on this cot thing, and he gave me a shot of the same stuff right here." Wid rubbed his left buttocks and pulled a face as he did. Eight faces winced with him. "Then they said I should just lie around there for a while at the clinic so they could watch me. And look what I got to keep." Wid reached to his back pocket and pulled out a fat wad of gauze that smelled like the typhoid shots. Carefully he unwrapped his token, a slender hypodermic needle and a test tube with a rubber cap. "Watch," Wid said pointing the hypo at Little Wooster. A jet thread hit and ran down Little Wooster's neck.

"Hey, Wid," he giggled. "How'd ya do that?"

"Easy. You just plunge into this tube for ammunition and shwoo—better 'n any squirt gun ever."

Little Wooster cocked his head to miss the next stream, laughing and shutting his eyes.

Wid reached his handful toward him. "Here, Little Wooster. It's for you. I told the nurse I had a cousin who liked to needle me all the time."

Little Wooster's forehead drew inward and he looked at Wid with narrow eyes. "Needle, Wid?" he said, perplexed.

"Yeah, needle. That means you're always getting to me."

"To you, Wid? Is that good?"

Wid reached closer to Little Wooster, nodding and smiling as he did when he read something he really liked. "Yeah—in this case. Plenty good."

CHAPTER NINE

What Wid told James that night was that he'd practiced all afternoon till he could hit the basin drain from clear across the room. And he was sure that with all those other hypos lined up on the counter, one less wouldn't matter at all.

The next day as Isabel waited for Katie to come out and play at the Moss Village, she asked Wid, "Well, are you going to be all right? Will you have some effects after?"

"Nope. I don't think so. He just said to take it easy today. And I've been thinking. How about if tomorrow we go over to Lost Canyon and see if we can find Tony? Then we could take some rides together on him and Goldie.

By now all of the cousins had gathered on the front porch. None of them liked to admit how much they dreaded riding double on the back of Little Wooster's saddle—especially when they galloped. Holding on was bad enough, but inner thighs rubbed raw were a disaster. Still, they all rode there sometimes. But they had learned how to suggest shortcuts and a slower pace to Little Wooster, who would have taken every turn at a polo clip, with or without a rider.

To have Tony back would mean riding him in the soft firmness of the hand-tooled saddle that had sat all summer on the railing that ran around Uncle Wooster's porch and to his parking place. Sometimes Katie had slipped away for a long sit astride the still saddle imagining herself a cowboy herding up the dogies they sang about when the cousins brought their instruments to a bonfire or a porch and sang "Home on the Range," "Big Rock Candy Mountain," "Red River Valley," and the sixteen verses to "Clementine." They whined around three basic chords on their ukuleles or the mandolin that Grandma had given James, their singing a drone of fuzzy improvisation. But on Katie's rides—imaginary or otherwise—she moved her lips to harmonies rich as hornet humming, and just as exclusive.

Thinking about the hike to Lost Canyon she urged, "Let's start first thing in the morning. How come we've waited this long in the summer to get him back?"

"But what if he's not even over there?" Charles said. "It'll sure be a waste of time to spend a whole day hunting."

"Why a waste of time? The hike up from the deer lick's worth it by itself—any day," answered James.

It was. The trail up the lower mountain was thin and not very steep as it wound off from the pink block of salt by the stream. Mister Davis kept the lick renewed. The deer, with their long rough tongues, wore smooth craters in the block as they passed it between getting water and bounding back up the trails to Lost Canyon or wherever they disappeared to. It took the cousins only about half as long to reach the ridge as it did to get to Echo Point. At the top they looked down Lost Canyon. Because it had no stream, there was no V cut through its bottom, and foliage was uniform from one side to the other. Standing on the rounded ridge, holding their lassos, the cousins waited to hear the sounds that they had come to hear. Out of the initial hush bubbled an unbelievably melodious cacophony—meadowlarks strewing "Salt Lake City is a pretty little place" from one brace of mountain mahogany to another, squirrels swallowing the day with their nibbling, a finch stretching one note past the swirls of an almost invisible breeze, the hubbub of unseen hooves somewhere leaving or entering a hiding place, bees taunting the Indian paint-brush, acres of moving green where sound told only part of what was there.

Finally Katie said in a whisper that she could not have explained, "If Tony's in there, it's sure going to be hard finding where. He could be anyplace."

"Yeah, we can't ever cover this whole canyon—and you can't see inside anywhere to get a clue," Wid said almost to himself. He was glad the top had been as easy to reach as it had. Even so, his skin felt tingly and he was trying to cover up a difficulty in breathing.

"Maybe if we fan out," James said scanning the canyon. There was an uneasy silence. The cousins thrived on joint adventure, but no one was eager to move into strange territory unaccompanied. If "fanning out" meant thrashing through the tight growth of serviceberry bushes, oak, sumac and haw-thorn—all thorny and dense, with no view of the ground except in scattered clearings—no one leaped to the opportunity. Katie prickled at seeing herself camouflaged and out of touch. But the notion that somewhere in there Tony might be munching on the long grass that was still sweet in the shade made the back of her scalp stand up in excitement. "If we just keep calling to each other, we'll know where everybody is," she said. "We could make a lot of noise and scare out Tony as easy as pie."

"Yeah, and scare what else? How do we know what might be down there in those bushes?" Isabel said, looking over the wavering green below that seemed to pulse with what they all felt inside.

Katie had begun to be positive that Tony was there to be found. If Mister Davis said he was there, all they had to do was look. Just because Wid had had some bad adventures didn't mean that anything would happen this time. "We can all be just like we're together—like always. It'll be worth it. Just think how great it'll be to have two horses to ride." She knew they all felt that way too; but, more important, there was something else that held them silent and unmoving.

None of them wanted to say anything about what it might be like trying to catch the pony if they did find him. Lassoing would be far from easy. He had always been a fiery little beast. Shetlands were not known for their temperate dispositions, and Tony had given everyone fits—as Mother called it—when they tried to catch and saddle him even in Uncle Phillip's field. He kicked and bit and never seemed to have his ears up. But once caught, he clipped along beside Goldie with any one of them on his back, perky and determined, taking three steps to the big mare's one. What would he be like, though, after being lost in the wilds since last summer? For almost a year everyone had expected him to wander out and be found, and Uncle Wooster had sent some men to look for him, but so far only Mister Davis had seen him. To Katie that was all the more reason to prove they could find what others couldn't. After all, whose canyon was it? And who should be able to do anything up there?

It was Wid who finally started the hunt. "Let's give it a try. What've we got to lose? And think how great Little Wooster would feel if we found him." Little Wooster and Goldie were doing their waiting this time at the deer lick.

"You stop there," Wid instructed Charles, who was the last to start down. "James, wait till you're about...here, to drop off. Then Katie—and then everybody else about that same distance apart. When I get situated on the other side, I'll yell and we can all start moving."

"What the heck do you think we're gonna do in all that brush?" Charles complained. "It's not like its soft stuff." But the others were on their way and by his remark more inclined than ever to plunge into the thickets of barbed green.

When they were spread across the canyon floor, Wid yoohoo'd and they each yoohoo'd back. "Now!" he called and they began thrashing their way toward the other end of Lost Canyon. They were never out of touch. They called and whistled and yodeled back and forth using their rounds of rope to scare up the sources of the sounds they had heard but not seen. Katie felt as if she were in John Burrough's darkest

Africa on the safari in the travelogue her class had gone to see in the Tabernacle on Temple Square. Her hiking stick became a machete and she could hear water buffalo screeching over the aspen.

She found herself now stomping through the brush in a rhythm, the kind she invariably set for herself in any kind of repeated action. It was like watching windshield wipers or jumping the rope, steady, insistent, conjuring up rhymes to match the meter that pounded through her. She began mouthing something to suit the moment,

"Don't think of snakes
And they'll never appear,
But be ready for anything
When it is near."

She had said it over three times when a deer did suddenly bound across her periphery, startling her into a whoop for the others to watch for it. It vaulted over the shrubbery fifteen feet at a span and disappeared into a brace of oak in a series of reports like a silenced gun. "How could anybody shoot one?" she thought. "How could you stand to?" Then the words began bouncing again in her head to the rhythm of her stride,

"Then how could anyone
Hurt such a thing
With all of that bounce
And life in its spring?"

She tried leaping like the deer but only crashed into the bushes that grabbed at her feet and ankles and scratched her face even when she held an arm and her lasso up for protection. It seemed a long way to go.

At the far end of the canyon Wid reassembled the group with yelping yoohoo's. "I guess he's gone," he sighed.

"Boy, I sure thought we'd find him," said James.

"What'll I tell Little Wooster?" Wid wondered out loud as he sat down and stared.

James plopped down, too, part way up the low mountain that they would now have to climb to get back into their own Canyon. "I guess all we can do is go back. He's not in there or we'd have seen him for sure," he said.

"But what about another day?" Katie persisted. "Just because he's not around one day doesn't mean he never is. Gosh, he probably roams all over in here. He could've just been out hunting for some different food or something. Gee, tomorrow...."

"No, not tomorrow, Katie," Wid said abruptly. He was tired. More tired than he could remember being for a long time. All he could think of was the long pull back up the mountain and then down again—all in the hottest sun there had been all summer. "He's probably traveled a hundred miles from here since last summer. We were crazy to think he'd still be anywhere around," Wid muttered with disgust.

"But Mister Davis said he saw him—just a couple of weeks ago."

"Months, Katie, not weeks. And besides, when did you start believing Bill Davis on everything?"

Katie had never heard anyone call him Bill Davis. Not even Father when he was talking to him. It was always *Mister* Davis. If Mother had heard Wid say that, she would have said, "Wid, someone older than you has a lot of reasons to be called Mister. Give him the dignity he deserves."

Katie watched Wid run his handkerchief around the back of his neck and over his face. He looked pale and flushed at the same time. Behind his ear she could see a red splotch. "He shouldn't have come on a hike today," she thought. "It's too soon. Oh, Wid, you crazy pill, what's going to happen to you now?" She felt like Mother and was mad at herself for being ticky.

She knew how Wid would hate it if he thought she were being ticky. Like the time he had the wood tick in his hair. Every night Mother inspected them for ticks after they'd been in the bushes and dead wood. In the beginning as flat as moles, the ticks were mostly harmless, and if they were discovered early, they could be urged out of their holds with a hot needle on their backsides. But if they were missed and made their way under the skin, their heads became imbedded and they began to bloat with the blood they were sucking. It took both heat and alcohol and often a pull with the tweezers to get them out. Then it was important to keep an eye on where they'd been in case part of them was still in there and could cause infection. The wood tick in Wid's curly tight hair had eluded even Mother's careful inspection until it was swollen and fat and sticking straight up from his scalp. For days after its removal Mother kept vigil for after effects until the children began to tease her about being "ticky," a word she had used until then to describe close needle work, a word that implied to Katie everything laborious and bothersome.

"We've got to take it easy going home," Katie said, "I've got a kind of ache in my side and going up hill fast really gets it. We've got plenty of time anyhow. We can end up at the gate and wait for a ride up the canyon."

The lower end of Lost Canyon was directly over the mountain from the gate. The cousins hiked up a deer trail until it slanted south toward the deer lick on the other side. From there on they had to make their own trail to the ridge. Nearing the top Katie watched Wid three hikers ahead of her. He was slow, stopping every few steps to stand straight and take a deep breath and wipe his forehead and neck. She was sure everyone else must be noticing, but no one questioned him about it.

As they came out of the brush and onto the low ridge, Wid stood up again. This time he stared across the gulf of Armchair Canyon. "Wow, what's that!" he said as part of his sigh. On the other side, above Mister Davis's place smoke rose in whiffs that hugged the mountain side and had not yet made it to the skyline.

"Is that a bonfire? Up there?" Wid asked, as the others trailed up beside him and followed his squinted gaze.

"It can't be," Phillip said. "Who'd have a bonfire this time of day?"

"And up on the mountain like that?" Isabel said. "The only place anywhere around there is Mister Davis's. And he sure wouldn't be having a fire with everything so dry."

155

But there was no mistaking the smoke, and it was far enough away that they could not make out any activity. James looked at the sun, still well up. Mister Davis would be somewhere up the canyon making his devious way back from his daily trek. And there would be no one coming through the gate for some time since it was Wednesday and the first of the fathers wouldn't be up for another two hours at least.

"We better get down and see what's going on," James said. "Nobody but us could possibly see that smoke."

He plunged down the Armchair side of the mountain with the others right behind him. Katie looked at Wid, who sighed heavily again and plunged with them. They didn't stop until they came to the stream, a mile down the road from the deer lick where they had started that morning. James led them along the creek until there was a fallen aspen to balance across. They scrambled up the other bank and were on the road just above the gate.

From there they never would have seen the smoke. Willow trees and birch spread across the reaches of the low dogwood and cut off the sky to give no view of the mountain behind Mister Davis's. The smoke must have been rising on the thin wind that barely moved the leaves, because there was no sign of it from where they peered into the trees.

"Sure a crazy place for a fire," Smithy said. "If it isn't a bonfire, what else could it be? Sure isn't from any lightning." The sky above them was the deep azure of a cloudless day.

"We better hike up there and see what's up," James said. "No telling what could happen if it was a fire in the brush. It could really take off."

"Like the Happy Home fire," Katie added. "Mother said they fought that for three days. And it was just lucky that it didn't get any more of the cabins."

They jogged up the road to Mister Davis's bridge. None of them had ever been across it. They had been told not to go to his place and that had made it all the more intriguing. But a journey over there would have to be taken when everyone wasn't around; maybe a pair might have dared it, but being alone this far from home was not something any of them sought. There was only a moment of hesitation before James and Charles led the line that clomped across the two planks crossing the creek about fifteen feet below.

From there they cut over to the bank and zig-zagged two switchbacks up it until they felt as if they were right below where the smoke must have been. The climb up the rugged hillside was in fine dark soil that gave with their lunging so that they had to take three steps to move up two. About fifty yards up the hill they could smell smoke. Another ten and they could see it, red twitches of flame seeping through the sage and privet, snatching at stems and branches and licking up their leaves. It was as if it were hiding, sneaking up on a wider and wider area, crackling softly and sending up only cloudlike smoke to blend with the hot August day.

The cousins stood marveling. "What in the heck..." muttered James. "It's a fire! It's a real fire—going after the canyon."

"What'll we do?" Katie asked, baffled by what seemed like something out of Jack Armstrong or Little Orphan Annie. There couldn't be a real fire there in the canyon eating its way toward their cabin.

"We could beat it out with our shirts maybe," suggested Jody Sue in a pale tone that said she knew the fire was way past that kind of dousing.

"We better just head for some help," Wid said, panting to where the others had been for several minutes. "Somebody go flag down a car in Parley's and tell them to get the fire department. And somebody better start up the road to warn the people in the cabins. It could spread really fast in this dry stuff."

Already the flames were charring a swath through the brush the length of two football fields, almost twice as big as when they had first spotted the fire. "Shouldn't somebody stay here to watch and give reports on what's happening?" James proposed. "Seems like it's all going up the canyon with the wind. Nothing coming down. So it'd be safe just standing here and keeping an eye on it."

Wid was already running down through the brush toward Parley's, and the others, except for Katie, were slanting off toward the road. Wid called as he ran, "No, don't stay, Bruv. The wind could change any time. Just head up the road. You better get on back of Little Wooster and make it up there as fast as you can to tell Mother."

Katie followed Wid to the road and turned down as he did.

"How come you're coming this way Katie? You'll have to go past the gate."

"So will you," Katie said.

"I've already been past it so much it waves at me coming and going. You better stick with the others." Wid kept running.

Katie was at his heels. "Two of us can do better flagging a car," she panted. "Besides they'll always stop for a girl."

They passed the gate, around its short end. Katie glanced at the notches. "Boy, what a long time since the ceremony," she thought. She touched the end post as she rounded it and then ran her fastest to keep up with Wid.

They set themselves on the downhill side of Parley's Canyon road, Highway 40. Three cars passed, all with their lights on indicating they'd been traveling a long way. The fourth, its lights out, pulled to a dusty stop in the gravel beside the road.

"What's up kids?" the driver asked, leaning out of his window.

"There's a fire," Wid called. "It's up there, on that mountain see? It's pretty big and spreading like mad. We gotta get the fire department."

The lone man squinted at the mountain and then nodded. "You're right, kid. That could get bad. I'll head for the phone at the first-aid station by the gravel pit."

"Thanks!" Wid shouted over the grating of tires and turned to Katie. "We better stay by the gate and wait for 'em. Maybe we could do something to help—give some directions or something."

They walked across the highway, went over the bridge, and cut through the long grass to the gate. Wid grabbed the crossbar and swung up to sit on the notched aspen. Katie did the same. "Wid, you look sick," she said examining his drawn face. "Awful sick. And what're those blotchy places all over your neck? Some on your cheek too." She touched the spots on his face and he drew defensively away, careful not to do it too fast.

Wid rubbed his hand over his skin pausing to feel more carefully when he ran onto a red area.

"Can you feel it?" Katie inquired.

"Something," Wid answered. "Something itchy."

Once he started touching the splotches of red, he couldn't quit. As his hand passed over them, he began to rub, then to scratch violently.

"Hey, you better not do that. It's looking worse. In fact terrible!" Katie warned.

"Boy, there's no way to stop! I never itched so bad in my whole life," said Wid beginning to squirm and scrunch his neck against his spine and his arms against his body. It was as if all his surfaces were alive and demanding attention.

Not waiting to be asked what she was doing, Katie slipped down from the gate and called back over her shoulder, "I'm gonna go get us a ride up the canyon."

"How? You can't just go out there and ask somebody to drive in here and take us up!" Wid shouted as she ran. "Besides we don't have a key!"

Katie didn't answer. She crossed the bridge and stood at the edge of the road ready to tackle any car that rounded the bend.

The first one that came was Uncle Wooster. Katie couldn't believe it. "Uncle Wooster! Gee am I glad to see you! There's a fire. And Wid's sick and itchy. And we've gotta get up home!"

Uncle Wooster's black touring car had stopped by the bridge. "What's all this, Katie? A fire? Wid sick? Where?"

Katie didn't even wonder why Uncle Wooster was up in

the middle of the day. She just opened the door, slid in, and slammed it before she answered, "The fire's right up there! Up above Mister Davis's. And Wid's by the gate."

Wid opened the gate with the key Uncle Wooster handed him. "Leave the gate open," Uncle Wooster instructed. Wid got in the back seat by crawling past Katie. He didn't even ask to ride on the runningboard. Uncle Wooster was all business, too. He shifted and turned without a single joke. Now the smoke was visible over the tallest trees but still blowing up toward the ridge.

"We've got to get people out of the cabins," Uncle Wooster said. "If that wind changed, a fire could wipe out a whole mountain side so fast..."

"Does it look like it's heading toward the cabins?" Katie asked, ducking to look out of the other side of the car.

"It's hard to tell. With just smoke to see, it looks like it's still going toward the ridge, but there's never been a fire that held one direction for very long. What we need is men to fight it. And where are we going to find them this time of day?"

"We hailed a car in Parley's, and the man that stopped was going to call the fire department from the first-aid station." Katie said.

"Good. That's good thinking. But even if they headed right out from Sugar House, it'd be half an hour before they'd be here. And their hoses wouldn't be much help up on that mountain. What we need is lots of men—to chop the brush and make fire lanes to cut the fire off."

"Well, who can we get? All us kids could help—really help. We know all the hikes and we know how to chop and stuff," Katie volunteered excitedly.

Uncle Wooster smiled and reached for her shoulder. "You're all right, Katie Barton. You're all right," he said.

Wid had not said a word. When Katie looked into the back seat for affirmation about what the cousins could do, her stomach went tight at what she saw. Wid was rolling around on the seat twitching and shrugging against the upholstery as he dug his nails into his hair and arms and legs in the wildest

160

scratching Katie had ever seen. It made her itch too and her own shoulders shuddered against her neck. "Wid," she exclaimed, "what in the world is it?"

Wid didn't answer. He just shook his head and ground his teeth.

"Boy, will I ever be glad to see Mother," Katie said to Uncle Wooster.

After the deer lick, there was no sign of the smoke. The road wound through its tunnel of green and looked as calm and inviting as ever. Katie tried to feel the way she always had coming up that road. There was the Third Rat House, the Second, Rabbit's Head, Daniel Moon's, the straight stretch to their hill. It all looked just the same. And that made the feeling worse. If only the smoke could still be seen, or better still, the fire. Then she could understand why she felt so funny. Everything was different—and yet so wierdly the same.

Uncle Wooster drove to the top of Maple Fork and backed into the highest parking place. Katie was out before he stopped. "The others must have gotten a ride, too," she thought, "or they would have been on the road. How long were we down there? They didn't have time to hike all the way back up."

But they had. In the slanted, arm-swinging gait they used on short hikes to make record time, they had raced with long strides the two miles up the canyon following Little Wooster and James on Goldie. Jody Sue said her side nearly split and all of their chests burned like soldering irons, but they had made it back to alert the cabins.

They loved to hike like that—especially if there were someone to show off for. Once when one of Father's friends had brought his daughter up for a visit, Katie had offered to take her on a hike. The girl was in a dress, a fluffy pink one, reason enough for scorn, but she also carried a fancy fan that she swept across the mountain air in flutters that piqued Katie's deepest sense of the appropriate. Katie had recruited Isabel and Jody Sue for the hike and the four had started in the flat meadow below the platform. The three canyon cohorts fairly ran up the switchback trail, not stopping to talk or breathe until they reached the needlepadded entry to The Crow's Nest a mile straight up. They had never gone quite that fast up the steep mountain to where the white latticework framed the planking and railings of the structure so familiar to them that they could have drawn a map of every set of initials in its twenty-foot flooring. From it could be seen the whole canyon, every cabin, the Armchair, the Divide, the Old Mine, and to the West, ridges of five mountain ranges clear out to Great Salt Lake.

On arrival Katie, seeing Jody Sue and Isabel do the same, swallowed her panting and casually looked back for the first time to see where their guest was. Her pale dress was moving in spurts along the trail, visible only now and then through the oak. The three watched for a moment and then Katie called, "Hi! How're you doing, Vanetta? We thought you were right behind us."

The run back down was much the same. Except that the cousins went even faster, grabbing the smoothed trunk of any oak that marked a turn. As they flew around the corner, their feet left the ground and the hand holding onto the turning post trees slid around and off to spill them several feet down the path, running to keep up with their momentum. At the bottom they waited by The Platform where Mother and her generation had danced under the pines to the lilt of a fiddler. Again, the visitor was far behind as the three cousins relished in silence their own proficiency and tossed pine cones at a tree trunk while they waited. Finally, Vanetta arrived, her frail dress torn, her white shoes full of dirt, her fan clutched in one hand and the other clinging to any hold she could find to brace her uncertain descent. Isabel and Jody Sue announced they had to go home, and Katie was left to walk to the road and up the hill to the cabin alone with Vanetta.

"You are a very good climber," Vanetta said to Katie.

"Thanks," Katie nodded, "so are you."

"No. I'm not. But I would like to be."

"Have you ever tried it before?"

"No, not really. My parents seldom do things outdoors."

"What do you do for fun then?" Katie asked, disbelieving.

"Oh, I read, and play the piano."

"Do you sew?"

"Sew?"

"Yes, you know, make things—on the machine—or do handiwork—you know, embroidery and things like that?"

"No, but I like to play jacks."

"Jacks? No kidding? Where?"

"Oh, on my front porch. Or on the kitchen floor. Anywhere that's smooth and hard."

"Hmm," said Katie. "That's amazing." She thought of how she loved to play jacks at home with Corinne, almost every day for hours and hours, right after bathing their dolls.

"Vanetta?" Katie was chewing on her cheek and making her mouth work. "Hiking can be more fun than that was today."

"How? I don't see how. I just loved watching how you did it—so fast."

They were almost to the top of the hill. "You want to empty your shoes and maybe straighten up a little before we get there?" she asked Vanetta.

"Oh, I don't really think so. Even though my father might not like the fact that my dress is torn, he'll be glad when he hears what a good time I had."

Katie didn't want to go home at all. She felt almost sick to her stomach.

"Katie," Vanetta said turning to her and stopping their slow steps. "It might seem kind of silly to you, but I'd really like you to know how much this has meant to me. Would you mind keeping my fan? I know it couldn't seem like much, but I'd really appreciate it if you would." She held out the closed fan. Katie took it and ran her fingers up and down its ivory smoothness, not opening it.

"Thank you, Katie," Vanetta said and started walking along the last part of the path to the porch.

Katie never showed the fan to anyone. She put it with her treasure box and her turquoise ring. Sometimes she hid it inside her shirt when she went to her secret place. She would open it and look at the carved figures on it and check to make sure none of the bindings were working loose. Then she would fan herself slowly, elegantly, as she read.

After that Katie never hiked fast that she didn't think of Vanetta, whom she never saw again. She even thought of her now, knowing how quick the cousins had been in getting up the canyon with their warning. It all seemed like years and years ago.

Uncle Wooster and Mother were having a conference halfway up the path. Katie ran past them to talk to James. He was getting things ready to go fight the fire. He had his canteen filled and slung over his shoulder and was tying a sweater by its arms around his waist. Davy was doing the same. "Where's Wid?" was James' first question.

Katie had forgotten all about poor Wid writhing there in the back seat. "Oh my gosh," she cried, jolting her head forward and hitting it with the heel of her hand. "I can't believe me! I forgot about Wid! And he's in awful shape!"

James and Davy ran with her out the path toward the car. Mother was leaning over the back seat talking to Wid telling him to ease out of the car and come up to the house where she could have a good look at him. As soon as he was out, Mother took him by the arm and Uncle Wooster started the car down the hill.

"Where's Uncle Wooster going?" Katie asked. "Aren't we going with him to fight the fire?"

"Yeah," said Davy. "Aren't we going to fight the fire."

"He's gone to try to scour up some help from the cabins up above and to try to find Mister Davis," Mother explained. "And we've got plenty to do ourselves right here."

Mother put Wid in her bed and went for the Witch Hazel. "Nothing like this for itching," she explained as she began soothing the cool, nostril-widening medicine over Wid with equally cool fingers. She gentled it into the angry red

164

that now covered him. He had begun to swell, all over, to puff up until his eyes were nowhere and his ear lobes sank into his cheeks. "You must be awfully uncomfortable," Mother said to Wid. "Nothing worse than itching. It looks like the hives. But it has to be a reaction to the anti-venom medicine they gave you, and it should clear up within a day."

While she stroked the witch hazel on Wid, Mother gave instructions to everyone else.

"James, you'll be the only one going with the menfolk. Plan on being up there for some time. I never saw a fire in the mountains get put out fast—especially in August. And Katie," she said to Katie who knew what she'd say to her. "I'll need you here. Fighting fires is men's work. Keeping everything going while they do is women's work." Katie jammed her jaws shut as Davy asked, "What about me?" dangling Wid's canteen that he had filled when James had his. "I'm a menfolk. And I can chop like everything."

"So can I, Davy," snapped Katie. "But let me tell you, that doesn't make any difference!" Katie banged out of the living room, through the kitchen where she didn't hear Lena's hello, and out to the path leading down to the lower level and the swing. She flopped herself over the notched seat of the swing, her stomach down so that she swung like a Raggedy Ann. The blood ran to her head as she pushed off with her toes and dangled her fingers in the thick dust while she passed back and forth. "How come?" she kept asking herself. "How come I can do everything the boys can except the big stuff?"

Davy must have been standing there behind the swing for some minutes before he moved into her vision and asked, "Katie, how long will it be before I get to be like Wid and James?"

Katie just shook her head and continued her passes at the dust.

Davy waited, then said, "Katie, does Mother really know everything?" Katie closed her eyes and then opened them to her view of Davy's boots, still without answering.

Finally she said, very low, "Seems like it—most of the time. Sometimes I wonder, though." Her eyes smarted from a hotness that licked her inner sides. "Go somewhere else, Davy," she managed to say just before tears turned everything to water.

CHAPTER TEN

Katie found there was plenty to do for those who stayed home. First, there had to be food prepared for the men. She and Lena made peanut butter sandwiches, cut up oranges, stripped carrots and filled the canvas water bags that hung from bumpers on trips. The fire department came more quickly than she thought they possibly could have, and soon after them came two truckloads of CCC boys. Dressed in their khaki outfits, they looked just like Mister Davis, only young. They all started from the Barton cabin because it sat well up on the mountain, higher than any around. This gave them a headstart in hiking up with their picks and axes and shovels to circle around the lower part of Rattlesnake Mountain and approach the fire from above.

Uncle Wooster directed the movements of everyone, even the fireman in charge. He sent Charles and James to show them where to go, with instructions to keep coming back for supplies and more directions. Before sunset, word had spread to most of the men in the city whose families lived in the canyon and they were up on the mountain too. The families in the meantime had been instructed to stay put and wait for further word. No one was to congest the road with downhill traffic unless it became dangerous to stay.

Katie and Davy made every trip they could to pass the clearing by the wood pile where Uncle Wooster was marshalling the forces. The other cousins had been asked to stay in their cabins, except for Smithy and Phillip, who became runners to the spring and to other cabins for more water and food. Little Wooster was the only one to remain in the clearing. He sat on Goldie, straddled and ready to go, watching his father and waiting for an urgency that would demand the speed that he and his horse alone could offer. It was Little Wooster who first spotted the sheriff making his way up the hill with unusual caution. From behind the fire truck a gangly man with bloomery pants stalked up to the clearing.

"What started it?" the man asked Uncle Wooster as soon as he saw who was in charge.

Uncle Wooster glanced at him and shook his head, not interrupting his instructions to the last of the CCC boys who had straggled up behind the others.

"Well, you gotta have some idea," the officer persisted, almost insolently.

There was a long pause as Uncle Wooster watched the CCC boys follow Charles up the mountain. "To tell you the truth," Uncle Wooster finally said with an irritated sigh, "I haven't given it a single thought. Maybe when it's out, huh?" and he turned to greet Mr. Edmunds and Mr. Morgan who had come from farther up the canyon to help.

Little Wooster eased Goldie over to where he caught the attention of the sheriff. "Whadda you think started it?" he asked the man.

The officer looked the boy and horse over and said, "Frankly, kid, I got no idea. But I'm gonna find out. I gotta."

"Is that how come you came up here?" asked Little Wooster.

"It's why I started out. But so far it looks like I'm not gonna have much cooperation." He breathed in, looked back disgustedly at Uncle Wooster, and then shot a glance up toward Little Wooster. "Hey kid, that horse reminds me. I just had the craziest thing happen. Just picked up a wild horse—not a mile down canyon."

"A wild horse?" said Little Wooster, his mouth dropping open.

"Yep. Just mindin' my own business, comin' up slow—lucky I was—this horse pops out in front of me. Damn near hit 'im. But I didn't. I jus' stopped like he done, both of us jus' right there starin' at each other. I noticed he had on this halter type thing and there was this rope barely danglin' from it, so I figured he must b'long to somebody, so I got out and he jus' stood there and I went up and grabbed this here frayed rope, and then I sez to myself, 'Leslie, what in Hell you plannin' to do with this here horse?' and 'course how did I know? So I just took a piece of rope outa my car and tied it to the one that was on him and then tied the whole kit and kaboodle to my bumper — and there he is." The sheriff pointed to where his car was, down the hill behind the fire engine.

Little Wooster never had tried to get his mouth closed through the whole story. Now he stared where the man pointed and let the situation sink in.

"A horse? On the road? Maybe one of Marcus Evers' got loose," Little Wooster pondered out loud. Just then Katie and Davy passed very slowly en route to taking a tin cup of water to Uncle Wooster. Katie excused herself excitedly as she sidled between Goldie and the sheriff. She had never been that close to a policeman, and she was so intent on trying to see what was on his badge that it took a minute for her to hear what Little Wooster had said.

"A horse? On the road?" she repeated.

"Yep. And he's tied to my bumper—right down there," the sheriff answered, important at last. He pointed past the fire truck.

Katie was already on her way, Davy at her heels. When she saw him standing there, dappled, calm as could be, his head in the long grass by last year's golf course, she squealed, "Tony!" He raised his head for only a moment and dropped back to the grass. Katie threw her arms around his neck forgetting his penchant for nipping and called, "Hey everybody, it's Tony! He's back! Still even has on his old halter—and the rope we tied him with!"

Little Wooster reined Goldie in beside Tony and dismounted. He took some stiff steps toward the pony just as the little horse laid back his ears and snapped his teeth at Katie's arm. At the same time he twisted around and began his familiar kicking with both hind feet as if he were practicing bucking. Little Wooster took two more steps and had hold of Tony's halter. In a soft voice he began talking as he ran his free hand down the horse's nose and scruffly neck. Katie had jumped clear of the bite and stood watching Little Wooster with his horse that had been gone for nearly a year.

"Hold it, ol' boy," Little Wooster kept saying. "Hold it. Hold it, ol' boy." The horse whinnied and seemed to quake, his eyes were frantic, but Little Wooster didn't move or stop talking.

The sheriff had come to see. "Man alive, what a crazy horse! What got into him? Did you see him kick! 'n try to bite! If I'd a known what kinda blasted critter he was, I sure wouldn't a picked him up."

Katie saw Little Wooster nuzzle the pony with his own face and hug his head to him. Gradually Tony's ears came up and his skin quit twitching. Katie didn't dare move or speak. Little Wooster worked his way down Tony's neck, his cheek against the tufted hair that had always been so sleek, his arms around the matted mane patting and pressing. "Ah, Tony," he said, "where ya been?" Katie could see Little Wooster's shoulders start to heave.

"Sir," she said huskily to the sheriff, "would you mind coming back up here and telling us about what happened?" She put her arm around Davy and steered him toward the clearing. He didn't look back as he would have any other time, but walked close to Katie watching what she was saying.

When Katie heard the sheriff's story, she rushed to tell Wid that all their efforts in Lost Canyon had not been worthless. "I just know we flushed him out of there! Just like with a quail or a pheasant," she said, sitting on the bed where Wid only nodded and continued his writhing. Katie knew that it would be useless to try to divert him with even that kind of story right now. Having the hives was bad enough, but having to miss the fire fighting would be something he'd regret forever.

For a while Katie received a running account of things on the mountain. James and Charles were back and forth until dark blacked out the trail they had worn. By then Father had come up and had gone off with the others. Katie, Davy, Mother, and Lena had dinner in the little kitchen where there was room for only a card table and two chairs. They ate there sometimes when there was a reason to hurry. Mother tried never to act as if she were in a hurry, but it was easy to tell when she was. She pursed her lips and hustled—as Father called it. The night of the fire Mother was in and out of everywhere, packing a suitcase here, wrapping a treasure there, sending loads to the car with Davy or Katie. They knew that no one could organize like Mother.

Soon after dark they began to smell the smoke. At first it was faint, like being in the vicinity of a bonfire. It grew more and more noticeable. By nine o'clock when Mother told Katie and Davy it was time to go to bed, it seared their eyes and they needed rubbing. "Just hop into bed," Mother said in her cheeriest tone, "and by the time you wake up it will be a whole new story."

The last thing in the world Katie wanted to do was go to bed. How would she know anything then? Davy felt the same reluctance, but when Mother told him he could sleep in Wid and James' bed he brightened immediately. "Oh boy! Right by Katie. I'll get all the news!" he chortled.

After Mother tucked him in, she sat on Katie's bed. "You know those prayers we said just now will do it, don't you?" she said to both of them. They knew it. They never doubted her. It always had been all right. Like when she tapped the old barometer in the front hall at home, the one that Grandpa Ruskins' father had brought across the plains. She knew after the tap what the weather would be like—as surely as she knew what would be for dinner. If it looked all right, she nodded at the barometer and claimed the day. If it was somehow contrary, especially if someone dear to her was "on the road," she would recheck the arrows on the faded face of the oak-rimmed barometer, tap it once more, and then turn away to begin working on the weather. She worked the same way on anything that needed it.

She sat for a while on Katie's bed reminiscing about when she was a girl and the other side of the canyon had burned. She talked a little about the Happy Home Fire, remembering from before Katie was born. Then she gradually switched to other stories until Davy could be heard breathing sleep breath, and Katie felt drowsy even in her excitement. "Mother," she asked, "how'll we know if the fire is out?"

"They'll be coming back. They're cutting wide paths up there to try to hold it. It takes time. It's all brush where the fire started. And that means it's racing. But they'll keep it from crossing the road and then keep it in the lower part of the canyon where there are no cabins. There's no need to worry. Just go to sleep. Why, with all those men—they have the electrical men working too, you know, all of them were in on the blasting up there on the mountain. There must be at least seventy or eighty men up there right now."

"I wish I were," Katie said not dreamily.

"Up there working with the men?"

"Sure. I could do any of it."

"Oh, Katie, you little pill. You always have to be in on it, don't you," smiled Mother squeezing Katie's toe. "And you always have to ride the wildest horse to get there. What in the world will become of you?"

"I'll grow up like Grandma, I guess. She rode a wild horse—all the time. She tells me about it when I sleep with her."

Mother smiled again. Even in the dark Katie knew she was smiling because her voice changed. "Oh, dearie, how I'd love to have that happen," she said bending over Katie and

172

kissing her. "Now get to sleep and let yourself be taken care of. It's really not too bad a thing to have happen."

When Mother left, Katie lay on her back counting the joists in the exposed ceiling that was the floor upstairs. She could hear Mother and Lena moving around and could feel the smoke on her eyes. It felt good to close them. "What if the fire came right down here?" she thought. Fire was the one thing she had ever had a nightmare about, and she'd had it several times. In it she saw flames coming out of her closet, their pointless ends wrapping around the door and charring it into falling. When it fell, the space behind it was a turmoil of black crawling with orange that sprawled out onto the floor and began to chase her. Wherever she ran, it followed. But it stopped when she stopped, never really catching her, only being there, shuddering with waiting. When she turned to see if it was still behind her, its smoky breath raised into brief, horrifying outline her room, her clothes, her dolls, the whole house and then consumed them. Usually she awoke trying to run, panting and sweating, her hair stuck to the back of her neck.

Now that there was a real fire it seemed less ominous than those that had beleaguered her in her sleep. Even with the smoke in her nostrils, she could not imagine the canyon actually on fire. Maybe the best thing she could do would be to get out of bed, slip up the path, and go watch what was happening, maybe even help out without anyone seeing her or missing her. Half awake, she drifted past the ceiling and was there, wielding her axe, a phantom of speed and proficiency. "Who's that?" the fire fighters all asked. "No one knows. But it looks like a girl! Look! She's walking right into the flames! She's cutting the flames down! They're sinking back! The fire is afraid of her! She's done it! She's put out the fire with her axe! Now she's riding off on a pinto pony— right up into the smoke!"

Katie opened her eyes and was not sleepy at all. It sounded quiet upstairs. Lena had gone to bed in the room through the wall from her. She knew Mother would not have gone to bed but would be mending or reading in the living room beside Wid. Poor Wid. To be missing the most excitement of any summer ever. She began smelling the smoke again. It seemed less dense. What if they had the whole thing out and she'd never even been in on any of it. She turned to her other side and turned her pillow with her to get the cool side up. Her hand touched the moccasins under her pillow. Uncle Wooster had brought them to her from an Indian reservation in New Mexico and she kept them where she could bring them out and fondle them as she went to sleep. She pulled them out and pressed them to her mouth and nose. She had forgotten how they smelled of fire like bacon and how much they felt like soft leaves between her fingers and lips. As she snuggled for a more persuasive fit into her pillow with her hand holding the moccasins, her fingers began to tell her head what she had to do. Why not? Why not be where she ought to be? The moccasins were it. They were the answer.

Katie slipped out of bed in her wooly pajamas and reached for her bathrobe. Of course the reason she hadn't thought of this sooner was that her clothes and boots were upstairs where she always undressed by the fire. Her boots would be set by Lena or Mother in the warming oven in the morning so that when she went to put them on in the cold they'd be toasty and a little bit stiff. Of course she couldn't have thought of going to the fire without clothes—especially without boots. Who'd ever get near Rattlesnake Mountain even in the daytime without boots? And who could climb over all those rocks barefoot? Not even the phantom.

Now, though, there was another way! Katie edged out of the bedroom to the small screened downstairs porch. Stealthily she inched open the door to the lower level and stepped through. The stoop was cold and slivery on her bare feet. She sat on a step and pulled the moccasins on. They were totally different from slippers. Slippers were slow and not meant to go anywhere, just to move from sitting to lying down. Moccasins had running in them. Katie's toes touched the ends and curled against the soft giving of the soles. She tied the thongs around her ankles and put her hands to her nose. Now her fingers had the moccasin smoke on them. She was ready.

Having feet tender from ten and a half summers of wearing shoes, Katie knew better than to try climbing over a rocky route in moccasins. Instead, she ran through the long grass to the parking place, then down the steep hill. She knew the ruts by heart and walked up over and down them, sinking into the deep dust, aware of her footprints. It felt like putting the heel of her palm into the flour that Mother let her sift and shape in the big bread pan. At the foot of the hill she could see the amber orange glow over the trees to her right. She began jogging down the road that was clearly visible in the eerie light from the fire. It seemed almost like daytime, except that the trees moved in their shadows and the creek sounded like a rush of rain.

She passed the lower Ruskin cabins, still meeting the dust with the soft feet of her moccasins. There was Daniel Moon's. She slowed to search both sides of the road. The curve pushed her into a faster run. She could hear the padding of her feet—and something else. The cabin beyond the trees was dark and she was almost to Rabbit's Head. The stream crashed into its rapids below the mammoth red rock formation as the road closed into darkness.

This was the tunnel part of the canyon, the longest straight stretch, arching with trees that met each other in the holding that Katie loved in the daylight. The one time that she had ridden down the canyon at night with Father to take a message to Mister Davis, this had been her favorite part of the drive. The car's headlights had pierced the tunnel of green and turned it into a cave of shimmering. Father said this is where he often saw deer on his early trips down in the morning. One would bound out of the underbrush onto the road, stand for a minute in bewilderment, and then bounce sometimes for half a mile ahead of the car, too afraid to leap off to where it had to go. Katie knew that she should watch for deer now. They were often roaming at night. But if one were there, there would be no seeing it in the dark.

Only a few more curves after the straight stretch and she'd be even with the edge of the fire where everybody would be working. It would be light there too since the trees opened up and let the road out. Katie's eyes were on swivels pivoting to every rustle in the bushes. She thought of playing Black-Out with the cousins at parties when they put out the lights in the basement playroom on Crystal, of the urgency not to be caught, of the terror of even a single hand on a shoulder or foot. "Blind people must be very afraid," she thought. "How would it be not to be able to trace sound or anticipate silent motion?"

Just before the Second Rat House, Katie's spine wrinkled. There was something moving across where she knew the bridge was. She slowed her jog trying to look straight ahead while her eyes ferreted the blackness where the sound was. "I'll just run past—fast—and before anything could even see me I'll be where the fire is," she thought. It had to be very close. Smoke was part of the darkness. Only it moved. Right above the next curve would be Father and James and all the men. Katie wondered why she hadn't picked up her hiking stick as she left. It was dumb to go anywhere without a hiking stick. She was almost past the Second Rat House. All there was was the stream running and her running through the dark. But there was something else.

She rounded the curve where she and Jody Sue had flown on their bug past the unbelieving ladies in the car. She tried to remember how it felt to laugh. Beyond the curve the sky opened red and furious, like the blood on Wid's head from Little Wooster's pick. Most of the smoke was still rising, now in great poofs that ate each other. Katie stood panting, her moccasins still in the powdery dust, her pajamas sticking solid to her back.

Now what? The fire was there, gigantic and real, but somehow it seemed almost friendly, at least glowing, magnetic and warm compared to whatever it was in the dark behind her.

176

She inched backwards not wanting to have her back to anything. She had to pry the expanse illuminated by the fire to see where to head next. The bank of the road was steep, and from its lip the forest looked denser than she had remembered, towering over her unless she moved back to the far side of the road and looked beyond it. Then she could make out some silhouettes against the sky here and there, but they moved like phantoms themselves, too far away to identify. Spurts of flame snatched at the sky. There was snorting and a hollow bellowing. Everything was in motion, pulsing and pulling, alive as the fires in her dreams. Katie was caught in the same anguished fascination. She couldn't move. She couldn't yell if she wanted to. She felt herself dissolving, floating on a phantasmagoric inertia.

She had never had any plan as to what she would do when she got to the fire—only that she would get there. She must have thought about seeing Father and James and the others, but that all was as hazy as the horizon that wisped now and then above the smoke, black against the sky. Trees crackled and broke and there was a roaring somewhere like water from Mountain Dell Reservoir where they hid under the spillway.

Katie hardly noticed that the front of her was hot and the back of her so cold she kept shivering. Her face blazed and her eyes had to stay only partly open. Transfixed, even her mouth was unmoving. The fire heaved and pitched like a giant breathing, like the snakes on top of each other in the grotto. It was like striking every match in the world and holding them at finger-tip.

Gradually she was sure she was not alone. There was no rustle, no sound at all except the fire. But the smoke and night air drifted about her heavy as fog, and in the vapors was a stench of something not of the fire or the dark. It oozed into her pores and scuffled with her composure until she waited limp and dry, knowing she should run but more unable than ever in her worst dream. She moved into the void that was her own body and could hear only her breathing. Then somewhere someone was breathing with her. She tried looking around without turning her head. The effort brought her mouth closed and started her tongue and lips moving. Her nose too. In the acrid bite of the smoke was a sweet, rancid blend of whiskey and tobacco.

"Mister Davis?" she braved. "That you, Mister Davis?"

There was a suggestion of dark against dark moving down the road toward her. "Mister Davis?" she tried again.

Then he materialized, standing over her plain and actual, puffing his pipe between clenched teeth. She had never seen him with his hat off. Close in the firelight his bald white forehead gleamed and even his stubble showed.

"Whatcha you doin' here, girl?" he asked peering at her in a new way. "Ya hadn't oughta be around here, ya know."

"Oh yes I should, Mister Davis. Father told me to meet him right here—at exactly this time."

"What time, girl?"

"Oh, this time. He said he'd pick me up right here on the road and we'd go home together. He's up there fighting the fire and he said for me to be right here."

"Mighty funny place to plan to meet. Seems to me ya been sneakin' around all by yerself."

Katie slid one foot ahead of the other to ease forward where she could begin running. If only she had her hiking stick. She could use it like a scythe. Maybe somebody would come down to the road from the fire. No wonder they couldn't find Mister Davis earlier. He'd been somewhere drinking. Suddenly his hand grabbed her wrist. It felt like the sandpaper in Wid's vice that they used to hold their boards solid while they planed or filed them when Mother was teaching them to build things.

"You let go!" she hissed at Mister Davis, who was breathing like the fire. "I'm going to meet my Father now—and probably Uncle Wooster too. And then I'm going home. And if you don't let go, you'll be in real trouble."

"I'm not gonna hurt ya, girl," Mister Davis said in a greasy voice. She could hear his teeth click as he took the pipe out with his other hand. "I just wanna talk."

Katie knew she could not get away. Her temples hammered and nausea started her mouth watering. "What did you want to talk about, Mister Davis?" she almost squeaked.

"About a lotta things. Now I'll tell ya what. Ya just do what I tell ya and I'll let-cha go—fer now." He wrung her wrist tighter. She could feel her hand begin to go numb.

"OK, Mister Davis, just tell me what you want me to do?" Katie swallowed.

"You come to my cabin tomorrow—when the fire's all put out—when everybody's forgotten all about it, and I'll show you." She knew he was smiling that smile that looked like he hurt somewhere.

"OK. Fine. That sounds just fine. And then you could tell me about the lure you have for my cat, too, that good stuff that draws animals from anywhere, remember?"

"It ain't gonna be no lure we'll be talkin' about, girl." He paused and started to chuckle so far down it sounded like crying. "But then again...maybe...maybe. The chuckles took over and he squeezed her wrist again and she thought it would pop her hand right off. "You remember now. Tomorrow—inna afternoon—after everything's died down about this fire. Ya don't show up—and you'll be one sorry sorry li'l girl."

"Oh, gee, Mister Davis, I'll be there for sure. You can count on me."

"An' don't you tell nobody how good I was to ya here tonight. Why, ya mighta run onto a snake—or a mountain lion—or anything. They all been scared outa that up there." He jerked her arm to point toward the fire.

"Oh, don't worry, Mister Davis, I won't tell anybody. I mean, I know how great you're being. I'll just see you tomorrow." Katie felt his grip loosen a little on her wrist. She began turning her fist and pulling away. Suddenly he wrenched her back.

"Now don't ya go thinking you're leaving till I'm good and ready to let-cha, ya hear?" he said threateningly.

"OK. Fine. Just fine. But my father should be here any time and he'll want me to leave with him." She could feel him faltering. She knew he didn't believe her about Father, but maybe he just thought it was a bare possibility. Someone could come up or down the road—or down from the fire.

"Awright. Ya go now. But none of this waiting fer yer daddy. Just head on home and remember what I told ya." Mister Davis let go and rocked back a little as Katie sped up the road into the dark tunnel, past Daniel Moon's, past the spring, up the hill to the cabin. She crept through the downstairs door, relieved that the light was still on only in the living room and on the upstairs porch. No one had come home yet.

In bed Katie trembled between the cold sheet blankets and waited for herself. She felt unarrived, disembodied. Her arms and legs were floating and lifting her whole body away from its moorings. Her head was nowhere. Her bathrobe and moccasins were still on—sealed to her. The only thing she could sense was a burning in her wrist and a great weariness.

Katie woke up to James shaking her shoulder. "Move over Katie. I gotta talk to you," he urged, chattering and shivering in the dark.

Katie fumbled for consciousness. "What time is it?" she asked. "What are you doing back? What about the fire?"

James crawled under the covers and curled up to get warm. "It's about morning. We've been up there all night. Boy, did it get cold!"

"But what about the fire? Did you put it out?"

"Not really. But we did what they call 'contain' it—it won't go any further, but it has to burn itself out where it's already burning. Boy, did it spread! It got all the foliage from Mister Davis's to the First Rat House. All on the same side of the road, though. And we dug out a huge lane clear from the road to the ridge so it couldn't jump across there either. Some of the men 're still up there watching to make sure nothing else breaks out, but I don't see how it could."

James sounded strange. Katie couldn't tell if it was

because he was trying to whisper or because his voice was funny. "What did you do the whole time?" she asked.

"At first Charles and I just carried stuff back and forth and took messages to people. After everybody got sort of established, we helped spell off the men. They got really tired. Boy, was it work! Mostly it was trying to do it so fast."

"Why does your voice sound like that?"

"Like what?"

"Like you've had a cold forever."

"Does it sound like that?"

"I'll say it does. Are you sick?"

"Not really, I guess. Maybe the earache I had last week has got to my throat or something."

"Earache? You never told me about that."

"No reason to. They always go away. Anyhow Wid was under the weather, and one's enough at a time." James tried to straighten out and lie on his back. As he pushed his legs down he sucked in his breath and let out a subdued grunt. Katie could feel him tense up.

"What was that? Did something hurt?"

"Nah, not really. Just my hip. On one trip down just before dark I slid on some rocks and landed pretty hard. I guess I banged it. It'll loosen up by morning."

"Boy, this sure has been the accidental family lately. Lucky everybody heals up fast."

"Katie."

"What?"

"Something a lot worse than a little fall happened up there tonight."

"What?"

"Well, you know Daniel Moon."

"Course I know Daniel Moon. Was he up there with the fire?"

"Not exactly."

"What do you mean, 'not exactly'?"

"Well, he wasn't there at all, not really. But two of the fathers from down the canyon were talking right where I couldn't help hearing." James raised his arms and put them under his head. Katie felt sure she didn't want to ask him anything. After a long time he said, "Mr. Shaw was talking to Mr. Harris. He said, 'I guess you heard about that Moon boy—what's his name?' Mr. Harris said that he hadn't. So Mr. Shaw said, 'He committed suicide—they found him hanging in the ice house that his father owns.'"

Katie felt heavy all over. Her ears were hot and her eyes were so wide open she could feel her eyelids inside her head. Nobody she'd ever known had really died. Nobody she'd ever even talked to—except Grandma Barton and she was pretty old and had been sick and had a glass cover over a sore on her leg for a long time. And Darlene Brown in the second grade who sat on the other side of the room and got hit crossing Highland Drive, and they put a light in on that corner after that. And Aunt Clarice, but she could just remember her as being quiet-voiced and very queenly. But Daniel Moon. Somebody really alive. Really right there. And somebody she had never been very nice to. In fact, not nice to at all. In fact, really awful to. And now he was dead. And he did it himself, committed *suicide*. Nobody ever did that. That was the worst thing you could do—ever—except maybe kill somebody else or be a Son of Perdition and deny Jesus. What did he look like? Hanging there? Were his eyes open or closed? In shows they had to close people's eyes or put pennies on them. How could he manage to get somewhere to drop from? And how could a rope hold him? He was so fat. But he was dead. Daniel Moon. Daniel Moon really dead? Why? Why would he do that? What did he mean by it?

Katie's mouth felt like the rocks by the grotto.

"Katie?"

She ran her tongue along her lips so she could answer. "What?"

"Did you hear what I said?"

"Yes."

"Wid sure will feel bad."

"When're you going to tell him?"

"Maybe after I talk to Father. I sure do wish we could've talked to Daniel Moon that time."

"Yeah, 'cause now there'll never be a chance. There'll never be a chance to do any of it. And he'll never have a chance to do anything at all. He won't even walk up the road. Or have a drink of water. He won't ever grow up and find out what it's like. He won't even remember how the wind feels. I wonder if he'll remember anything. I wish..."

"There's no use wishing, Katie," James said sadly. "All you do is get yourself in trouble. Hoping is just fine—that's what you're s'posed to do, I guess. But wishing...boy, that's just no good at all."

The room felt stuffy with old smoke. Katie blinked over her burny eyes. "Do you think Wid'll be able to figure it out?" she asked in almost a whisper.

"Probly. I know Father will."

Katie listened to James breathe for a long time. She could tell he wasn't asleep, but she knew he was through talking. He lay mostly still except for his head. If he moved his hip, he moaned under his breath. The whole time he sounded strange—sort of rusty—even when he wasn't talking.

Katie thought finally. "No wonder there was a fire."

She turned on her side and saw the sky becoming white. In a few minutes the pink would start. Then the orange. Then the sun would hit the top of Crow's Nest Mountain and work its way down to the smoldering black where men still moved around with their shovels and axes. This was the first time in her life that she had been awake already when the sun came up. A few times Mother had awakened her to go on a big hike and it always seemed exciting, but now her eyes burned and the morning was colder than she ever thought it could be. She looked at James and wondered if he were seeing the morning too. "I sure am glad he's accident proof," she thought. "Especially now that the fire's out." She was trying to figure out why she didn't want to talk to James about Mister Davis when she fell asleep.

CHAPTER ELEVEN

James was gone when Katie woke up, and Davy too. The bedroom was warm from the sun hitting the screen window, and she was wringing wet. Her pillow was soaked and her curls flattened against it. She started to throw back the covers to get up but then remembered the night before. She felt for her moccasins that still clung like skin to her feet. She pulled up her knees and without looking swung her legs on top of the covers and lay back letting the moccasins move her toes and draw her back into the night. The same feeling of suspension began to crawl through her. With her left hand, she touched her right wrist. It was tender. She didn't want to look at it. Mister Davis loomed against the ceiling, his forehead shining in a miasma of orange and black. Katie wanted to go back to sleep, never to get up at all, to just sleep and sleep. She tried to close her eyes but saw the same scene on the backs of her lids. Then she remembered James and what he had told her and how strange he had sounded. She rolled off the bed and headed for the upstairs, trying to moisten her mouth with a lot of swallowing.

"Well, there she is," greeted Mother on the porch, "rosy cheeks and all. And in the bathrobe that she slept in all night."

"Bathrobe?" A look down confirmed the observation.

"Yes, you little goose, you wouldn't let me take it off when I came down to tuck you in last night."

"When were you down?" Katie asked uncomfortably, aware of her moccasins and of her feet swollen inside them.

"I came down to kiss you after James got settled. You were rolled up like a chipmunk and wouldn't let me budge your robe."

That must have been way after the sun came up, Katie thought. "What time is it now?" she asked, "and where's Wid? How is he anyhow? Did he itch all night?" For some reason she didn't want to mention the fire or even James. In the daylight all of last night seemed exactly like one of her nightmares, gone and irrelevant.

Mother was mending in the stilt rocker, something she usually did at night, and she hardly looked up from her needle to answer Katie's questions. Her matter-of-factness meant there was something big to worry about. "It's ten thirty. And Wid is now sitting up in the dining room having a very late and very big breakfast. He heals as easily as he gets hurt —luckily." She turned her marble darning egg around and started stitching across the same area she had just covered. "James is in the poster bed in case you're wondering. All to willingly, I'm 'fraid. The day that little boobie stays down with just an earache..." Mother had quit talking to Katie and was pursing her mouth around words that were almost going back in. "The fire was hard on everyone anywhere near it."

"How? Where's Father? Did he get home? Did they put it all out?" Katie felt the fire coming back, seeping through her. "I can smell smoke like anything," she said looking past Mother to the filmy air beyond the porch.

"They got it all out, and Father had to rush down to the city on some business with Uncle Wooster. They're trying to help the firemen find out how it started, and they still haven't been able to locate Mister Davis."

Katie's temples went concave and her stomach dropped into her legs.

"Where do they think he could be?" she asked.

"That's the mystery. Nobody knows. Not a soul saw him yesterday or last night. And you know how regular his days usually are—at least as far as where he is in the canyon at what time. But..." Mother brightened with a full-busted and determined sigh, "never mind for now. They'll get the whole thing straightened out. The main business for us today is to get everybody back to normal around here. We'd better start with a little girl getting something hot in her tummy to start the day." She nodded Katie toward the dining room and was back puckering at her mending.

Mechanically Katie started down the porch. She noticed that the double doors to the living room were closed, something they never were in the daytime, even when it was raining. Her feet throbbed when she tried to stand on her toes to see through the glass at the top of one of the doors. All she could make out was a hump in the bed. "Don't go in for now," Mother said distantly, "I want James to get some sleep. That's the best thing there is for any ailment you know."

Something was way out of kilter to Katie. Mother was on the porch, Wid was eating without her, and even as tired as James must be, she'd be very surprised if he were really asleep. Davy came wheeling around the corner from the outside, the screen slamming behind him. "Hi, Katie!" he exploded. "Boy, was that an exciting night! Father said he'd take us up to where the fire was and show us it. And next time I bet they'll let us two go fight it with 'em. Father said they needed every bit 'a help they could get. In fact, he said they really coulda used me, being as I'm such a good chopper and hiker and all." Davy was slicked up for the day except for his hair which had been slept into a point and made him look like an elf. He never got by with going across the path looking like that, but he was out the door again and calling, "Wanna have me tell Isabel and Jody Sue when you'll be over?"

"Never mind, Davy. I have to do some other things first," she called, knowing he was too far gone to hear. If Mother saw her start for the bedroom that had been Grandma's, she didn't say anything. Katie walked casually as she could on feet that suddenly felt like raw stumps. Her head was a stranger to her, filled with abrupt comings and goings, blurred perceptions. It was like dreaming just before going to sleep.

She kept thinking she couldn't really be awake and feel this way, swarming with premonition and remembering, almost dizzy with an overwhelming impulse to run somewhere. Maybe she had never been really afraid in her whole life before. Was this what it felt like? Nothing in place, everything swirling and mixed up? Every day that she could remember she had liked getting up. It was as full of promise as stretching—that languid expulsion of sleep that left everything alive in its wake. There were always excitements waiting. But this day was so ruffled and uncomfortable that all she wanted to do was disappear, not to be anywhere. Even one of her favorite things—putting her boots on—sounded awful.

Katie looked down at her feet. Her moccasins were shredded and broken in their seams. The beading was still there on the tops of them, but there was hardly anything left of the front part of the soles. For the first time she let herself feel her feet hurt. She limped to the bedroom that jutted out from the porch and in one movement jumped on the bed, sprang high to reach a rafter, and swung over it to sit up next to the roof. Her feet were knives. Walking along the beams into her shingled playhouse was like walking on sharp rocks. When she sat down on the afghan, she crossed her leg and examined her right foot. Taking off the moccasin, she saw that it was cut and bruised all across the ball. The left one was the same. She could hardly stand to touch the soreness. She knew Mother would have those feet soaking in soothing hot water the minute she saw them. But what could she tell her? How could she explain feet like that? Nobody got anything that sore just doing normal things. The funny part was Katie couldn't remember her feet hurting at all. Yet she must have run right through her moccasins coming home—right up the middle of the road where all the rocks were. And there wasn't a way ever that she could tell Mother anything about any of it.

It wasn't that Katie wasn't used to the usual kinds of camouflage. When the cousins made moss villages and went searching up Grandma's gully for the thick rich moss that grew in the shady stream below Castle Crags, they often had to wade to get to where they could peel it off in huge dripping sections. Or they were forced to slosh in the pond below Hickman's where the waterfall crashed and then ran into the trough to the water wheel. The bottom was either slimy or rocky—either way better with boots on. So when they were headed home, they followed a careful route that took them through the deepest dust in the canyon, ending at the foot of Maple Fork where they'd cake their guilty boots with stomping in the dust until they looked as if they'd been only on a very long hike. Mother being constantly on the alert for precautions made wet feet a highly dangerous indulgence, one never admitted. How had she missed noticing Katie's moccasined feet and Davy's morning-after hair?

She knew Mother was worried about James. That's why she hadn't noticed. Mother had had that cheerful preoccupied look that meant she was about to take some kind of drastic action about something and make it seem like an everyday thing. Katie could hear her now straightening her way to the room below. She could picture her tidying as she moved across the porch, picking up, rearranging "plumping" everything in her path.

"Katie, you'd better come and get dressed and have some breakfast so Lena can clear. And I want you and Wid to have some spelling this morning."

Two mornings a week Mother held school at the dining room table, usually on days when there was plenty of time—or when there was something going on that she wanted to divert the children from, like the milk truck. The Arden Dairy truck and its driver, Mr. Post, made the run on Tuesdays and Thursdays to bring dairy supplies, bread, and—to those avant-garde enough to have ice boxes—ice. When they could, the cousins met the truck down the canyon and then hung on its open bed by the supports to the roof and rode up, wheedling half pints of chocolate or orange drink out of gangly, toothy Mr. Post as he made his stop-and-run journey to every cabin. Mother heard of their successes and promptly began her pedagogy in the very middle of the route. "Never be cheeky," she admonished before their first lesson. "Pay or work for what you get. What you get for nothing is nothing."

From then on, there were hour-long lessons reviewing arithmetic, handwriting, reading, and spelling, capped by either an art lesson, with Mother getting out her layered palette and letting them experiment on canvas, or a lesson in building where Mother instructed in the use of the round saw, the plane, the chisel, the ways to put together things sanded to silken smoothness. It wasn't that they minded school, it was just that Mother was too good at reading their minds and knowing exactly when to hold it. And the worst was spelling. Katie could do the rest and like it pretty well, but spelling? Ugh!

A lot of the time Katie simply made up words when she couldn't spell the real ones. Making things up was as natural as finding finger places in smooth screw holes. She liked to watch Mother watch her when she was reciting and improvising on something that she'd taught her. At home she'd say it just fine, but in Primary opening exercises Katie would give "Polly's Dollies" or "A Mortifying Mistake" an extra line or a few different phrases that would be sure to make Mother purse her lips and shake her head. When she was Persephone in the Ward play and was supposed to hold hands with Pluto in the finale, she knew she had to do something in order not to have to hold Maylan Miner's gooey palm. So with an impromptu flourish of net and flowers, she waltzed out of the grand promenade leaning to a hand cupped around her ear, chirping "Demeter is calling! Demeter is calling!" Off-stage, Mother, trying to be solemn, had greeted her with "Is she calling youOOooOOooo?"

Once she was the reader and James the curtain puller

for "Hiawatha" at Highland Park Grade School. Father had said James had one of the best parts because every time he pulled the curtain everybody applauded, so during the performance Katie invented lines that had James pulling and pulling. If Miss Peterson smiled, Katie never knew it.

Katie began remembering now how even when it got her in trouble she liked making things up. Like the time she told Rosalyn about having a new blue bike—and then trying to act as if she did, when no one in the family had ever had a bike. It never seemed like a lie—only like pretending. And it was so much fun to see Rosalyn so puzzled, Rosalyn who always had a nickel or more to spend on candy at the store across from school, and who had a room all her own with pink metal furniture and who beat Katie in the hopscotch tournament when Katie had beaten her every day at recess.

Maybe the night before was all made up. Maybe it was just one of her travelogues and Mister Davis had not been there at all, and Daniel Moon was still alive.

She pressed her foot to make sure it hurt and then called, "Mother, do you think it would be all right if I got dressed up here?"

"Why?" asked her mother who now stood just below her looking up.

Katie slid her feet under her and dived onto her stomach so that her head was downward and she was leaning over the edge of the old shingled roof to talk upside down to her mother. "Well it just seemed kind of cozy to be up here with my children to get dressed. Would it be too much trouble for you to hand me my things? My boots, too?"

Any other time Mother would have recognized Katie's efforts to change the wind, but this time she answered, "All right—if you scurry and hop right down here after." She added perfunctorily, "We need to get your hair curled."

The boots on her swollen feet felt like Mister Davis's grip on her wrist. Katie laced them loose but still didn't see how she could possibly walk without a noticeable struggle. As she swung down onto the bed from the rafters, she almost buckled but decided she absolutely couldn't let anyone know anything about it until she'd had time to work out a way that it could have happened—maybe somewhere today, doing something fairly acceptable that she could report back about in the nonchalant fashion she had learned from her brothers.

She walked on her heels to the dining room, saying, "Have you ever tried getting across a puddle like this? It's the neatest way. Doesn't get your soles wet at all—and your heels don't matter if they get wet 'cause they don't soak through."

Wid was still swollen and fairly red, but he said he didn't itch any more and Katie could tell by what he'd eaten that he felt better. She wondered if he knew about Daniel Moon. She bet he didn't. James would have waited to tell him till they could have some time to talk about it.

"Well, I guess we missed just the best thing that's happened all summer is all," she said to him, plunking down on the bench where her place was. "How do you feel?"

"You mean about that?"

"No, about how you feel. How're your hives?"

"Not bad. Not bad at all. I figure that's it. That's the last of getting anything wrong. From now on, the dopey stuff is just not going to happen to me." Wid seemed sad. Not the mad kind of sad that he sometimes got when things went wrong. More older sad. Like he was a grown-up or something. Katie nodded and looked at the bowl of oatmeal Lena had set before her. It disappeared beneath the cream she poured over it. She would have put another spoonful of sugar on it if Mother hadn't been within appearing distance. Maybe Wid did know about Daniel Moon.

"When did you get to talk to James?" she asked him.

"James? Not ever. I was already out of bed when he came up this morning and Mother had him right back in her bed before we said two words. I hope he wakes up soon so we can hear about the fire." Wid didn't really seem interested in the fire though. He was thinking of something else, Katie could tell.

Her mush tasted worse than usual. Katie stirred it like mud pies and made herself a peanut butter and honey sandwich with the bread on the table and tried to make it go down with big gulps of milk. She couldn't understand why Wid wasn't up doing something. Even if he still felt a little sick, he'd never just sit around with her there and think. She used her knife to make the salt shaker chase the pepper around her glass. Finally Wid leaned forward on his crossed arms and sighed the biggest sigh Katie had ever heard. "He knows about Daniel Moon," Katie thought. She swallowed but the peanut butter stuck to her throat.

"Wid," she swallowed again. "I know about Daniel Moon."

Again, Katie could smell the smoke and she heard the maples scraping the edge of the roof in front. Wid kept his eyes on the blue and white oilcloth and lowered his chin to meet his folded arms. After a long time he said, "I figured you did."

There was another long pause, then he said, "I wonder where he is."

Katie let herself wonder, too, and then realized that's all she'd been wondering about Daniel Moon. She wasn't wondering about why he did it or about his folks or about any of the things she'd wondered about last night. All she could think was I wonder where Daniel Moon is.

"Where do you think he is, Wid?" she said softly.

"The funny thing is, I think I know, but when it comes right down to specifics, I sure don't know much," Wid answered in the same tone. Then in a minute, "On the other hand, it seems like I know that more than I know anything else in my life. It's crazy."

Everything Wid said always made sense to Katie even when she couldn't understand it. She wanted to ask him what he thought about if the fire was because of Daniel Moon or anything, or if he thought there would be something else bad happen, but it all seemed settled, like this was the end, not the beginning of anything. Maybe it would be. Maybe all the unaccountable business had worked itself out—and now the canyon could start to be itself again.

Mother came through the kitchen from the living room and reported that James was supposed to sleep as long as he possibly could and that nothing, absolutely nothing, was to disturb him. Wid and Katie looked at each other and Wid got up to help clear the table for the school session. Katie tried to do the same but couldn't stand on her feet. They throbbed inside her boots and any weight on them felt like razors in her bones.

"I'll lay out the tablets," she offered to Mother, sitting back down on her bench. "It really sounds like a good idea to have spelling today—to keep us sort of quiet for James and all."

Mother curled Katie's ringlets before the school session with more than her usual carefulness, as if flattening the light hair around her forefinger with the brush were a kind of settling. It was the one thing that was in place that morning. Everything in school seemed forgettable, almost nonexistent. "I'll go for water today," Katie volunteered when it was over. "Or I'll rake the path, or take the milk back down to the creek." She knew Mother would notice her limping if she stayed around the house for her jobs.

Mother was stacking her mending on the red sewing box by the stilt rocker. She had on her best smock and under it a city dress, so Katie knew she was ready for a not regular day. Katie suddenly longed for a normal day, and more than anything for Mother to laugh. Mother had always laughed. Once even at a Ruskin reunion. There were so many relatives there that the reunion had to be held in the recreation hall of a ward, and the program, representative talents from all branches of the family, was on the stage. Mother held out pretty well for most of it, but nearly at the end a boy began a trumpet solo of "The Lost Chord." Katie was sitting next to Mother and could feel it begin to happen. The chord was very lost; in fact even Katie, whose musical ear was not exactly exact, was pondering where it had gone. First, she felt

Mother start to jiggle. She darted a glance at her and saw her fist rolled up at her mouth, her cheeks puffing and her eyes watering. They were sitting on the solid bench that surrounded the hall, in plain sight of all the relatives. Katie tried to look somewhere safe—at the vaulted ceiling, at the rear doors, at the leaded windows across the field of heads. Nothing worked. She could hear Mother stifling snorts of air and knew that James was doing the same on the other side of her. The bench began to quiver and Katie knew the piece had better end soon—the whole program had better end. "We always disgrace ourselves," Mother had said time and again. "And it's all your fault," she'd smile, paddling one of their bottoms and starting to laugh again remembering. Sometimes they managed to make it to a safe ending, where Mother would daub her eyes and nose daintily with her lace hanky as if she had been terribly moved, and sigh back into control. But at the reunion the end failed to come soon enough. Just before the final phrases of the trumpet, Mother had burst out with what she would have labeled a most unladylike noise. The whole audience had turned to watch as Mother led the procession of her disgraced family out for a drink of water.

How long had it been since Mother had laughed—really hard like usual? How long since anybody had? Even she and Jody Sue had not practiced their three laughs for a long time. They had laughs that they had developed over several summers. Any time they felt particularly in need they would look at each other and go to Jody Sue's bedroom where they would take turns moving up the scale. The first laugh was gutteral and brought with great effort from the stomach. It sounded a lot like the ominous laughs on John Dew The Magician, but by the time it had run its breathy course, the two were laughing for very real. The second rose in tone, in fact ran the gamut from high to low like the laughing lady at Salt Air. By the time they had pushed that one through, the two girls were forced to lie down with their aching sides. But they had to get to the third laugh, which was high-pitched as mouse talk and wound down only with the loss of breath. At its end, Jody Sue and Katie were rolling on the bed, their cheeks paining, their sides screaming in a doubling up that found no relief except in separation. They would end up crawling away from each other and reeling off to recover. Then it would be hours before they could see each other again without starting all over.

Katie picked up the dipper and the milk can from the table, tested to see how much water was still in it, and asked Lena if there were any milk to go to the stream. She knew she would never laugh again. Walking was like being on cut glass. She bumped the can in front of her with her knee to distract any attention from her feet that she slid along the floor. As she passed the kitchen door to the living room, she pushed it open a crack and could still see only an outline of James in the bed in the room with no windows.

Lena handed her the tall quart bottle about one-third full of milk and patted her shoulder. Lena looked tall and thinner than before in her flowered print house dress. And her feet looked curlier than ever. She had some problem with bunions—big swellings Mother explained—and her shoes rose and fell like the shape of dried squash rind. Katie watched her walk across the linoleum and thought how much they must hurt her—all the time. "Think how it must feel to stand and iron," Katie thought, picturing Lena at the board placed on the backs of two straight chairs taking the flat irons off the stove and pressing the steam out of the shirts for hours at a time. She wanted to offer to help with the morning dishes but they were already done. Lena did things like James ate—so fast that it was hard to believe there had ever been anything there.

It was painful going down the hill. Katie had to stop often, hoping she wouldn't meet anyone. She dreaded arriving at the road and knew she would never get to the spring for water this morning. She crossed the road looking both ways and went down the slope on the other side sitting down. She landed near enough to the cooler that she could reach the milk bottle in, and then she waded across the shallows to the moss village. In the shaded coolness below the platform, the stream ran in rivulets. Between them and without the boys this year she and Isabel and Jody Sue had patted moss into hills and valleys and constructed villages and playgrounds. There were roads for their tin cars and swings for their fairies. She sat gingerly on the bank where it was only slightly damp, eased off her boots, and let her feet dangle in the tiny icy river that ran through the park of the town.

It took only a minute for her to go numb. "Remember Fairy House?" she thought. "Remember when you found out the fairies didn't really live in there?" Fairy House was a vacant one-room brown cabin built just off the road below L. G. For years the children had been convinced that the couple who built it for a honeymoon had mysteriously disappeared and that after that fairies had come there to preserve the lovers' privacy for them. Until two years before, no one had dared go near Fairy House, let alone enter it. On their hikes they had skirted around it and pointed it out from the top of Castle Crags, but it was sacred and not to be fooled with—like the Darning Needles that twirred around their heads sometimes at night and would sew up their mouths unless they kept them open the whole time the buzzing insects were near.

Finally the cousins had decided they needed a clubhouse the year they were cowboys and had to have initiations, and none of their huts was big enough. So gradually they had braved the drooping screen door of Fairy House to find a splintery floor and unpainted walls with stuffing from the chair scattered everywhere by mice and squirrels. That year they fixed it up, pilfered paint from their cabins to make sections of color, screened the high windows, repaired the door, built shelves, and packed in furniture borrowed from wherever might least miss it. Sometimes Isabel and Katie played dolls there; most of the time all of them just came to eat their lunches en route to somewhere else. But Katie was always a little sorry about the fairies and hoped they liked it all slicked up and busy.

She had to pull her feet out of the cold. Besides, sitting

was no good. It just let things get bigger. She tried to pull her boots on, but her feet seemed more swollen and she couldn't lace the boots at all. She hooked them loosely and tied the laces around her calf. Where could she go? Not back to the road. No telling now when he'd show up. Or where. There was the trail along the stream up to Uncle Wooster's. It would be steep in places and lots harder to climb than the road, but safer. It was out of sight almost all the way.

Katie made a slow trek along the narrow path wishing she were somewhere very quiet just lying down. Before she was aware of traveling any of the familiar ground, she was at Grandma's, hobbling across the hollow wooden porch and yoohooing at her door. One of Grandma's ladies, Sister Boshard, came to the door smiling her powdered gray look. "Is Grandma busy?" Katie asked. "Oh, no thank you, I'll just wait right here for her," she answered when Sister Boshard opened the door. She leaned and then sat on the railing waiting for Grandma, who started talking as soon as she came into view down the long screened porch.

"Why, if it isn't my little honey bunch!" she smiled. "Who in the world would I rather be seeing? And how was all the excitement at your house?"

Katie knew that Father and probably Mother too would have come over to report everything to Grandma as soon as they could, and she also knew that Grandma would have been just like Mother in trouble—calm and sure as the sun over Pinetop.

The minute Grandma opened the door and stepped out, Katie was in her arms sobbing. Grandma held her to her stout bosom and eased her around to the back of the cabin where they would be alone. Neither of them said anything. Katie could feel the velvet flowers on Grandma's dress and was not even afraid that her tears would spot them. "There, there," Grandma finally said. "Come in here."

She led Katie limping toward the back door and into the little kitchen where no one worked but Grandma. She perched Katie on the high stool that James had made and sat herself next to her on the cane-bottomed chair by the table. "It was a pretty bad night, wasn't it," she offered. "I guess we were all mighty frightened." She let it be silent for a bit. Katie shook in spasms of crying that seemed to come from somewhere that had never been before. Grandma got up and handed her a drink of water. After a gulp, Katie began to breathe herself into quiet—exactly as she did after laughing with Jody Sue.

"Grandma, what were you scared of?" Katie said imploringly. She couldn't imagine Grandma afraid of anything.

"I was scared of the whole thing, Honey—the fire, the chances of its getting to the cabins, what it might do to the canyon—and to the men up there fighting it. Mostly I was afraid things would never be the same." Grandma held Katie's head against her again and pressed her hand along Katie's forehead and hair. "It seems like the scariest thing of all is thinking you're on the brink, ready to drop into the unfamiliar. Especially if the familiar is everything you love and have loved forever."

"But, Grandma, it seems like you'd know too much to be afraid. You've probably...well, it doesn't seem like anything could be new to you," Katie said, shaking her head as she leaned against the velvet flowers.

"Oh, Katie, my little Katie. How I love you. So many things are as new to me as they are to you—no matter how many times they might seem to have come around. I remember when I was a little girl and I thought that by the time I was twenty everything would have happened to me and I'd be ready for a repeat of any of it. It took me a long time more than that to get ready, and I'll never be where everything's happened. Varieties of the same thing maybe, some repetition, but mostly surprises...even now. But being ready doesn't necessarily make you not afraid. Sometimes the expecting is the scariest part. Even if the expecting is kind of felicitous." Grandma paused and Katie tasted the word "felicitous." Grandma gave her words all the time, no matter what they were talking about.

"What do you do when you're scared, Grandma?" Katie

asked after a minute.

Without hesitation Grandma answered, "Work. For all I'm worth. Always have. Best medicine there is. Sit around and think about it and you're sunk. Get to work on something—anything—and you're saved. You can always tell if something's twitching in me by the shape of my house. The shinier it is, the more gumption I've been looking for under dust and behind cobwebs."

"Are you pretty clean around here this morning?" Katie half-grinned.

"So clean! Would you like to check?" Grandma drew away and held Katie's chin in her hands. "And how about you? Would you like a job—a dandy of a job?"

Katie nodded, sober again. "I might just need the very biggest job you ever could find." Her shoulders sagged and her feet started to hurt again. "In the meantime, could I please take off my boots?"

Grandma leaned to help undo her boots. As she started to pull them off, Katie winced. "What's this?" Grandma asked, stripping away the wet stocking. "Oh, my little sweetheart, what have you done to your poor feet?"

Katie started to cry again as Grandma rubbed gently over the swollen, discolored feet. "Grandma, oh Grandma. How was I so dumb? I did the dumbest, stupidest thing I've ever done—and the worst. And there's no way I can go home. There's no way I'll ever feel right again—as long as I live. And Mother's so worried about James...and I don't know what's wrong with him, but it's got to be something huge to have Mother that worried." Katie gulped and blurted, "And Daniel Moon committed suicide. Did you know that?"

"Yes, I heard."

"Oh, Grandma, what if it was 'cause we were so bad to him? And the fire too. What if it started all by itself just to show us? And Daniel Moon—he'll never get up again—or see the canyon—or go to a bonfire. And last night I went to the fire—I got up when Mother thought I was asleep and went to the fire—and ruined my feet. They probably hurt so much to let me know how wrong I was for not minding. And for being so bad." Katie trailed off into sobs.

"That's a mighty big load for a little sliver like you," Grandma told Katie when she paused. "No wonder you're a bit frightened. Now the question is, what do you do about it?"

"You tell me," Katie implored.

"No, I don't quite think that's the system. Maybe we'd both better go to work for a while and see what we can see." Grandma tightened the strings of her long apron and went back to the enamel bowl she must have been mixing in when Katie came. She began beating with a wooden spoon in the rhythm that Katie adored. Holding the bowl under her left arm on a tilt that would have poured the batter out, she whisked the spoon around the bowl and combined whatever ingredients were in it with a fervor that kept the mixture suspended and rotating like the whir of a propeller. Katie wanted to be able to smell the buttermilk and yeast that only Grandma used in pancakes. The rhythm began pounding when Grandma added eggs to the batter which turned pale yellow over and under the spoon. As Katie watched, her scalp picked up the meter. Her breathing eased to match it and her skin felt attached to her body again. Gradually she let things fall back into her head and ripple to her feet that had faded away in the hot water. It was like waking up after a dream just before morning.

"Grandma," she said at last. "You don't think the fire was because of Daniel Moon, do you?"

"Land no," Grandma answered, still stirring. "There was some natural cause that we'll all find out about. And for Daniel—there was some natural cause there, too. Pity it had to be his own. But don't you go trying to take responsibility for anybody else's notions of what they should or shouldn't do with themselves. Goodness knows, its hard enough to be responsible for your own. Just you make good and sure your own notions include not making somebody worse off than he already is, and you won't be doing anything the Lord would disapprove of, let alone punish you for. I can't help thinking we make our own punishment, right here and now—and that all the Lord can do is suffer with us."

"But that's the thing—we made Daniel Moon lonesome—and that's making somebody a lot worse off than he might have been."

"How did you make him lonesome?"

"Well, we never played with him, or invited him to anything. Or even talked to him." Katie hesitated. "We just plain hated him."

"Why did you hate him?"

"Because he ruined everything. No matter what we made, he ruined it, and he beat up on James."

"Why do you think he did?"

"I don't know. I guess 'cause we weren't nice to him."

Grandma paused and looked far out the window over the sink. "Maybe," she said. "I wonder. What starts things going in us? Does one grief have to breed another grief? Some people say it takes money to make money and happiness to make happiness. And I guess for folks that's pretty true. The sad thing is that it's so much easier to keep grief all to yourself — while it's about impossible not to go out and share happiness. And grief all by itself can fester—and become so tender that not even the one who has it can stand to touch it. And he jumps if anyone tries."

"But Grandma, Daniel Moon saved Wid you know. And Wid and James tried to go see him and say thank you, but they never found him. Do you think he would have jumped—or been too sore to get near?"

"Who knows, Honey? But you can't go blaming yourself—or the Lord—for what happened to him. You probably could have been nicer. Glory knows, nobody's ever really nice enough. But all you can do now is watch for another chance somewhere to be that much nicer to somebody who needs it. That's all the Lord expects of any of us—I'm as sure of that as I am of my bob in back." She reached to secure her long bone hairpins into the thick, still partly brown knot near the top of her head.

202

"And in the meantime don't go blaming yourself for this kind of thing happening to somebody else. If Daniel had grown up to be a fine happy man, would you take any credit? I hardly think so. Then why should you blame yourself if he didn't? We're all so quick to accept the blame for problems around us—and to give blame to others for what we do to ourselves all by ourselves; but who do you ever see rush in to say, See—look what somebody else did all because of me—when it's something good? Now listen to me, little honey bunch, you can't go blaming yourself or the Lord for fires or Daniel Moon or death or a rigamarole of other things that just plain happen without you—or Him—being in on it at all. But as for not minding your mother and leaving the house when you weren't supposed to—that's a different matter. That you *can* be responsible for—how you handle your own affairs. You rest a while and then scoot over home and tell your mother exactly what happened. And I promise, you'll be surprised at how much better everything will be."

Everything was better already. Katie had four pancakes with streams of butter and hot syrup over them before she left, and her feet fit her boots fairly well in the stockings that Grandma had dried on the stove. She could walk if she went slow, taking the weight on her heels. Now all she had to do was figure out what to do about Mister Davis and his cabin. She almost wished she could have talked to Grandma about that, but it seemed like something too strange to even have a natural cause, let alone cure.

Katie walked down the path from Grandma's to Uncle Phillip's field and along the stream where she had seen Daniel Moon watching James and the bonfire. She wished she had asked Grandma where she thought he was. Beyond the stream and through the bushes, brown and white Tony was munching hay with Goldie. It seemed unreal that Tony had ever been gone. Katie wished she were riding him now lunging up the road—but thinking about it only made her feet hurt. She walked back to where she had left the milk can, filled it, and went up the hill to the cabin hardly limping.

CHAPTER TWELVE

By evening James was moaning almost constantly. When Mother asked him to identify where the pain
was, he pointed to his ears and his right leg. He couldn't talk
at all. He just gritted his teeth and rolled a little, always with
his eyes shut. Mother had planned to take him down to see
Uncle David, but it was such agony for him to move that
she decided she had better get Uncle David up to see him
first. Isabel's and Jody Sue's mother, Laura, had offered to
drive down to give the message since Mother wanted to stay
very close to James. When Katie came home from Grandma's, she knew she could tell Mother anything and it would
be all right, but she decided to tell Wid instead and not
bother her. Even so, she and Wid hardly talked. Somehow
James lying with his eyes closed in the living room was more
oppressive than the fire had ever been. There was nothing
anyone could do about him—only stay around.

Uncle David drove up the hill at the same time Father
did. It was after dark, and as they parked, their headlights
swung across the greenery like four spider eyes. At the
bedside, Uncle David listened and probed with his intent
thoroughness. Only Mother and Father were in the room,
but Wid, Katie, and Davy were observing through the glass

in the doors. Davy was standing on a chair beside Katie. "What's wrong with him?" he asked over and over and received only a shhh from Katie. When Uncle David was through, he stepped into the kitchen with Mother and Father. With his usual dispatch he was almost immediately in his car and headed down the hill.

"Mother and Father gathered the children and explained that Uncle David had found some infection in James and that he had started draining it off with a hypodermic needle. It might take several days and James would be extremely uncomfortable since it had caused a very high fever. But they couldn't afford to move him for fear of spreading the infection, so they would do everything they could to give him some relief and wait until Uncle David came up again tomorrow. They had a short family prayer around James' bed. Sometimes it seemed as though Father had already had his conversation with the Lord and only needed to confirm it out loud.

In bed later, Katie realized she had forgotten all about her promise to Mister Davis. In fact, she hadn't even asked Father if they ever located him.

The next morning James was worse. Through the glass Katie could see him writhing and Mother putting cold packs on his head. He gathered the sheets up in his fists and wrung them as he shook his head back and forth on the pillow. Katie could not imagine anything hurting that much. Mother said no one was to slam a door or walk heavily across the floor because he could feel every tremor.

The cousins came from across the path to see how things were and stayed only long enough to dawdle in the needles under the fir and stir in the dirt with their boots. Little Wooster sat on Tony and patted him constantly on his curried rump as the horse ate the long grass by the swing. No one even talked about the fire.

Katie spent most of the day in her rafter playhouse right above James. Toward afternoon he began to moan loud enough that she could hear. Every now and then he screamed

—like there was something terrible attacking him. Katie wanted to scream too, to run to him—or to someone—and do something to make it not happen again.

Mother carried on as if everything else was normal. She and Lena served dinner at noon and had supper ready by six o'clock. Mother held school for an hour, instructing between visits to James. Late in the day she asked Katie to sit by the bed while she went to get Grandma in the car. They were back almost before Katie had time to wring out a new cloth for a cold pack.

Grandma felt James' head and pulse and turned back the covers to see his body. He had doubled up some at first, but now he lay rigid and straight, pushing from his elbows and heels to move. "You little scallywag," she admonished lovingly, "what trick are you up to now?" But even Grandma could not look or sound facetious. She and Mother consulted on the porch, both looking at their watches and talking about Uncle David. Then Grandma went to sit by James while Mother got everyone to the table.

Dinner was almost silent, with only Mother injecting an airy remark or question. Wid looked almost normal again and Katie's feet were forgotten. After their dessert of bread in milk with sugar, Davy asked Wid to play checkers, and Katie went to help Lena with the dishes. It seemed like three years before Uncle David and Father arrived.

This time Uncle David came out of the living room looking drawn and very serious. When he left, Mother and Father called everyone together and explained that James had an infection of the bone that was spreading as Mother called it "like wildfire." It had been at first in his ear, then in the hip he had injured, and now seemed to be moving into his knee. Uncle David was on his way to the first-aid station to call for an ambulance to take him to the hospital. The draining was not helping, in fact not even keeping up with the infection, and he could not be moved except with the most care possible. For some reason the disease went rampant if there was motion. Besides, even with the shot Uncle David had given him, James was in so much pain that he could not stand to be touched, let alone lifted or held. "So sore that he can't be touched," Katie thought, feeling alien and helpless.

Father and Mother stayed very close to each other, Father with his arm around her or she holding the back of his belt as she did when they walked together. He looked so very big, and she so small. Together they prepared for taking James away. It was very different, despite their overt cheerfulness, from taking Wid down those times. Why? Katie kept asking herself. Wid was in trouble both times—he was plenty sick. But even Davy sensed the difference. "Wid," he said over the checker board, "did you hate going past the gate when they took you down?"

"Yes. Sure I did. It wasn't in the plan at all. But heck, I knew I'd be right back up and it wouldn't even count."

"But what if you hadn't been, Wid? I mean...what if you had to stay? What if you couldn't ever come back up?" Davy bit his lip and scowled in perplexity.

"Well, that wouldn't ever happen. We all know that. We'd all—any of us—get right back up here, no matter what." Wid sounded his most convincing.

Davy missed the jump that Wid had set up for him and said he needed a drink. Katie, who had been watching over his shoulder, reached down and jumped three men as Wid began putting the checkers away. He and Katie looked everywhere but at each other as Father put an arm around each of them and guided them in to kneel beside James with Grandma, Lena, Davy, and Mother. This time Father said it was Mother's turn.

If Father's prayers seemed sometimes perfunctory in his having been there already, Mother's never were. She conversed as if she had just been granted permission for a one-time audience with the one who could make all the difference. She prayed in a low, intimate, far from formal voice that assured a hearing. As they all knelt around James she began, "Dear Father in Heaven, thank Thee for this beautiful day and for this heavenly place to come to, and for each other, and for Thee." Katie always imagined her talking to her own papa with reverence and joy in the supplication. "As you know," Mother continued, "we have a special problem tonight. Our James is ill enough that he must be taken to the hospital to be cured. Please, Father in Heaven, help us to be all You intended us to be in this. Help us to be strong and to bring our best selves to whatever it takes. Help us to truly utilize all we have been so generously given to make it go well.

"And please bless those who will stay here that they will never forget how blessed we all are—with love and hope and faith — to get them through the darkest thing of all — waiting. Please help them to take care of each other and to feel the love we have for them, and never to forget how happy they make us—You and their father and me." Mother squeezed Davy's shoulder, tightened against Katie's arm that was through hers, and went on: "Especially tonight and in the days to come, please bless those who will attend James. Guide their able hands and minds. And bless James in this that he will be manly in all that that means—able to cope with the pain and sure that the treatment he receives will be for his best good. Please let his father's sense of fairness remain his ally, so that he will know he can play by whatever rules he has to. And help him always to remember and rely on Thee. Who knows better than You what a boy he is!" Mother paused only briefly and slowly added, "what a fine …funny…loving boy he is." Katie could see James squeezing Father's hand trying not to flinch or moan. "Let him come back to us, Father in Heaven, whenever You can. We need him and we do love him. Oh, we do love him. In the name of Thy son Jesus Christ, Amen."

They all said amen fiercely, even James through his teeth.

Two men in white jackets and pants came up the path from the parking place carrying a stretcher between them. In the living room they maneuvered the stretcher beside James and then asked him to try to lift or roll himself onto it.

209

"It will be better if you aren't lifted," Uncle David explained.

Katie watched James hike himself up on his elbows and try to shift over. He fell back with a yell that ran through her temples. Next he tried moving his legs first and inching his hips over the edge of the stretcher. He was covered with sweat and had never once opened his eyes. With his hips partially on the stretcher, he gave a furious shove with his arms and slid with another scream almost to where he needed to be. "Now just pull with your left hand and you're there," Father urged. He was white with wanting to help.

Mother drew the cover up over James' flannel plaid pajamas and ran one last cool cloth across his face. Without a tear she kissed him, assuring him that she'd be right beside him and so would Father, and that he was going to be just fine. Grandma patted his blond hair, kinky with sweat, and told him that she was going to be staying with the others and not to worry about having Mother and Father stay with him.

Wid barely punched him on the arm as they carried him past and said hoarsely, "Stick in there, Bruv. Remember how quick us Bartons get back in the game."

Davy and Katie were on either side of the doorway as they moved around to make the turn. Davy stood with his mouth half open and then closed, swallowing in rhythm and riveted to James. One side of the stretcher bumped the door frame and James screamed that same way. Katie lunged forward and threw her arms around his head. "Oh, James, don't hurt!" she blurted and then drew back, tears searing her face as the stretcher and James, with his eyes closed, eased down the path to the ambulance.

"Will they turn on the siren?" Davy asked following the entourage of Mother and Father and Uncle David as they disappeared into its cavern. "And how about the red light that flashes?" But it was an almost silent and very dim shape that made its way down the steep hill with only its red brake lights shining in the dark behind its eyes that pierced the green sheltering the road.

CHAPTER THIRTEEN

The next evening Father came up with word that James was going to be operated on. Dr. Tyree, a new bone specialist at the clinic would try a procedure on him that was the best that had been developed for osteomyelitis, the bone disease that had apparently been eating away at James for longer than he knew. Uncle David said Dr. Tyree was the best man in his field and that if anyone could fix James, he could. Father told them all about the hospital and the fine care that James was getting, and mostly that he was now having lots less pain with what they could give him under trained care.

"And what have all of you monkeys been up to today?" he asked as they sat down to Grandma's Johnny Cake and potato soup.

Katie's day had been a blank, the longest of her life. Wid said he had ridden Goldie with Little Wooster, and Davy said, "I been throwin' football in the field with Matthew. I can catch while I'm runnin'—even hard ones."

"Maybe when you get good enough you can play in the finger bowl," Father joked. Davy looked puzzled but smiled.

"I want to catch it like James does when Wid throws. He's the best runner ever—and Wid's the best thrower."

211

"Did you get your jobs done?" Father asked quietly. "All that debris cleared up where the men dropped their equipment after the fire?"

Wid nodded and Katie thought about how the men must have come back down the hill behind their house to drop their picks and axes and shovels in the wood pile for distribution to the places from which they had been borrowed or brought. All of that had happened while she was asleep or talking to James that night. So much could happen without a person even knowing about it.

"Did they ever find out what happened to Mister Davis that night?" she heard herself asking.

"As a matter of fact, yes. He must have been in Sugar House. Uncle Wooster saw him getting off the train by the gate the next night and he said he'd had an emergency—a toothache I think — and had to get down to have it seen to — had been gone all day and overnight. Why he didn't even know about the fire. And it started right behind his place."

Katie stared at her soup. Wid said suspiciously, "Yeah, and the funny thing is that from what I hear it started from hot ashes. At least that's what Phillip said his Father said. And who in the heck else would have put hot ashes by Mister Davis's outhouse?"

"Now, Wid, nobody knows that for sure—at least as far as I know; and it's not good to go spreading rumors—especially the kind that could really hurt someone—even if you think you know for sure. It's kind of too bad to spread anything that's going to make unhappiness." Father looked the unhappiest Katie could imagine as he reached to rub Wid's shoulder but was looking at the maple outside the screen.

"Candland," Grandma said quickly, "you need some rest, and so does everybody else. Let's get you to bed."

"Good idea," answered Father, "just as soon as I read these kids a great story I have in mind."

After dinner they all clustered in the living room. Nobody sat on the bed. Father opened to a chapter in the *Bible Story Book,* whose lavendar-shaded illustrations were as

212

familiar to Katie as the hands that held it. He began reading "David, the Hero of Israel." It was about David the shepherd boy killing a lion, about David and Saul and the songs David played on his harp for the troubled king. "Yeah, and his friend was Jonathan," Davy injected coming to sit in Father's lap after he started.

Father nodded, pulled him in, and kept reading. His voice went deep and he seemed to be reading what wasn't there. Katie hardly heard the words that she already knew. Sitting with her armless rocker next to Father's she watched his boot push him back and forth as he read: "The boy David said to the King, lord, do not let your heart fail because of this Philistine. Your servant David will go against him and take away the reproach from Israel..." Father's arm brushed Katie's uncombed curls as he rocked and read: "David told the king, 'God delivered me out of the mouth of the lion and out of the paw of the bear, and he will deliver me out of the hand of the Philistine! And Saul said, 'Go, David, and God be with you.'"

"And he smote Goliath with his flipper!" Davy said triumphantly sitting up in Father's lap and aiming an imaginary stone through an imaginary flipper at Goliath.

"That's right," Father smiled, "but how do you think he managed to 'smite' the Philistine—when he was only a boy?"

Wid, sitting cross-legged in front of the stove, stared into the fire. Wid could concentrate like no one else could. One night when he was reading the funny papers on the floor, lightning had struck so near the cabin it had actually rocked it. Later he said he thought he felt something as he knelt over his reading, but he had not even looked up when the strike had come. Now he said very quietly, "David knew why." The only sound was the soft snapping of the flames.

Katie's throat was clamped shut. Father, looking only at the book, had moved on without her hearing. "My cup runneth over. Surely goodness and mercy shall follow me all the days of my life: and I will dwell in the house of the Lord forever." It was as if he had invented the words. They rolled over Katie in a huge sadness. She wanted James back, and Mother. She wanted not to have to think about anything but David and Goliath, to have it just a story with a picture of a boy stooping to pick up pebbles in a stream to sling at a giant shouting from a hilltop in the distance.

"James woulda done just like David," Davy said wistfully. I know he would. He woulda flipped the rock so straight—and so far..." He gazed at the bear skin on the floor. "He woulda killed him just like you killed the bear," he said to Father.

Father shook his head and smiled. "No, Davy, I think he'd do a lot better than I did with the bear." Davy had chosen to forget that Father had explained that his killing the bear had been a very fishy fish story.

"Wid would do it too. A cinch." Davy looked surely at his biggest brother. "Couldn't ya, Wid?"

Wid sighed, "Ho! Sure, Davy," and stood up. He looked at Davy for a minute and then reached over to give him a light punch on the arm.

In less than two weeks summer would be over. It would be time to pack the car, shutter the cabin, and go past the gate to the city. Katie kept thinking of all the things she still wanted to do before then, but even working on the new swing in Grandma's gully seemed hard to get to. The cousins had it all up but were working on stabilizing the platform and building a retaining wall to hold back the soil and make a flat landing place for getting off. She tried the swing a few times, pushing up from the high platform against the mountain, the rope between her legs and the stick under her. The first swing out was better than the roller coaster at Lagoon, flying at least forty feet above the ravine and swooping back to barely clear the pine trunks surrounding the cleared hillside. Wid and Smithy and Phillip could flip off the seat at the swing's highest point and hang onto the rope to dangle and whoop like the real Tarzan.

But Katie's whoops had gone out of her. She spent time

talking to Grandma and riding Tony sometimes with Little Wooster on Goldie. Little Wooster was just right because he liked riding through thin trails where single file precluded talking. He didn't talk much anyhow, but once he did say when they stopped for a drink, "I bet James sure hurts." Katie wondered which kind of hurt he meant. She knew he knew about lots of kinds.

No one had seen Mister Davis. Evidently the fire had started for sure at his place, and it had been found to be his fault for dumping hot ashes out all right. Wid said he had heard that Mister Davis was having to go to a hearing about it and that he might not be back at all.

Katie believed him—thoroughly, felt exonerated, reborn — almost exploratory again. Maybe she could find Shadow before the end of summer. That at least would make things end with some sort of rightness.

But Shadow saved her the trouble of hunting. Three days after James had gone, she and Davy were making mud pies out of the sifted red dirt behind the house.

"Listen!" said Katie, raising her head from the wood block covered with perfect rounds of pancakes. "Did you hear that?"

"I didn't hear nothing," Davy said, not looking up.

Katie stood with the tray in her hands waiting. This time there was no mistaking it. The meow was loud and low and coming closer.

"Hey! I do hear!" Davy whispered excitedly. "Do you think it's a mountain lion?"

Just then a sleek black cat about a foot high and two feet long strolled onto the path.

"It's Shadow!" Katie exclaimed huskily.

The cat stopped, her long tail rippling and her head high. Her sides sloped in from her backbone and hung like drapes, giving her the slender litheness of a panther.

"Wow!" Davy breathed. "She's a giant!"

"And beautiful," Katie added. "Twice as beautiful as her mother."

Shadow's mother had been Katie's cat the year before. She and three of her kittens had died in the canyon last summer. The mother, Twinge, had been caught in a trap set under the house, and James and Wid had buried her before they told Katie about it. One of the kittens had fallen off the roof on the high side, another had gotten in a fight with a squirrel, and the third had started being sick and chasing itself all day and Mother had said it must have found a tick or something. One afternoon after all their funerals, Katie had been lonesome and had wanted to see one of them again, so she had dug up the one buried by the swing. It had been buried only a few days, but when Katie took the lid off the shoe box, the furry kitten was white with maggots. Katie had slammed the box closed but could remember every detail of the white swarm no matter how hard she tried not to. Shadow had been her only cat then, and had disappeared the very day they were to move down in the fall. Black except for a white splash on her head, long-haired and still small, she had been Katie's favorite. Now she stood swishing her tail and examining Davy and Katie.

Katie restrained her first impulse to start toward her. She held Davy back too and just watched. Shadow was as still as the stone lion at the Capitol.

"Wait here, Davy," Katie whispered. "Don't let her out of your sight. I'll go get some food."

She was back quickly with a dish of cream left from breakfast. She set it carefully down and stepped back, pulling Davy with her. Shadow stayed still.

"Farther back," Katie whispered at Davy.

When they were halfway across the backyard, Shadow moved toward the bowl. She whiskered the surface of the milk and then her pink tongue dipped in and out of it. It was gone and so was she before Katie could figure her next move.

"Darn! We shoulda grabbed her," Davy said.

"No, I bet she'll be back, Katie answered. We'll just have to keep something out for her. Did you see how she gobbled that cream!"

216

She was right. Shadow made more visits—three that day. The next morning Davy and Katie were watching the bowl when she came, trying to establish some easiness that would allow them to approach her. This time, though, when she finished, the big cat didn't stride away. As Katie and Davy knelt over their mud pies acting as if they were not noticing, Shadow crept toward them. "Don't look at her!" Katie warned. The cat padded past Davy and began to rub against Katie's thigh. There was not a sound. Gradually Katie reached down and stroked Shadow's silky back. Out of her came a purr so close to a growl that Davy edged up to Katie and eyed the cat suspiciously.

"She won't hurt you, Davy," Katie assured him. "Come on over and give her a rub."

Davy put his hand out toward Shadow and she was off. In two bounds she was up the bank and into the brush.

"What'd I do?" Davy puzzled. "I just wanted to pet her."

"She'll come back — and you'll get another chance. I guess she just remembers me 'cause she was mine."

Within a few minutes the cat was back, but this time very different. She walked toward Katie and Davy until she had their attention and then turned and strolled toward the wood pile. Within a few feet she stopped, looked around again, and waited.

"She wants us to follow her!" Katie observed. "Watch. I'll bet she won't go without us."

The cat stood examining them. Katie took a few steps toward her. Shadow turned and again headed for the end of the path that went up the gully. Katie stopped. Shadow stopped and looked back until Katie started walking again.

"See, she's expecting us," Katie said as Davy caught up with her.

"You really think so?" Davy marvelled. "Can a cat be that smart?"

"Shadow can be. She's a ripsnorter—that's what James used to call her."

The two followed Shadow as she led them up the trail

in the gully, slithering through the stream bed and bushes until they were at the old tank that had been their clubhouse. "What if she's going after another rattler—like the one Mister Davis said he saw her kill?" Davy panted, trying to keep up.

"Don't worry. She wouldn't come all the way up here for that," Katie assured him. "She's got something else in mind."

The big cat leaped from the mountain side to the top of the tank and disappeared. "Come on. She's gone inside it," Katie urged as she scrambled up the pipe ladder. Peering down into the black of the opening she could see nothing. And there was not a sound. Davy leaned over the edge too, just as a thundering meow reverberated through the hollow room below. "She wants us to come in. Come on, let's swing from here and see what's down there."

Davy was blinking and asking who first, but Katie was already down and reaching for him. "Just hold the edge and then come down to my shoulders," she instructed excitedly.

He landed with a thump in the dark beside her, almost knocking her over. It was darker than ever. Gradually their eyes widened in the dim interior of the tank, and they could begin to make out shapes—the stool from Smithy's, the card table from Aunt Lucine's. In the far corner Shadow meowed. From the same corner came other sounds, tiny high squeaks and muffled movement.

"What is it?" Davy breathed.

"I bet I know," Katie exulted. "Shadow's got some kittens!"

"Kittens? Up here?"

"Sure. What else?" Katie started toward the corner and then thought, "Wait a minute! Kittens? How? What kind? Who could the father be?" She remembered Mister Davis's talk about mountain lions and about Shadow going off with the snake in her mouth, and she very much wanted a flashlight.

"Let's just take it easy," she warned Davy. "As soon as our eyes get used to the dark we'll be able to see them from here and we won't scare Shadow by going too close."

As their eyes adjusted, Shadow was outlined against the corner and small bodies could be seen lying against her. Katie took Davy's hand and tip-toed toward them. Shadow was growling her purr as the kittens nursed. "Oh, how darling," Katie said reaching for a black one that matched its mother. She drew it gently away from the nipple as she had done a hundred times with all the kittens Twinge had had. But this was no city kitten. It was small, but its claws came out and it hissed and bared sharp little teeth. Katie dropped it like a hot coal.

"Gee!" she exclaimed. "What the heck!"

"What happened?" Davy asked reaching for the hand that she had put in her mouth.

"That crazy little cat bit me!"

"Why? I never heard of a kitten biting!"

"Neither have I, but that one sure did. I wish we could see what they really looked like." Katie sucked her finger where the bite was, pondered a minute, and then said, "You know what we better do is go back home and get Wid and some gloves and maybe a gunny sack and come back up here and get the kittens and take them where we can domesticate them."

"*Domesticate* them?"

"Yes, you know—house break them and stuff."

Shadow had not stirred from her position of nursing mother. The dropped kitten was back in its place and the family looked calm enough. "Let's go," Katie said. "You can reach the opening if I give you a foot up."

It couldn't have taken more than half an hour to race down the gully to the cabin, yoohoo for Wid, who brought Little Wooster and Goldie tearing across the path with him, and pump back up the trail to the tank with the equipment needed. But the tank was empty. Katie shot the flashlight she had remembered into the corner. There was nothing left but an old sheet blanket that had been at various times a table cloth, a rug, and a pillow for the tank's club members.

It was hard to convince Wid that there really had been a cat and some kittens. He had never been around when Shadow had visited at the cabin, and even though Davy swore faithfully that there sure had been, Katie was not at all certain that Wid was convinced. In fact, she knew she had to produce the evidence to really persuade him. And she would.

Right then she began thinking about the lure that Mister Davis had tried to give her. He said it would work for any animal, surefire. And he was not in his cabin—not even anywhere around. She figured the lure could easily be outside. Why not go exploring down there and find whatever it was and then get Shadow and her kittens back? She knew how mother cats always hid their babies if they were disturbed. And Shadow probably had them in a place so tricky that nobody would ever find them again.

"I wonder why she wanted us to see them in the first place?" she thought. "Maybe she just wanted to show them off like any other mother. But she's hidden them now, that's for sure. And I'll never find them without that lure."

Every day Father came up with the news about James. His surgery had been as successful as the doctors could have hoped, but he was going to have to be in the hospital for at least ten weeks, and maybe longer. "Ten weeks!" Katie exploded. "That'll be clear into..." She counted on her fingers... "August, September, October! Why he'll miss half of school! And who'll be captain of the ball team?" Somehow she had expected that when they went down to the city James would be there, maybe in his knickers centering a football or walking the back fence from Sallinger's garage clear up the alley. At least he'd be in the house somewhere, wrestling with Wid in the front room or roller skating around the drain in the basement. Or at very least he'd be in bed there, getting well, maybe playing some card tricks or checkers. Ten weeks!

Katie tried to picture fifth grade without him. Who'd sing

off key in Miss Allman's class like he'd planned? Who'd be in charge of the soccers at recess? Who would she talk to about Euan and Betty, the two they liked and secretly met at the Ward show to sit with when the lights went out? Katie tried to picture James in the hospital, all in white, pale and peaked like the picture of The Little Lame Prince. All she could keep coming back to was the daydream she indulged all the time now: James was lying on a stretcher, but he got up and threw the cover way in the air and ran to slide safe into home. That's how it was going to be, that was all there was to it.

Most days Father brought letters from Mother telling them how much she loved and missed them and how brave they were to keep everything going — just like James, who was being the bravest ever. She stayed right at the hospital with him. She even slept on a cot Uncle David had them move in at night by James' bed. She was better than any special nurse they could have had, Father explained.

When they asked how James was doing, Father told them about his funny ways. He told about when James had had to take ether for his operation—of how he would count "one" and the nurse "two" and so on until James was just going zuzzz. Father said that had been the very worst thing for James, that he hated that most, not being awake. He told how James had come to ten hours later with a red heating lamp above him. He thought he was dead and when he saw the lamp he said, "What'd I do to deserve this?"

Father laughed telling it the way James had, and they could just hear him. But what was he really doing? And how bad was he hurting? And why did he have to stay and stay?

In one letter, Mother described the cast that had been put on James from his arm pits to his knee on one leg, and to his foot on the other. She said it itched so much that James had been poking tongue depressors down to scratch, and they were stuck everywhere under his cast. He was in a ward of boys covering half a floor at the hospital, and even when he was still "pretty dopey" he had gotten to know them. He said he felt lucky—that everyone seemed worse off than he was — except Peter who was up out of bed and walking around. James envied his being able to move, and especially his going to the window to put the shade up or down and control the light. "I wish all I had was diabetes," James had said. Then one day Peter went home and James was even more envious. But in two days the news was shushed around the hospital ward that Peter had died. Katie could imagine James as he was the night of the fire when Daniel Moon died—lying on his back and shivering. Only now what would he be thinking? It was good Mother was there. She'd get James home faster than anybody.

One night after James had been gone a little over a week, Katie heard Father and Grandma talking in the living room while she was helping Lena with the dishes. Father was saying Dr. Tyree was worried. There was something about the bone being all eaten away and the infection spreading. Grandma had her back to the kitchen door and all Katie could hear her say was, "He'll walk. He'll walk." And then Father was crying and Grandma was there there-ing him like she had Katie and Uncle David.

Gravel filled Katie from her mouth to her stomach. Her lips felt cold as she breathed and stuck together when she swallowed. Father cried quite often really—when he saw a sad show, or when one of the children did something really well, or when Mother had a birthday party for him and invited all his old friends to surprise him. But this was different. It wasn't just tears and lumps, it was something else so bottomless that Katie knew she never wanted to be a grown-up.

In her bed that night Katie reached for her moccasins. Rubbing them was different, even smelling them had changed. Instead of leaping with life in them, she felt herself knotted with apprehensions so vague that they swam like thunder clouds beyond a wavy horizon. In the swirling mist was a Daniel she had never known, collapsed but suspended against a fiery backdrop. There was Mister Davis

222

floating on a yellow smile, rising edgeless in the smoke from his pipe to hover over the red lights of an ambulance going down down somewhere below the spring. Katie pulled at herself until she was in a chipmunk ball, opening her eyes to stare closed the curtain that remained undrawn wherever her eyelids went. Then it came, the blackening, the obliterating of everything behind James, James running in his knickers, his head down and then thrown back to catch the ball that his arms reached for. James laughing as he ran everywhere she looked, his blond hair flopping, his left ear tucked into itself the way he made it stay when he wanted to distract a teacher. Weeping wrangled with her throat but ached into silence.

Katie turned to the edge of her bed and stood up on the cold floor. In her bare feet she went out the door, up the trail to the upstairs, walked across the screened porch, slipped past Davy's cot, and slid into bed beside Father. She was shivering with sweat. Before she was completely under the blankets, Father's arm was under her head, drawing her to him. His chest rose like a hillside under her cheek.

"Father."

"Yes, Bug."

"Does James open his eyes now?"

"Yes. Almost all the time."

"Does he talk to you?"

"Yes. And he kids—like always."

"Father?"

There was silence as Father cupped Katie to him, his hand holding her thigh as firmly as when he picked her up.

"Will James be all right?"

"James will be all right."

"You know what I mean—really all right?"

"Katie-bug, there're some things we just can't tell ahead of time, or even really figure out when they happen—like when—or if—James will walk again—or run. We just can't tell really what will happen. There's a chance that he'll be... different from how we've known him." Father took a long breath. "But some things we do know—if we let ourselves. And that's that even if it's the worst, it's all somehow all right."

"But will James be back?"

Katie could feel Father stop breathing.

"Will he be there to go to school with me? Ever?" Katie persisted.

"I don't know. I just don't know. But he'll try—like you never saw anyone try. And so will we. And you know, when you've got something like you and James have together—pals as you are—there's not a way that anything can ever change that. Not anything. Loving somebody is the greatest privilege you ever get—the greatest blessing—more even than having somebody love you. And no matter what happens, that feeling makes you holy, it makes you know more about richness and abundance and just plain rightness than anything else ever can. And you're one of the lucky ones, little sweetie, 'cause you've been blessed with a loving heart—and with people to give it to."

Katie felt the ocean welling up in her, washing in surging waves over the terrifying blur of her fears. Behind the waters, only James remained, ahead of it all, still running.

"Father, I want James back," she sobbed.

"Oh, my Katie-bug, you'll have him. Even if it's not in the way you're used to, you'll never lose him. None of us will. Don't you ever forget that for a minute. Somehow it all works out—even this. Somebody makes it. Only we're so darn short on foresight we can't see how sometimes."

Father stroked her hair and held her, his tears wetting her curls, rocking her as he had from the time she was a baby. Neither knew they had gone to sleep at exactly the same moment.

CHAPTER FOURTEEN

"We've only got three more days before we have to leave," Katie told Davy the next morning. "We've got to get that lure today if we expect to have time to entice Shadow back." "Entice" was one of Grandma's delicious words.

"You mean you're gonna take me to look with you?" Davy said, delighted.

"Uh huh. You'd be a good one. You could crawl in tight places, and I know you wouldn't tell the others—any of the cousins. They were there when he offered to give me the stuff and I know they all think it's a fake. But you believe in it don't you?"

Davy nodded till his hair flopped.

The two walked first clear to the gate. On the way Katie showed Davy the rat houses and the deer lick. Davy had never been past Rabbit's Head, so he made the trip an excursion, testing every bridge, running clear around every cabin. When the stream flowed wide just below Henderson's he wished he had his pole vault to sail over it. They all had poles made of sapling maples that they could plant in the center of the stream to flip them to the other side. Any place very deep or very wide was tantalizing, especially for Davy who had just learned to jump by practicing in Uncle Phillip's field, where he and Matthew went over the cross bar used by the older cousins for high jumping.

At the curve where Katie had been the night of the fire, she stopped to look up at the charred mountain. It was a tufted blanket of black where everything had been green forever. The smell had faded, but the trees were either black skeletons or gone. She pulled her eyes away. It couldn't be real. And she was sure that she had not really met Mister Davis there in the orange haze. He had been in Sugar House. In the daylight the road was soft and Davy was saying, "Golly! Wow!" as he saw the remains of the forest.

Katie pushed his shoulders downhill. "Let's run, Davy. Bet I can beat you to the gate!"

They ran the last nine curves and Katie hardly noticed the bridge leading to Mister Davis's. At the gate they examined their gray notches. "Boy," Davy said, "can you b'lieve that was just this year? It seems like a hunderd years ago."

Katie passed her hand over four of the notches and said, "Let's go."

Across the bridge to Mister Davis's was a path almost obscured by some kind of bushes that Katie had never seen anywhere else. They had leaves like willows but they grew upward and were drawn toward the ground only by weight, not inclination. Katie held one aside for Davy as she pushed through and suddenly felt a pain rip up her hand and arm. Between her first and second fingers was lodged the biggest thorn she had ever seen. She pulled it out and tried to make the puncture bleed by squeezing it. All it did was hurt more. It was as if her whole hand were pierced. It began swelling immediately, but she was too anxious to get to the cabin to bother with it. "Watch out for that stupid thing," she warned Davy.

The cabin hugged the mountain and looked sniveling—too tacky to matter at all. How could it be such a mess when he was up here all the time and with plenty of chance to keep it fixed up? The roof dripped over the sides. Nothing was painted. The screen was rusty and bulging. The yard was strewn with cans and bottles. Davy sidled up to Katie. "Boy, do you think he really isn't here?" he asked.

Sloth—that was the word Katie thought—one in *Anne of Green Gables.* "No, we know he's not. Wid said he won't be back." But Katie felt her eyes begin to search and she wanted very much to hurry. "Let's try back of the house first. That's the place he'd most likely want to attract animals."

They kicked their way through the yard to the backside of the cabin and began bending to look between the trash for something that might seem like a lure. "How about this?" Davy said pointing to a thick brown granular pile next to the house.

For Davy's sake Katie examined it closely, stirring it with a stick and picking up a pinch to smell. It smelled like Katie's favorite, Uncle Huck. "Nope," she said authoritatively. "That's just tobacco of some kind—probably out of his pipe— an ash tray dump."

They kept hunting. Katie went from a box of sawdust to a sack of salt, smelling and poking. Near the end of the porch she stooped to open a small wooden barrel whose lid was half off. "Look!" she called to Davy, "this sure is something weird."

It was then she smelled it. The same combination that infected the air the night of the fire. She raised her head to see Mister Davis standing over her, smiling around his pipe.

"Well, well," he smirked. "If it ain't. Now what might ya be looking for on my property, girl? I guess ya just figured ya'd keep your word. Kinda tardy, though, aren't ya?"

Talking very quickly Katie shuffled cautiously backward with Mister Davis taking the same steps she did. "Y-yes. You could say that, Mister Davis. We just came down to see if you were here. We wanted to find out about the lure you told me about—you remember—the one that will get any animal. I want to find my cat—Shadow, the big black one, remember? You saw her kill the rattlesnake up by Leigh's. And Father is going to meet us right out there by the bridge on his way up. He's been coming up early because of James. He's in the hospital, you know?"

"Yeah, I know. I know about all of it." Mister Davis smiled harder and kept backing her toward the steep bank that cut off an escape to the rear. She could see Davy standing next to the house watching.

"My little brother has to leave—right now," she said very loudly, signaling with her hand by her side to run for the path while Mister Davis was this far away from it. "He could go find some help," she thought, "and be back here before anything really bad could happen." But Davy stood eyeing Mister Davis and not moving.

With the same lunge he had used that night, Mister Davis reached for Katie's wrist, but Katie was prepared. She dodged and he stumbled into the bank. She would have run, but his boot caught hers as he fell and rolled her to the ground beside him. Before she could get away, he grabbed her arm and pinned her down. Her swollen hand ached to her shoulder.

"Now, lookie here, Miss Prissy, I'm not gonna hurt ya. Just get up nice and quiet and ya can come in the house and see what I had to show ya. The lure's in there besides. Ya think I'd be dumb enough to leave it out when I'm not home?"

Katie was on her feet and Mister Davis was trying to get on his. She could see Davy still standing by the house. "Why doesn't he run?" she thought. "He could be clear down to Parley's by now." She pointed again to the path with a jerky nod, but he just stood there.

"Mister Davis, how about if you tell us some of your stories?" she tried, wriggling her arm that was going numb in his grip. "I really like to hear about what happens up here. You sure do know a lot more about all of it than anybody else." Davy still stood there.

Mister Davis started for the cabin, leading Katie like a stubborn pony. "OK little lady, that's just what we'll do—tell stories. But I like to sit down when I talk—just come on in and be sociable."

Katie decided to go easy. She'd think of something on the way. Her chest was drumming, but she was more mad than afraid. She wanted to feel out the moment when she could smash her boot into Mister Davis. But he had such a hold on her that there was no maneuvering yet.

In an ecstasy of exerting physical force, he panted and lurched. He was entranced by something beyond Katie, something that compelled his pulling her as if neither of them really existed. He seemed to have forgotten that Davy was even there, watching at the edge of safety, waiting. "Oh, Davy, don't see this," Katie thought, shutting her eyes and being ashamed of the burning that she was not going to loose into tears. "Just run!" she wanted to scream. "Get out of here and get somebody! Be as smart as I know you are, you dummie!"

But she gritted her teeth and he only stood there brown against the brown boards, his eyes slices above his rigid mouth.

Mister Davis yanked Katie to the front door and into his kitchen, one of the two rooms that comprised the house. It smelled of whiskey, stale tobacco, food cooked too long ago, and a shirt that had needed washing forever.

As soon as they were inside the almost dark room, Mister Davis relaxed his hold on her arm. He swayed backwards and swept elaborately down in a deep bow, extending his arms to welcome her. Gradually, behind him, Katie could make out the wall. It was hung with calendars like the one in the barber shop by the confectionary that she and Corinne giggled past. They were all around the whole room, calendars, calendars, calendars, some faded, others bright and shiny, but all of them bursting with bosoms and bottoms that made Katie want to run for a towel to cover them.

"Like my girls?" Mister Davis smirked, looking at her looking. "Bet ya never saw a c'lection like this, did ya?" He giggled like a silly girl himself, all different from how he was on the road. But his hat was off this time too, and his wisps of hair rose like antennae from his white bald head, making him look electric.

Katie felt electric. Everything inside her was sizzling and ready to fly, especially her head. "You didn't lock the door, it's open. I'll get out. Just you watch, Mister Davis!" she thought, scattering herself to every possibility. "And you'll be mighty sorry for all this!"

"Ya want to see the lure?" he said in an oily voice that sent a sudden control through her.

"I don't believe you have any lure," Katie dared him. "You just talk big. You couldn't catch a chipmunk—not with a bear trap." She watched him straighten up as his smirk faded. She continued, pushed into loudness by her presumption, "If you do have something that works, why don't you hurry up and show me—before my father gets here."

His face squirmed in unsettling indecision and then broke into a smile, crinkled and stained. Leaning toward her with his pale eyes, he sneered, "Ha! Ya think that dumb idea's gonna work again, huh? That bus'ness 'bout yer daddy? I know when he comes 'n goes. 'N no daddy's out there anywhere." He reached again for her left arm. "And ya think I don't have the stuff, huh? Think ol' Bill Davis don't have what he says he does, huh?" Every "huh" blew acid at Katie's eyes and made her stomach reel. "Well, girlie, we'll just see about that." He wrung her wrist and pulled her with him, not noticing that in her other hand she now held behind her the curved steel lifter from his coal stove that she had been standing beside.

Mister Davis maneuvered her toward the back room. There was no door to open, just a drooping paisley curtain to push aside. Katie couldn't look at what she saw. "Davy, where are you?" she agonized behind her eyes. In one glance she had seen too much. There was no place on the walls not plastered with hideous pictures. Katie could never have imagined anything so strange, so unbearable. Even with her eyes closed in revulsion she could see them wilting into the walls, all peeling and dripping as if they couldn't stand to be seen. Unlike the brazen showing off of the calendars in the other room, these curled like paper in a fire, into themselves and into her.

Behind her clamped lids she remembered James and how he couldn't open his eyes when he hurt so much. Back there in the squirming dark she kept seeing the insinuating pictures and knew she would never open her eyes again without them and the shock they paralysed her with. They flooded in waves and gyrations, their colors and details soaking into each other but staying so vivid that Katie could not diffuse them. Where did he get them? Where did anything like that come from? Where did anybody get pictures like that? And why? Whoever thought of such awful stuff? Who could? And who'd want to? And how could he stand to have them there, right there on his walls, right where he'd have to go to sleep with them and wake up to them? They danced like hissing flames on her brain.

Mister Davis had let go of Katie's arm and was standing in front of her swaying in a trance of overwhelming communion. He had watched her see the pictures. His smile had stuck to his brown-edged teeth and his eyes had a dull shine. His whiskers were wet under his glistening cheeks. His shoulders hunched back and his neck was thrust forward so that his body curved into his legs like a cobra.

"Ya like 'em, don't ya?" he purred. "They make ya feel good don't they? Like ya wanna dance or somethin'." Mister Davis slid closer to Katie. "Open 'em up, little lady, Miss Girlie. See how good it makes ya feel jes lookin'. See what it makes ya feel like..." He reached to touch her eyes.

His leather fingers touched her lids and Katie was awake, smashing the heavy end of the lifter into his forehead. It took him by surprise and he stumbled backward, both hands cupping the front of his head. But Katie's blow had come from too low to be direct. He was only dazed by it. As she shot back through the curtain to the kitchen, he was stomping and yelling after her. She raced across the kitchen, slammed out of the screen door, and was headed for the path to the bridge before she realized he was no longer behind her. Almost through the yard she hesitated and then heard from in back of her, "Katie! Come on!"

It was Davy, coming past her at his fastest. The door slammed and she knew he had come out of it too. He passed her up still shouting, "Katie! Hurry! Run!" She pushed off in the brown dirt and followed him through the tangle of thorny bushes and across Mister Davis's bridge.

At the road they turned down, racing for the Parley's Highway. They ran past the gate without slowing down, Davy still in front of Katie by half a stride.

CHAPTER FIFTEEN

The Hupmobile was stacked the same way it had been coming up, but some loads had been taken down earlier in the week by Father in the Auburn as he moved Grandma's things out of her place. Wid, Katie, and Davy lay on the quilts in the back seat, Wid and Davy ready to put their propellers out when they got to the highway. In front, Grandma and Lena sat with Father, and the windshield was open all the way.

It had been the quickest closing the cabin had ever had. Mother would probably have apoplexy Father had said, but this year Grandma let a lot of things go that would never have passed Mother's usual inspection. The rugs were rolled up without being beaten, the bedding was folded without a final shake, the dishes were stacked in cupboards and covered with dish towels, not packed away in tight wooden boxes, and some dry goods were left in the crocks with rocks on their lids. If the mice and chipmunks got in, they'd have a feast.

All the cousins had come to say goodbye, knowing they'd be moving down soon and that none of them would really be together again until Thanksgiving and Christmas. Leaving was always full of quietness, but this year not one so much as talked about the next get-together. Katie wondered if the leaves would even be back on the trees next year.

"Goodbye, cabin," she whispered, taking her last load down the path and looking back at the sprawling white place that never changed.

"Goodbye, path." Her boots took the familiar trail without direction. "And watch for Shadow, OK?" She climbed into the car knowing Shadow was somewhere else.

"Goodbye, hill." Down the hill with her came the Auburn with Wid and his snake bite, its dust was on her moccasins.

"Goodbye, spring." She was spraying jets with Jody Sue and swallowing her prayer for Wid.

"Goodbye, steepest place." She jolted giddily down it, a brakeman in a cone of noise.

"Goodbye, Daniel Moon's Place." The clump of birch hanging by its roots was only a little closer to falling. What did it ever hang on to?

"Goodbye, Rabbit's Head."

"Goodbye, straight stretch."

"Goodbye, Second Rat House."

"Goodbye, and please grow, mountain where the fire was," Davy said solemnly, hardly out loud. Katie was surprised that he was noticing. She had to lean down over the quilts to see past him out of the window, over the edging of green, and up to the scorched mountain. Black scarecrows of scrub oak gnarled against the deep, almost purple blue of the sky, and puffs of clouds floated like batting across the ridge. "Who can number the clouds?" Katie could hear Grandma saying. And the next curve snatched the place of the fire out of sight.

"Goodbye, Deerlick."

"And Lost Canyon...and stay home, Tony."

The Hupmobile moaned down the curves where the sun fell hot and uninterrupted by the shading of growth.

Father drove in low to save the brakes, and the car fumed. There had to be one last hot spot. Father pulled off in a crunch on the lip of the highest place above the stream.

"I'll help," Wid offered, his first words in almost the whole day.

But Davy was already out and running with the dipper for water. As Davy clamored back in, Wid said earnestly, looking back, "Goodbye, hot spot."

Katie turned back and saw Wid peering at the top of Rattlesnake Mountain as it disappeared over the whir of his propeller. She saw him run the thumb of his left hand up and down his first two fingers, the swelling still showing fat around his nail. She tried to imagine how it was when the grotto was the scariest thing she could think of, and a snake a trophy. She remembered for the first time all summer how she had felt about Wid and the Moss Village. When she and Jody Sue and Isabel had worked on it, Wid must have been at the Rat Houses—or somewhere else—and she hadn't even noticed. And James too. James must have been somewhere else clear back then.

The car dived into the last tunnel of arching birch and maple, the chokecherry branches swaying and dripping leaves in its passing. Katie saw the end of the tunnel widen into the protrusion of Mister Davis's parking place above the bridge. There were the cousins after mumble peg, worrying about bugs and a fire. James was slicing the circle with his knife. She closed her eyes again, but the rest was there too. She knew it would be.

As the car moved past, she heard Davy say carefully, "And goodbye, Mister Davis." His vehemence was shaded with something she could never have expected.

"Even Davy," she thought, incredulous. "Even Davy. Nothing comes out with only one side, not even for him. Not even when he was the one who hit Mister Davis. Not even when he was the one who figured it all out and saved us." She clung onto her mind and shoved it into shape as hard as she could, trying not to remember, easing the awfulness away, only to catch it roaring over the dike of her resolve. "Oh, Davy, you little squirt, even you will always have it now, won't you?" she thought only half sadly. "But you did it. You had to. What if you hadn't been brave enough to go in there in the kitchen while he had me in the other room? And smart enough to stand on a chair by the wall next to the door? And quick enough to swing the poker just in time?"

Katie's remembering grabbed her back to the afternoon two days before which she had tried so desperately to blot out with the busy-ness Grandma had told her worked so well. She saw herself in the back seat of the car that she and Davy had hailed in Parley's after they escaped. The two men in it had volunteered to go back into Mister Davis's with them to find him. The gate had been open and they had driven back to the wide place leading into the path Katie sank at seeing again.

"I don't think I want to go in there," she had told them.

"I will," Davy offered, as excited as when Wid or James asked him to play catch.

Katie had stayed in the car. She thought she couldn't even stand to watch them cross the bridge. But she had. When they were out of sight, she pulled herself out of the car and walked slowly to the bushes on the other side of the road. She knew she was going to be sick. She leaned over and threw up. Mother would have said "lost her dinner." But this was vomit.

The reddish pink purge burned her throat and nose and turned her eyes to water. She fell to her knees and leaned forward on her hands, feeling her insides gather and retch. Finally the spasms subsided like the end of sobbing, and she sat back on her heels. She let her head fall back and pulled her eyes shut shivering.

When she opened them, she saw the splatter on the dusty bank below the chokecherry clump opposite the gate. she reached for the soil on both sides of the blotch and scraped it over the pink puddle until it was as concealing as the best camouflage topping of an underground.

She patted it, deliberate, hypnotized, and then mussed it up to look natural. For a moment she sat back and eyed the careful mound. Then she rose and reached a tiny limb of chokecherry, its leaves edged with ochre. She twirled it and smelled it slowly. Then she forced it into the soft dry earth and stabilized it with a little rock of sandstone on each side.

She had been back in the car by the time Davy came running ahead of the two men who were crossing the bridge on either side of Mister Davis.

Seeing him slumped and teetering on their arms, she again slid out of the far side of the car. Up the road, starting to stride at a pace even faster than on the climb with Vanetta, she had called to Davy, "Let's us walk up. We can make it by the time they get him to Sugar House. Just tell them to call Father, and he'll know what to do."

Now on their last trip down, passing that place, she could still hear Davy panting beside her on their walk up. "I told 'em what you said to me about what t'do with 'im. You should'a seen it, Katie. When we got back in there, Mister Davis was flat on the floor. He was as out as you can get. The poker musta really worked. In fact I was scared it mighta worked too good. But they poured water on 'im and slapped 'im 'n stuff and brought 'im to. And they're gonna take 'im down to the city. To jail prob'ly. Maybe to the pen in Sugar House. And maybe we'll get to see 'im lookin' out through the bars. Outa those windows you can see over the wall."

Katie knew Davy would never know much of it except the poker part. And he was already feeling funny about that. It wouldn't be something he'd talk about. And she knew she'd never tell anyone — not even James or Grandma or Father — about Mister Davis — about the night of the fire or what was in his place.

In the middle, on top of the quilts in the back seat of the Hupmobile she swung around to watch the turn smother the brown shape of where Mister Davis's cabin was lurking without its smoke beyond the cottonwoods and willows. The wound of the mountain behind it was being closed off in the tinged green of their going, as if the curtain she'd wished for were finally being pulled.

Katie twisted back to look over Father's hands on the steering wheel and out through the windshield as the car approached the gate. She noticed the sun as orange as fire spreading up the Parley's mountains ahead. The gate raised its knotty triangle across the road.

"Here's the key, son," Father said, handing it over the seat to Wid. Davy was with him, both of them out of their doors slowly, with the reluctance of more than leaving.

When Katie hesitated to get out to swing on the gate as always, Father turned from the front to pat her hair that had not been in ringlets since Mother had left with James. Grandma didn't turn, but looked into the rear view mirror on the dashboard to put her view level with Katie's. After a minute of holding her blue-gray eyes that had narrowed in seeing, Grandma said softly what Katie had heard her say before, "Being old and full of days is not easy, is it Love?" Then she added, "But the gate's still there."

Katie felt Grandma's brown eyes in the mirror like rays in a prism, gently finding every corner of her. She got quietly out of the car and walked to the gate. Wid had loosened the cross bar, and they both gave it a shove and jumped on. Katie lifted herself by her arms straight up from this year's notches, her hands covering almost five years' worth as she swung open with Wid and Davy and the gate. The day smelled like fall—tangy and nippy. She could hear the leaves scrunch under her boots as she walked back to the car. She hadn't noticed that the leaves had started to color, even drop. "Heavenly Father," she began to herself, and then realized that she had used up every promise she had on getting Wid better.

The canyon lay above her, already cool and foreign. Not a place was secret. Not a place was known. Except for Father's refrain which drifted through her like the changing air. "Oh Danny Boy, the pipes the pipes are calling, across the glenn and down the mountainside. The summer's gone, and all the leaves are falling...."

She climbed into the empty space, and the Hupmobile rolled silently through the gate, tossing dust over its own tracks.